Titles by *Langaa* RPCIG

Francis B. Nyamnjoh
Stories from Abakwa
Mind Searching
The Disillusioned African
The Convert
Souls Forgotten
Married But Available

Dibussi Tande
No Turning Back. Poems of Freedom 1990-1993
Scribbles from the Den: Essays on Politics and Collective
Memory in Cameroon

Kangsen Feka Wakai
Fragmented Melodies

Ntemfac Ofege
Namondo. Child of the Water Spirits
Hot Water for the Famous Seven

Emmanuel Fru Doh
Not Yet Damascus
The Fire Within
Africa's Political Wastelands: The Bastardization of Cameroon
Oriki'badan
Wading the Tide

Thom
Tale of an A

Peter Wutel
Grassfields Stories
Green Rape: Poetry for
Majunga Tok: Poems i
Cry, My Belove
No Love L
Straddling The Mungo: A Book of F

Ba'bila Muti
Coils of Mortal Flesh

Kehbuma Langmia
Titabet and the Takumbeng
An Evil Meal of Evil

Victor Elame Musinga
The Barn
The Tragedy of Mr. No Balance

Ngessimo Mathe Mutaka
Building Capacity: Using TEFL and African Languages as
Development-oriented Literacy Tools

Milton Krieger
Cameroon's Social Democratic Front: Its History and Prospects as
an Opposition Political Party, 1990-2011

Sammy Oke Akombi
The Raped Amulet
The Woman Who Ate Python
Beware the Drives: Book of Verse

Susan Nkwentie Nde
Precipice
Second Engagement

**Francis B. Nyamnjoh &
Richard Fonteh Akum**
The Cameroon GCE Crisis: A Test of Anglophone Solidarity

Joyce Ashuntantang & Dibussi Tande
Their Champagne Party Will End! Poems in Honor of Bate
Besong

Emmanuel Achu
Disturbing the Peace

Rosemary Ekosso
The House of Falling Women

Peterkins Manyong
God the Politician

George Ngwane
The Power in the Writer: Collected Essays on Culture, Democracy
& Development in Africa

John Percival
The 1961 Cameroon Plebiscite: Choice or Betrayal

Albert Azeyeh
Réussite scolaire, faillite sociale : généalogie mentale de la crise
de l'Afrique noire francophone

Aloysius Ajab Amin & Jean-Luc Dubois
Croissance et développement au Cameroun :
d'une croissance équilibrée à un développement équitable

Carlson Anyangwe
Imperialistic Politics in Cameroun:
Resistance & the Inception of the Restoration of the Statehood
of Southern Cameroons
Betrayal of Too Trusting a People: The UN, the UK and the Trust
Territory of the Southen Cameroons

Bill F. Ndi
K'Cracy, Trees in the Storm and Other Poems
Map: Musings On Ars Poetica
Thomas J   Fighting Sailor Turn'd Peaceable /Le marin
                  battant devenu paisible

n Toure, Therese Mungah
hombe & Thierry Karsenti
nging Mindsets in Education

les Alobwed'Epie
Day God Blinked

D. Nyamndi
Yar Symphony
osing, Whether winning
Tussles: Collected Plays
Dogs in the Sun

Samuel Ebelle Kingue
Si Dieu était tout un chacun de nous ?

Ignasio Malizani Jimu
Urban Appropriation and Transformation: bicycle, taxi and
handcart operators in Mzuzu, Malawi

Justice Nyo' Wakai
Under the Broken Scale of Justice: The Law and My Times

John Eyong Mengot
A Pact of Ages

Ignasio Malizani Jimu
Urban Appropriation and Transformation: Bicycle Taxi and
Handcart Operators

Joyce B. Ashuntantang
Landscaping and Coloniality: The Dissemination of Cameroon
Anglophone Literature

Jude Fokwang
Mediating Legitimacy: Chieftaincy and Democratisation in Two
African Chiefdoms

Michael A. Yanou
Dispossession and Access to Land in South Africa: an African
Perspevctive

Tikum Mbah Azonga
Cup Man and Other Stories
John Nkemngong Nkengasong
Letters to Marions (And the Coming Generations)

Amady Aly Dieng
Les étudiants africains et la littérature négro-africaine d'expression
française

Tah Asongwed
Born to Rule: Autobiography of a life President

Frida Menkan Mbunda
Shadows From The Abyss

Bongasu Tanla Kishani
A Basket of Kola Nuts

Fo Angwafo III S.A.N of Mankon
Royalty and Politics: The Story of My Life

Basil Diki
The Lord of Anomy

Churchill Ewumbue-Monono
Youth and Nation-Building in Cameroon: A Study of National
Youth Day Messages and Leadership Discourse (1949-2009)

Emmanuel N. Chia, Joseph C. Suh & Alexandre Ndeffo Tene
Perspectives on Translation and Interpretation in Cameroon

Linus T. Asong
The Crown of Thorns
No Way to Die
A Legend of the Dead: Sequel of *The Crown of Thorns*

Vivian Sihshu Yenika
Imitation Whiteman

Beatrice Fri Bime
Someplace, Somewhere
Mystique: A Collection of Lake Myths

Shadrach A. Ambanasom
Son of the Native Soil
The Cameroonian Novel of English Expression: An Introduction

Tangie Nsoh Fonchingong and Gemandze John Bobuin
Cameroon: The Stakes and Challenges of Governance and
Development

Tatah Mentan
Democratizing or Reconfiguring Predatory Autocracy? Myths and
Realities in Africa Today

Roselyne M. Jua & Bate Besong
To the Budding Creative Writer: A Handbook

Albert Mukong
Prisoner without a Crime: Disciplining Dissent in Ahidjo's
Cameroon

Mbuh Tennu Mbuh
In the Shadow of my Country

A Legend of the Dead

Sequel to *The Crown of Thorns*

Linus T. Asong

Langaa Research & Publishing CIG
Mankon, Bamenda

Publisher:
Langaa RPCIG
Langaa Research & Publishing Common Initiative Group
P.O. Box 902 Mankon
Bamenda
North West Region
Cameroon
Langaagrp@gmail.com
www.langaa-rpcig.net

Distributed outside N. America by African Books Collective
orders@africanbookscollective.com
www.africanbookscollective.com

Distributed in N. America by Michigan State University Press
msupress@msu.edu
www.msupress.msu.edu

ISBN: 9956-558-70-2

DISCLAIMER

The names, characters, places and incidents in this book are either the product of the author's imagination or are used fictitiously. Accordingly, any resemblance to actual persons, living or dead, events, or locales is entirely one of incredible coincidence.

Contents

Part One

Chapter One 3
Chapter Two 9
Chapter Three 23
Chapter Four 31

Part Two

Chapter Five 35
Chapter Six 45
Chapter Seven 49
Chapter Eight 67
Chapter Nine 79
Chapter Ten 91
Chapter Eleven 103
Chapter Twelve 109
Chapter Thirteen 113
Chapter Fourteen 119

Part Three

Chapter Fifteen 127
Chapter Sixteen 131
Chapter Seventeen 149
Chapter Eighteen 159
Chapter Nineteen 165

Part Four

Chapter Twenty 177
Chapter Twenty-One 185
Chapter Twenty-Two 193
Chapter Twenty-Three 205
Chapter Twenty-Four 211
Chapter Twenty-Five 225
Chapter Twenty-Six 237

Epilogue 243

Thus forever with reverted look
The mystic volume of the world they read
Spelling it backward, like a Hebrew book
Till life became **A Legend of the Dead.**

(Henry W. Longfellow:
The Jewish Cemetery at Newport)

FOR MY BELOVED PARENTS

Edward Asong
And
Francisca Njiondock (of blessed memory)

Part One

Chapter One

If a man will begin with certainties,
he shall end in doubts;
but if he will be content to begin with doubts,
he shall end with certainties
          (Francis Bacon: *Advancement of Learning*)

*T*HE GOVERNOR sat at his desk without saying anything, either to his wife or his two sons noisily flipping over the pages of some football magazine on a desk in the corner of the spacious office. He thought of it, and that would have been the best thing to do. But he could not summon the courage to ask his wife to leave until he had finished talking over the phone. He turned as if in excruciating pain and, gnashing his teeth, moved his eyes towards the open window and stared outside with a fierce earnestness. He could very well have been looking at a projection of his own perturbed mind for, in some strange way, the atmosphere matched his thoughts and feelings - a bewildering mosaic of foreboding images. Over the burnt sky-scraping eucalyptus trees to the right, and, entangled in their rugged, craggy, naked branches, floated shrouds of thick mist like the shreds of some sinuous mourning garment.

Farther up and near the sky, fragments of clouds, undoubtedly rain clouds, crawled away in silence towards the distant left. Many more at the centre, thicker, darker, heavier. As though too tired and too weary to drift either to the right or to the left, they had begun to pile one upon the other in curious masses. So unnatural they looked, so distinct, so sharply cut that they seemed less a work of nature than that of a titanic Michelangelo at work on the canvas of the heavens. They hung on, sombre, ominous, pregnant with rain, yet uneasily withholding it as though it were a basket of eggs that would fall to the ground and shatter.

3

It had rained before, and it would rain again. That was typical of the period between the end of April and the beginning of May. Some thunder moaned from over the hills and the wind suddenly started to blow. It was not violent, but noticeable all the same. The young leaves and velvety pansies in the pot at the window had begun to shiver voluptuously under the quick pressure of the breeze, even as he was watching.

***

Governor Abraham-Isaac was an administrator of great repute, having served the country in that capacity for about five years. He had higher ambitions though, of one day becoming the Prime Minister. He was just about sixty-five years old and huge in stature. His hair grew scantily on his head and he had a wide forehead, such that the initial impression a stranger got of him was that of baldness. But he was not bald. It was just that his hair retreated very far above the forehead. He had large eyes which had the tendency to dilate from time to time when he spoke, giving him a permanently frightened look. At the same time his thick brows rose at an oblique angle, so that he also looked angry or confused each time they pulled together. Heavy folds of skin descended below his eyes, emphasizing their wide open nature. It would appear his eyes had a slight defect because they never looked exactly in the same direction. Two gorges of age-lines descended from both sides of his broad nose. His lips, thick, were upturned, making the presence of a smile virtually difficult, unless forced. Spanning the area between the bridge of his nose and the irregular arc of the border of his upper lip was a moustache, a Hitlerian patch of hairs. His neck was so thick that it was just enough for him to lower his head and you would not see the entire front collar of his shirt.

Ninety degrees Fahrenheit, the radio had announced the temperature barely five minutes earlier. Inside, the office was cool and refreshing - the air conditioners worked round the clock. Yet the Governor felt very uncomfortable, and with good reason: he was listening to a piece of news which was building up tension in him that was finding expression in a sudden and intense rise of his body temperature. He had already taken off his cotton jacket, a relic of his trip to Britain one winter eleven years ago. It was hanging from the backrest of his chair. Bubbles of cold sweat, icy cold sweat, were visible over his thick fleshy neck above the collar, on the tip of his heavy nose and across his forehead. He was leaning forward on the table, his head inclined on his left hand. His fluffy cheek pressing hard against the knuckles of his tightly clenched fist, twisted his nose and mouth, distorting the entire left side of his face. It now gave him a severe comical look.

He listened, pipe in mouth, first with his usual sceptical indifference, then with a growing concern and finally with an admixture of fear and horrified amazement.

"The DO was burnt to death, Your Excellency," the Captain continued. "Beyond recognition," he reiterated, but with no intention to shock anybody.

"What was the motive?" the Governor inquired preposterously, and as though there was any motive that could sufficiently justify the atrocities.

"We don't know, Your Excellency. We have so far only heard that he was involved in the sale of the statue of a god."

"They still talk of statues of gods at this point in the history of mankind?" the Governor wondered aloud.

There was silence from the other end of the line.

"And his wife?" the man inquired superfluously, eyeing his own wife who now seemed to lean forward, perhaps with the intention of eavesdropping.

"Clobbered to death," came the Captain's retort. The voice was so loud that the woman could hear everything he was saying from where she sat.

"She was found naked and very dead in the yard of the burning home."

"He had children, nnoh?" the Governor asked. He threw a glance at his own children playing.

"He did, Your Excellency. Two. We have met his son and daughter who attend college in Likume. They say their parents had two children with them. One three years, and another six months."

"But there was no sign of them?"

"None, Your Excellency. None at all."

"Could they have been abducted or how?"

"Unlikely, Your Excellency. Unlikely. They too were killed."

"The Reverend Father?"

"Killed, too, Your Excellency."

"Shit?" the Governor cursed exasperatingly. That was his expression for the most severe condemnation, for the most severe expression of disgust.

"Shit!" he said again, his mahogany face completely contorted with rage. "And they killed their own Chief!"

"Chopped to pieces, Your Excellency. Together with some six or seven members of his council."

"Who did the killings?"

"The killings, Your Excellency, are said to have been planned and sanctioned by a rebel Council of Elders under the leadership of a certain Ngobefuo. The actual killings were said to have been executed under the personal direction and supervision of a man named Ngangabe. They are both still in hiding."

"No arrest?" the Governor gasped, his bulging eyes squinting with wonder until nobody could tell where he was looking any more. He looked across at his astonished wife.

"None, Your Excellency. Not before I was dispatched," the officer said.

"No war," he grunted between an affirmation and an interrogation.

"None, Your Excellency."

"No resistance, armed or otherwise?"

"None, Your Excellency."

Sighs poured from the Governor's gaping mouth like water from a tap. He lifted his head from the listening position with great effort, unclenched his fist and rubbed hard at the lobe of his broad ear with the back of his left hand. His right hand was still lying on the open file before him, a Parker pen clenched between his sweaty fingers in a motion for writing. He had initially thought of making a few personal notes prior to having a full-length report made when all the facts would have been known. He had placed the itching nib of the pen on the top left hand corner of the blank sheet of paper. It still stuck to the paper at the end of the grim report. The dot he had made had now turned into a large blot.

True, he ruminated with a terrible self-bitterness, he could never be held accountable for the outrage. It had come unexpectedly, like a thunderclap, without anything which could be regarded as a warning he would be blamed for having ignored. Yet its consequences on his political career were far-reaching. They were bound to affect his candidature for the much-sought-for office of Prime Minister.

And the elections were only eleven months away. He had protected his reputation until that fateful hour, with matchless and deliberate cunning. Yet, and yet, that was what it had come to! No possibility anywhere for him to help foment a rebellion in the provinces of the other Governors who were his rivals, just so that they could be even with him on records! What's done is done and can never be undone, he thought. It was useless to sit back bemoaning his fate, or beseeching divine intervention. He must work out a solution that would stand up in his defence. It must never look like some neglect on his part may have been responsible for a crisis of that magnitude.

"Kill nobody," he said resolutely. "If there is no resistance, kill nobody. Bring such members of that so-called Council of Elders as you can lay hands on. Especially that man Ngobefuo. Alive. I repeat, alive. I want to talk to them first."

"Your Excellency," the voice responded. The Governor could hear the speaker click his heels.

***

"Just what is happening?" his wife entreated him.

"Well, well," he vainly tried to cover it up. "Just one of those small things. Some nincompoop trying to stir up trouble in Small Monje and make life difficult for innocent people."

"They killed who?" The national daily which she read had not reported the killings, so she was learning of it for the first time.

"Anyway," he seemed to evade a direct answer. "Things are under control. They are control."

Chapter Two

Le hasard c'est peut-être le pseudonyme de Dieu,
quand il ne veut pas signer.
>   (Anatole France, *Le Jardin d'Epicure*)

IT WAS a little after six. Darkness was still a long way.
Heavy rain had fallen in the early hours of the afternoon,
but the sun was now shining. It had been shining for the past
two hours. Now thick columns of vapour could be seen rising gently
from the smoking earth, winding up in grotesque curly spirals towards
the amber sky. Termites, invaded in their subterranean castles by
floods of rain-water, crept out in ones and twos or even threes and
fours and launched themselves lustily into the air. Not for them that
whatever goes up must come down. Sparrows, clock birds and
countless other species of birds perching on mounds and tree tops,
chirping and chiming away the hours of the day, sprang voraciously
at the defenceless insects.

A greenish long-base Land Rover, not in the newest of conditions,
rattled up to the rear gate into the Governor's lodge and stopped. A
policeman on duty (the truest porter of hell's gate) had been dozing
off for the past hour in the shed inside the compound. His rifle,
loaded, lay discarded at his feet. The noise of the Land Rover woke
him up. He shook his head with the briskness of a cock bathing in
saw dust and turned reluctantly in the direction of the noise.

For one brief moment he was afraid. Switching agility into his
slumber he grabbed his gun and shot up. It was no Government
vehicle, he realized. His feet instantly seemed to be weighted with
lead. It must have taken him not less than five irritating minutes to
make the short distance of ten metres between his shed and the
barred gate.

Two men climbed down from the vehicle and strode with an air
of importance, possibly calculated to offset the idea that they had
approached the house from the rear. The policeman scrutinised them

9

as they came towards the gate. One was in a charcoal-grey three-piece suit, an unlit pipe sticking tenaciously to his lips. He must have been in his fifties or even sixties, for his face was wrinkled, and his hair was already greying around the edges in a manner that could only be ascribed to age. He stood probably one and three quarters of a metre in height.

The other was slightly shorter, and wore a very colourful gown. It reached down midway between his knees and ankles and was gorgeously decorated along the hands, neck and bottom. The outfit gave him a look of wealth and respect. He looked just as old as the first man, but he walked with greater consciousness of his own dignity.

"Good evening, officer," the man in suit greeted through the bars.

"Evening," the officer answered in his throat. It was actually a snarl.

"Is this the Provincial Governor's residence?" the man asked.

"Yes, it is."

"Is he in?"

The officer leaned against the barrier and looked down appraisingly at the man's shoes. He then lifted his eyes along his profile to the head and said sourly.

"Yes, he is in."

"We like to see him," the visitor said.

"We who? You are who?"

The man in suit searched his breast pocket for his identity card which he presented through a gap in the barrier. The officer looked from the picture in it to the man's face. Then he read the details:

NAME: .... Blasius Betong
BIRTH PLACE: .... Yegoh
DIVISION:.................................... Biongong
DATE OF BIRTH:...................... Around 1913
RESIDENCE: .... LIKUME
OCCUPATION: .... Businessman

He did not return the card to the man. Instead he held out his knotted palm towards the other man. The man understood and gave him his card.

NAME: .... Marcus Anuse
BIRTHPLACE: .... Small Monje
DIVISION: .... Biongong
DATE OF BIRTH: .... Around 1917
RESIDENCE: .... LIKUME
OCCUPATION: .... Businessman

"You want to see the Governor for why?"

No answer.

"You want to see the Governor for official wok or for personal?"

"Is offisial," the man called Anuse said. "We come with all the Palamount Tsiefs of Biongong," he announced, pointing to the Land Rover. "Tshey hafe important tsings to discuss with the Gofnor. About Small Monje."

"What?" the officer jerked to attention. He had not been listening. Anuse repeated.

The man opened the side gate and went out to meet them.

The three then walked back to the Land Rover.

"Good evening sirs," he greeted the three old men slouched in three separate seats in all the kingly accoutrements he had ever heard of: large black caps with red feathers and porcupine spikes stuck to the front of each; large and colourful beads around the neck and bangles from carved elephant tusks on the arm, then huge multi-coloured and multi-layered gowns.

There was no response. They did not understand the officer.

"His Highness, Goment's man is greeting you," Betong told them with very great reverence.

"Tell him that we are also greeting him," one of the Chiefs said in a deep sonorous voice. Meanwhile the officer was going round the lorry. Along the side in conspicuous white paint against the blue background was written Anuse's motto - MAN LIVES BY MAN. Then he got attracted by the load on the carriage.

"You want to see him with all this?"

"Yes," Anuse beamed. "Tshey are all for him, officer. Tshe two Seeps, fife fowls, tshe two goats, tshree bags of egusi."

The Officer seemed to smile. It was one of the unwritten laws of his duties that nobody with a gift for the Governor must be turned away.

"Come in first," he beckoned to them before asking: "Is he expecting you?"

He did not hear or care to listen to what the answer to his question was. His attitude had changed and he spoke with far less aggression.

Betong walked behind him as he entered through the side door while Anuse went back into the Land Rover and waited until the main gate was pulled open. Then he drove in and went to halt in front of the officer's little room.

"Come down with them and follow me," the officer told Anuse.

They all climbed down and walked into an adjoining building. As soon as the Chiefs were shown where to sit, Anuse pressed and was shown where to off-load the gifts even before their presence was announced to the Governor. From his past experiences in giving bribes, he knew how crucial the gifts were in determining the Governor's attitude towards their extremely delicate mission.

The gifts were delivered. The officer then filled in the necessary formalities in the Visitor's Book for seeing the Governor, and made them sign in the place of the Chiefs before he went out to inform the Governor.

"The Elders of their Council or their Chiefs?" the Governor asked furiously.

"The Chiefs of Biongong, Your Excellency. Three of them. Two businessmen from Likume are with them. And two sheeps, two goats, with fowls and bags of egusi."

The Governor's brows had risen abruptly but gradually settled more or less horizontally over his eyes. A little thrill seemed to steal its way into his heart. When he next spoke there was an overture of friendliness in his tone. His first instinct had been to ask the officer to tell them that he only wanted to see the Elders of the Council of Small Monje, and that they should be sent away at once. But the mention of the gifts seemed to have struck a note of excitement. As though it was the one thing necessary to set the logical processes of his mind in motion, it instantly occurred to him that they might indeed hold the key to the solution of the bloody incident. He decided to meet them.

"Take them to the waiting room."

"Your Excellency."

When he came in later Anuse and Betong introduced themselves. Turning towards the Chiefs Betong began:

"This is His Highness Chief Fuobefuo, Paramount Chief of Nonudji. He is father of all the Paramount Chiefs of Biongong. This is Chief Moneki. He is second in command to Chief Fuobefuo in the hierarchy of our Paramount Chiefs. And this is His Highness Chief Yagu, Paramount Chief of Jungo. They have come to see Your Excellency."

In point of fact, Chief Fuobefuo was not the highest in the hierarchy of the Biongong Chiefs. He was merely the oldest. But it did not seem to matter. Besides, he looked old and respectable enough to pass for the highest of the Chiefs. The important thing was that the detail helped their case very much.

The Governor nodded, sat down and crossed his legs. "They are aware of what has happened in Small Monje, not so?" he inquired with gravest concern.

"They are, Your Excellency," Betong answered.

"Does their coming have something to do with it?"

Nobody said anything.

"They are all understanding me I hope?" he said.

They do not understand English, Your Excellency. They brought me to interpret. They know all about the trouble in Small Monje. From the beginning to the end. That is what has brought them here today, Your Excellency."

This was completely false. The trip had been undertaken mainly to serve Anuse's own ends, and perhaps, those of Betong. Marcus Anuse, an evil genius, was born with a craving for power that was vicious and destructive in its intensity. He had been born third among the sons of their father who was the ruling Paramount Chief of Small Monje. But Anuse believed that he ought to be the one to succeed their father. He hoped, prayed and wished for something to happen, some disaster or the sudden death of his two brothers, to leave the way open for him to become the new Chief. Nature would not oblige him. They lived on, healthy and strong, to take care of him, for it was he who became the sickling.

He next prayed for sterility in the wombs of their wives. This way, upon their death, the succession would devolve on his own offspring. Once again the consequences of his prayer turned on him. he became the only fatherless man among the princes of the throne, while the two others shared between them eight children, all sons! This happened within the first eight years of their marriages.

Unbearably frustrated, Anuse departed from Small Monje to seek his fortune down the Coast. He was twenty then, and it was to Likume that he went and lived. There he joined some of his other tribesmen who had migrated before him. He had come there determined to find in Likume what fate denied him in Small Monje - power, influence. but he soon learned that he would never get power unless he had money. He then decided to assemble all his wits to get money.

He began as a Park collector. His duty was to loiter about the lorry station, collecting passengers and their fares for drivers, in return for a small fee just enough for his daily bread. It was a mean job by all standards. But he could never have hoped for anything better because he had never gone beyond Standard Four in School. Besides, it gave him one very important satisfaction - he saw money, touched it, counted it, smelt it, and even licked it. He soon discovered too that if he used his brains well, he could make a really good start. He would impose charges on the luggage of passengers, far above the amount he later gave to the drivers concerned. Some days he made about four thousand francs that way.

Again this was not much money, even by the standards of the time. But it was better than nothing. He did this job for five years, saving every little franc that he earned or smuggled, and living entirely off the generosity of his uncles and other tribesmen. He knew what a good reputation meant for a man's life and never trifled with his public image. Whatever else he was, he passed for a polite and honest young man who was not ashamed to work for his living. Park collectors were notorious for stealing passengers' luggage or even defrauding them of their fares. But no such complaint was ever raised against Anuse. Not that he did not steal. But he did it so well that he was never suspected, let alone caught.

He was a regular court-goer, and never missed a court session that involved fraud, misappropriation of funds, impersonation, and even armed robbery. Gradually and systematically he came to master all the techniques of fraud. And with this he developed a personal philosophy and a personal morality. To him, it became as obvious as a law of nature, as obvious as night follows day, that no human being could ever rise from obscurity to eminence without committing some major fraud or crime. Stealing, he would argue to himself, is an important asset to society. How would they tell a good Policeman, a good Lawyer, or a good Magistrate, if nobody put their talents to the test? How would Lawyers get rich? How would Policemen be promoted? The expression, now very much in common use - *A goat eats only where it is tethered* - was known to have been coined by him. And it was Anuse himself who was said to have modified it by saying that *some goats even die where they are tied!* He never forgot the story of Judas Iscariot and the thirty pieces of silver, if a man lacked money, nothing else that he had mattered. And if he had it, it did not matter what else he lacked. In fact, such a man lacked nothing.

All the tricks necessary for courting praise and acclamations he studied like a book. Among the families of all the rich members of his tribe and the entire Municipal Council, he was known to be a selfless giver. From his thefts of the day he made small gifts in various forms to the children of these people. And each time he gave a child something he insisted as a condition for future gifts, that the child concerned should show the gift to his or her parents. To the parents and their children Anuse became a synonym for generosity. In doing this he knew that at some future date he would require either their direct help or their endorsement of some request.

With his meagre savings he managed to bribe the Chairman of the Municipal Council to give him a job as an Office Messenger and Mail - Runner. This was when he first met his destiny. By cleverly removing stamps from letters given to be posted, and by smuggling bundles of typing sheets and file jackets from the store and selling them to his agents in town, he succeeded in accumulating enough money to be able to buy the office of Gate-Keeper.

The Gate-Keeper had a very important responsibility, and provided the Council with much of its revenue. He took tickets from the Council Office which he kept and issued to drivers each time a loaded vehicle was leaving the lorry-station. Each ticket was worth only one hundred francs. But the Likume lorry station controlled much of the traffic to other coastal towns.

Thus it was not uncommon for the Council to make sales of one hundred thousand francs on some very busy days. Anuse approached the man who recorded the number of tickets issued to him with an offer he could not deny. If the man noted down less tickets than he actually received, say twenty instead of forty, they would share whatever booty the twenty extra tickets fetched them. For thirteen years the two men plied their trade-undetected. During these years Anuse accumulated wealth in the bank.

***

For several years since their arrival in Likume, the Biongong tribesmen had always paid their taxes directly to the Municipal Council. But as their numbers increased every year, the council found that it could no longer assess the income of many of these people because it did not know all of them well enough. It decided therefore, that the Biogong tribesmen should come together and choose a man who would act as a liaison between them and the Council. Such a man would collect their taxes and pay to the Council. He would also receive new tax tickets at the beginning of each year which he would issue to the people, depending on his assessment of their income. He should be a man everybody knew to be honest. Must also have landed property so that in case of any fraud, his property could be seized as compensation. He must know his people very well, and he must have some general knowledge of the activities of the Municipal Council.

Only one man met all these conditions - Marcus Anuse. He had thus become the leader of his people. But he was far from being satisfied. Tax tickets cost five thousand five hundred francs each. But, depending on how well you respected and worshipped his authority as "the King of Likume", Anuse could make a man pay as much as twenty thousand francs income tax. He decided the rate, and his word was final. For the unfortunate individual, the alternative was to leave Likume. Anuse became literally a King in his own right, feeding fat on the labours of his less fortunate brothers.

And nobody could dare to openly condemn or challenge his actions. He was not only powerful amongst his people, but very popular with the police. Not that he could order the arrest of anybody. But if he ever did anything to anybody, and the matter was taken to the police, nothing was ever done. When he noticed that his wealth was drawing too much attention and that his activities in the Council were being trailed, he resigned and went into private business. As a private businessman, he managed by some devious means to procure a machine for printing tax tickets which he sold to his people.

All this money went into his pockets, and he explained to the Council auditors each time they looked disturbed by the decline in his sales that people were not paying taxes any more, because of mounting unemployment as a result of the economic crises. In the meantime he succeeded in making contacts with other tax assessor in other districts, to whom he explained the advantages of the deal. They co-operated with him fully, agreed to have him print tickets for them too for a fee and did not betray him. This business too he carried on for eight years - undetected. By this time his savings had reached fifteen million francs. His business rose astronomically, and so did his prestige and influence.

Whenever a Minister or any important Government official visited Likume, Anuse was among the V.I.P.'s to receive him. He had a seat in the tribune and there was no known Commissioner or ordinary policeman to whom he had never made an important gift, either in cash or kind. The throne of Nkokonoko Small Monje ceased to have any meaning whatsoever in his life. So did anybody else. He had become his own god, his own law.

***

But by the time the present crisis erupted in Small Monje, Anuse's business had begun to suffer very severe blows. A certain Police Inspector (there is always one such) had refused to be reconciled to Anuse's activities and had set out to painstakingly investigate the source of his wealth. His machines had been tracked down and confiscated. Anuse himself had been arrested, together with all his accomplices in the other districts. That same day, however, he had been released on bail, and nothing had been said to him thereafter. But half his capital had been squandered on his captors to destroy evidence against him. The office of tax-assessor and collector had been seized from him.

The throne he had previously thought of with scorn began to attract him. He knew that apart from the hundreds of daughters whose dowries could bring hundreds of thousands of francs, the crown of Small Monje had large estates of cocoa, coffee and bananas. All these, if adequately managed could provide him with the funds he so vitally needed to revive his crumbling enterprises. It became the only thing he could cling to. And he believed he could do it very easily when the crisis broke out and left the throne vacant.

***

This was the way things stood in his mind when by a sheer stroke of fortune the Chiefs played into his hands. He had gone to Nkapa to buy some produce when he ran into the old Chiefs. They carefully explained the purpose of their journey: they were going to Likume personally to send a delegation of their sons to Tetseale to protest to the Provincial Governor against the withdrawal of help that had been promised them.

By the time the District Officer of Small Monje was killed, three lorry loads of drugs for dispensaries and materials for schools in Nonudji, Moneki and Jungo had already reached Bejange, just about fifty kilometres from Small Monje. Small Monje in turn was a kind of gateway into the other tribes. The news which reached the drivers of the vehicles carrying the things was that Biongong had declared war on the Government and all its agents. They therefore fled back to Tetseale. But in the version of the news that had decided to withdraw all help from them because of the trouble in Small Monje. They therefore wanted the Governor to know how they were feeling about its conduct towards them.

Anuse thought he could exploit the situation to his own profit. He pondered over what they had said for a very long time. It would be more effective for them to go to Tetseale, he suggested, and talk to the Governor directly because the matter was to such urgent importance that he would not choose but listen to them. When they complained that they did not understand English and did not know the way to Tetseale he offered to help. He would take them there and also provide somebody to interpret their complaints. He even offered to lodge them in a hotel in Nkapa, at his own expense while he returned to Likume to prepare for the journey.

Back in Likume he approached Betong to whom he carefully explained his ploy. Betong should come with him and act as interpreter for the Chiefs. The Provincial Governor must be made to believe that their main purpose for coming there to see him was to beg him to put an end to all the bloodshed in Nkokonoko Small Monje by making Anuse the Chief. Whatever they said did not matter. If that worked, and if he became the new Paramount Chief of Small Monje, Betong would be the only buyer of produce from the enormous estates of the crown of Small Monje. He would in addition get a cash reward of one hundred thousand francs.

"Man leafs by man," he ended.

Betong could not resist the offer. The departure of Anuse for Small Monje as Chief would, moreover, leave him in sole control of the produce buying business in Likume, because Anuse was his only rival among the Biongong tribesmen. So that was what had brought him to Tetseale. His answer to the Governor's question as to whether the people knew about the trouble in Small Monje did not therefore reflect the thoughts and feelings of the Chiefs.

After speaking to the Governor Betong spoke to them for a moment on other matters and then said:

"Your Excellency, they say they know the story of Small Monje from A to Z and are ready to tell you everything about it."

"Let them tell me please," the Governor said. "I am listening."

Betong turned to the Chiefs:

"His highness, the Governor says you should now tell him all that is worrying you. The thing that brought you here. He is listening."

Fuobefuo spoke first:

"Tell him that if a man puts his hair in the fire, it is he alone who will hear the smell. Tell him that although we all come from Biongong and belong to one blood, we are not all of Small Monje. Small Monje is not us.

"Let him know that he should not allow the things that are happening in Small Monje to make him break his promises to us. Before trouble started in Small Monje we were promised medicines and zinc and also perenox for our cocoa farms. We were told to expect them in a month. We heard that the things were already being brought when he decided that he will not help us again because of Small Monje. Tell him that this is worrying us all. Tell him that our people have come to us and have cried. Our farms need a lot of medicines. The rains have not yet come. When the medicines are not put now, if we wait until the rains come, they will wash all away. And after the rains it will be soon time for harvest. So nothing will come of the labours of all our people if the perenox is not sent now.

"The walls of the schools the goment asked us to build have reached roofing level in all the places. They will be washed down by rain when it comes, if a roof of zinc is not put over them now. Our people will be very glad to hear that these things we are talking about have come back with us from Tetseale, or are following us. We had no hand in what took place in Small Monje. He himself knows that we had never said no to anything he had asked us to do. None of his men had ever been insulted in our land. Tell him that he should not let our people suffer because of Small Monje."

After the old Chief had finished laying their complaint Betong turned to the Governor with an interpretation that fitted into his purpose:

"Chief Fuobefuo was speaking for all of them, your Excellency," he began.

The Governor nodded.

He went on:

"They say that if anything happens in any corner of the whole Division of Biongong, you should know that they are in the best position to know why it happened, how it happened, and what can be done to stop it from happening again like that. Especially if it is something as serious as the things that have just taken place in Small Monje."

The Governor nodded again.

"They say it was for this reason that they have for the first time left their palaces at home, enduring all the difficulties, just to come and let you know how it came that blood had to spill to that extent."

The Governor nodded several times and leaned forward toward the speaker, giving him his maximum attention.

"They say they have looked into the seeds of time," Betong went on, "and have seen blood coming again in the near future. Unless Your Excellency takes their advice. They say all the three of them had gone to Nkokonoko Small Monje, first individually, then as a group. They said they had warned the late DO but he would not listen to them. They say they are sure that the Governor has some record here showing their importance among the Chiefs of Biongong, and that if the Governor too like he should not listen to them. They would return and sit back to see more blood."

The Governor found it necessary to interrupt him. He said:

"Let them know that what this country needs is peace. That is why the events in Small Monje have so disturbed the state. I will be defeating my main purpose for ever becoming Governor, because it will be working directly against the very principles for which we stand, if I overlook an advice from people of their calibre. I know who they are. I know what they stand for in Biongong. Let them know that they are talking to the representative of the Head of State."

Betong picked up the thread from where he had stopped and discussed with the Chiefs something that had nothing to do with their mission, all the time making sure that the name Ngobefuo and Anuse crept in. He then turned to the Governor and said:

"Your Excellency, they say the root cause of all the bloodshed is a certain man call Ngobefuo. This man is a slave who seized power in the tribe. They say you will see in your presence here a man called Anuse whom they have forced to abandon his business in Likume and come with them. They say the whole trouble began because this Mr. Anuse was rejected. He was the correct person to rule after the death of Chief Fuondee. They say that when that old Chief lay dying Ngobefuo deceived him into assigning him the powers of the caretaker of the tribe.

Then as soon as the Chief died, since Ngobefuo knew that slaves could not be allowed to rule he grew jealous, took bribes and changed the succession from the rightful Anuse to Nchindia. He gave it to Nchindia because he knew that being a small boy he would be able to use him any way he liked. They say that as soon as this happened too they hurried to Small Monje to speak to the DO about it."

"Are they therefore saying that it is Anuse who ought to be the Chief?" the Governor inquired.

"If there is ever to be peace in Small Monje, Your Excellency."

"Tell them that the Government is ready to take immediate steps to avoid any further trouble along any lines they will suggest."

Betong told the Chiefs:

"The Governor says that they are ready to let you have all your needs back if only there is the promise that you will never allow

21

what has happened in Small Monje to happen in your own areas. He says he had nothing at all against you people, and that the fact that those lorries came back did not mean that the Government had broken its promise at all."

"Your Excellency, they have made one more request; that they would be glad if you would arrange for the medicines and other materials which were already being sent to them before the trouble started, to be sent again. They say they heard that the drivers were running for their lives, but that Your Excellency should make them know that nobody can do anything to them in Small Monje..."

"The things will be sent back immediately. Tell them so."

Betong turned and said exactly what the Governor had said. The Governor then turned to Anuse:

"So you are the prince who was supposed to rule?" "I am, Ya Excellency. But Ngobefuo he will not want to see me. He will not even like tshe people to call me name..."

"Why?"

"Because he know tshat I do not like tshe type of confusion he is causing in the village.lk Because he know tshat if I am Tsief tshere will be peace, and when tshere is peace he will have no infruence. Ya Excellency I have been willing to saclifice my wealtshy business in Likume and so forth and go back home, if only my plesence will bling back peace. Bot he will not want to see me. He keeps torning tshe heart of tshe people against me.

"When tshe Revelend Fatsher and tshe DO tlied to convince tshat tshey needed a man like me who can hold tshe people together, he got the others and they killed the innocentmen. When tshe boy he had choosen to lule decided tshat he will hand over tshe thlone to me he also included him in tshe deatsh. I know tshat by now again he must have choosen anotsher child who he can use as tshe new Tscief of Small Monje, so tshat tshere should be more trouble."

"Not after I have learnt all this eh," the Governor told him.

"The State needed just this kind of very reliable information to avoid the error repeating itself eh."

Betong then explained:

"Your Excellency, the Chiefs beg you not to misunderstand these small gifts that they have brought to you. They say it is to beg you to understand that they are tired of seeing blood in Small Monje, and that you should put an end to it."

Chapter Three

The nearer the bone, the sweeter the meat.
(*Proverbia Communica*, 801)

When a cow gives birth to something rare,
it is helped in the suckling by it owner.
(Ngumbu Njururi: *Proverb From Gikuyu*)

THE DAY after the three Paramount Chiefs left Tetseale, Captain Abongo arrived from Small Monje. He was Company Commander who had been sent to quell the uprising. He was bringing with him three members of the outrageous Council of Elders which had carried out the brutal murders. They were Ngobefuo, Ndenwontio and Ntongntong. Four more were still in hiding, while three had already been killed by the enraged soldiers before they received the second order to bring them alive.

When the soldiers had just arrived at Small Monje with the instructions to "bring back peace there at any cost" still vibrating in their veins, they began an immediate hunt for the man called Ngobefuo who was said to be the leader of the rebellion. Before the Governor's second orders reached them three old men had been tortured in the process of tracking down Ngobefuo. The soldiers did not know what Ngobefuo actually looked like. Luckily for Ngobefuo they had only set eyes on him after being told not to kill him. The Governor had earlier on received information that the three Elders were being brought.

"Is Ngobefuo amongst them?" he had inquired in fury. He had been told that he was. So as soon as the three men were brought into his office he closed the filed he had been poring over and studied the old men critically.

In the forefront was a diminutive and decrepit old man. He was hardly up to a metre and one half in height, and with a much wrinkled body which showed at the exposed portions of his dress. He wore only a small coat with sleeves cut off at the shoulders and a loin cloth, black with dirt at the seams, which descended just below his knees. There was not a single hair on his head and though it was hard to guess his precise age, he was definitely very old. His brows were very thick and his jaws shrunken as though the flesh had been carved out with a knife. He had no teeth. His eyes, as tiny as those of a bat, seemed to glitter under his hooded brows like a diamond in the dark. His slightly protruding nose rose abruptly over his small mouth with the lips turned inwards with age. His tiny feet were now bare, but he had come dressed in an over-sized pair of discarded army boots which Captain Abongo had compelled him to leave outside the office of the Governor.

They are all new to this environment. But of the three the little old man seemed the most composed, and as soon as he stepped in he fixed an unblinking eye on the Governor. His left hand, as skinny as tanned leather, seemed stuck to a pipe which he fingered ceaselessly in the breast pocket of his sleeveless coat.

The man next to him was much taller. He was certainly over a metre and one half. He might even have been a metre and three quarters. He too was of an indeterminate age. But he was certainly as sold as the little man. Strangely enough, for all his age he had lost very little hair from his head. But his hair was grey, whitish grey. He had fairly bulging eyes below heavy greyish brows. He looked restless and uncomfortable. He would lift his eyes to the Governor, to the walls, and towards the others, even turning round, before looking steadily at the carpet in front of him. He stood, continuously and perhaps unconsciously shaking his left knee without moving his feet from where they seemed to be planted. He wore a dirty threadbare down-reaching velvet gown with a lacerated embroidery running from the neck to the bottom line.

The third man was literally a monster, the prototype of a Cyclops. He towered about two metres and had a large head, the shape of an upturned water melon, and with hair as scanty as a poorly burnt bush with elephant grass. He had only one eye which would have suited his figure better if it had been placed exactly on the space between the blind one and the eye with which he now surveyed the world. He too had very thick brows which drew first together before pulling apart again.

Everything about him seemed to be in proportion to his immense bulk - a broad forehead, a large nose with wide cavernous nostrils out of which a very unpicturesque remnant of snuff trickled down onto a heavy moustache. His mouth was broad and his lips thick and turned outwards. A large scar ran down his left jaw from the corner of his blind eye into a nest of beard under his chin. He wore an old black long-sleeved shirt which hung loosely over his huge loin cloth.

This was the true representative of the Biongong race as history and anthropology recorded them. It was at him that the Governor was looking when he asked through the interpreter:

"Who of you is Ngobefuo?"

Chevrons replaced the lines above the Governor's brows. The pygmy was Ngobefuo! A striking contradiction to what he had deduced from the type of information received about him. The Governor looked from one face to the other incredulously.

"Ngobefuo is that man, Your Excellency," the Captain came to the Governor's aid. He was supported by the interpreter.

"This man?" He was still not convinced.

"He is, Your Excellency."

"Do they have I.D. Cards?"

"They don't Your Excellency. But he is the one. He is Ngobefuo."

Still intent on doubting the Captain the Governor raised his eyes in the direction of the Cyclops and asked:

"Who are you?"

"Ndenwontio, Goment."

"And you?"

"I am Ntongntong, Goment."

"Leave them and the interpreter, with me," the Governor told the Captain. As soon as the door shut behind the Captain the Governor showed them where to sit. There were some five chairs along the wall to the right in front of the Governor. That was where they were to sit.

The taller man had taken two steps towards the chairs but halted as Ngobefuo began to talk.

"Goment. My mind is not here with me," he said. "I beg to talk to you on my feet."

If the Governor still had any lingering doubts as to whether the little man was Ngobefuo, they disappeared that very instance. Who else but such a notorious terrorist could dare to contradict a Governor's orders in that defiant manner. With his mind brimming with vile misinformation about Ngobefuo, the Governor told the others to sit down.

They very promptly obeyed. Turning to Ngobefuo, he said:

"If you choose to answer on your hands, it's your cross."

Ngobefuo did not stir. He looked at nobody. He merely felt his pipe quietly. It was in place. He did not talk.

***

The file for Small Monje had not left the Governor's table since the news of the crisis there reached him. He threw it open, glanced through a few pages and raised his head to address the three men:

"On the seventh of May you took the law of this Republic into your own wicked hands and killed the duly appointed District Officer of your area together with his wife and children. On that same day too you killed your own Paramount Chief along with seven members of his Council. Is that right?"

His voice was deep, resonant and vibrated with anger and threat. But that did not tickle Ngobefuo. He gave the interpreter just enough time to finish, then he inquired:

"By which Goment means the three of us here?"

"Yes."

Ngobefuo did not say he was wrong. He only said:

"On that day that Goment is talking about, the Council of Elders decided in the name of the eleven villages of the tribe of Nkokonoko Small Monje which it represented, to kill those people as punishment for what they did. Goment, that was what happened." He looked across at the others for confirmation.

They nodded their heads but did not open their mouths.

"But at any rate," the Governor resumed, "you three here were there, right?"

Again Ngobefuo did not confirm or refute. He said:

"We were members of the Council too, Goment."

"Meaning therefore that you were there, right?"

"I have said that all the members of the Council of Elders were there, Goment."

The Governor looked irritated by the man's way of responding to the questions. He had brought them to obtain specific facts about what had happened so as to see how it would fit into what he knew already about Ngobefuo.

"Where are the rest of the members?" he inquired.

"We don't know, Goment," Ngobefuo seemed to answer for them all.

"You in particular don't know or all of you?"

"I don't know, Goment. And if my brothers here knew they would have told me. But they have never. So I say we don't know."

"Give me the names of all the members of your council," the Governor requested.

After Ngobefuo had given him he pointed directly at him and asked:

"Who are you?"

"I said Ngobefuo, Goment."

"What position do you hold in your tribe?"

"I am the care-taker, Goment. I lead the Council of Elders."

"You therefore led the Council of Elders to do the killing, am I right?"

Ngobefuo munched his gums and remained silent. He did not like such a lead question. It seemed to demand only the type of answer which would make the need for further explanation unnecessary. And they had come to explain, not to confess guilt. They had come to tell why they did what they did, in detail. When the Governor's question was repeated he said:

"I was the caretaker at that time as I am now."

The Governor wrote down several points.

"Do you, Ngobefuo, belong to the royal line of the tribe of Nkokonoko Small Monje?" he asked.

Ngobefuo looked at the Governor and the interpreter uncomprehendingly.

"Are you a prince?" the Governor asked more precisely.

He remained silent. He owed nobody any apologies for what they had done. No people in their shoes would have behaved differently. Without any doubt, the Government owed them an apology for what the DO did, even though he was already killed. And now the Governor was raising the touchy topic of his background! Somebody must have told the Governor about it so that he should use it to insult him. Of course, he Ngobefuo, was not a prince. He was the grand son of a slave. But so what? He had acquitted himself with distinction in defence of the tradition of the tribe. He had done things no free-born, not even a prince, or an heir-apparent was capable of doing. Why ask whether he was a prince?

"I am no prince," he said defiantly. "I belong to no royal line. But I control the tribe. I control the royal line of Nkokonoko Small Monje."

The Governor noted down something in his file.

"Why do you not belong to the royal line?" he asked.

"A man is born into the royal line, Goment. I do not belong to it because I was not born into it."

"Who gave you that office then?"

"The Chief and the members of the Council."

The Governor's face creased and contorted into a sudden scowl. He drew in his lips and gnawed at them with a grin for a whole minute.

"Nobody gave it to you," he told Ngobefuo. "You seized it." He wanted to add: "You are a slave who grew jealous of the royal line and seized power from a dying Chief." But he changed his mind. It was too obvious to be mentioned.

"Seized from who, Goment?" Ngobefuo raised an enquiring brow.

Now that he was forced to tell the truth aloud, the Governor told him:

"From the late Chief when he lay dying,"

It was Ngobefuo's turn to be amused. There was first a faint crackle down his throat like that of a mother hen, followed by a hoarse cough. The tiny skinny orifice that was his mouth distended in a grotesque grimace of mirthless laugh.

"Haaaaaa!" he shouted. That was surely the Governor's ignorance betraying itself. He talked of the late Chief as though he was a care-taker. He talked of seizing power as if it was a cutlass?

"Goment, the office of care-take cannot be seized like that. It is given to the man in the market. It is everybody who gives it to him. Everybody. A man is care-taker of the tribe, not of his house. It cannot be seized."

The Governor lifted his eyes towards him as if to say "you are talking shit." And indeed it was shit. He had already got the real facts. He had asked the savages to come to see if he could make them confirm what he reliably knew about them already. He had been interested in knowing four things - whether Ngobefuo was indeed the leader of the rebel gang; whether Ngobefuo belonged to the royal line or he was really a slave. He had been interested in knowing whether it was the Council that decided and led the killing; and he had wanted to get the names of the members of the Council. The reason they could have for doing so was absolutely immaterial because they could never speak the truth. He decided he could start working out the measures he would take to solve the problem. He scribbled a few things into the file in front of him for a very long time, and placed his pen down. Summoning every nerve of his authority into his voice he bawled:

"Because you have proved beyond all reasonable doubts that you are absolutely incapable of managing your own affairs, the Government will step in now. You will be ruled directly by us."

"What, Goment?" the three men shouted simultaneously.

"The Government will rule Small Monje."

"Without our Chief?" The threat sounded familiar. Will someone tell the man that they had heard that before, and that the last time that happened somebody lost his head, Ngobefuo thought.

"What Chief? Have you not killed your Chief? I called you here to inform you that from now henceforth the Government will choose whoever he wants to rule you eh," the Governor said calmly but severely. "And the Government will enthrone such a chief himself. Go back to Nkokonoko Small Monje and announce that the Government will be bringing back the man who was supposed to rule since the death of your Fuo-ndee, and make him the rightful Chief. I am talking about Marcus Anuse whom you do know very well, Ngobefuo, as the man to rule."

Ngobefuo looked at Ndenwontio who first looked at Ntongntong before looking at the two others. They felt the same bitterness towards the Governor. Perhaps they were just dreaming. No, they were not dreaming. They were wide awake. They had killed the District Officer. Yes. But they had not done that in madness. They had been severely provoked. They had now come willingly to tell the Governor exactly why they had done so. That way the Governor would know what kind of advice to give to his future agents to that area. But the Governor seemed to have taken them for children or madmen, and had again bruised the scars of the wounds his DO had just inflicted on their traditions. That he had chosen Anuse to rule! That was just throwing excrement into the face of the whole tribe and its traditions. A man who had built a house in which he left rooms open for people to sleep with the daughters of the Chief for him to get money for his trade? A man who had insulted the throne in the market in Likume? What did the Governor mean exactly? He ought to be told immediately that even if it was a joke he was cracking, they had already chosen a new Chief before coming to see him. He told the Governor:

"Goment, we too will want to tell you that the crown, the bangles and the sceptre of the throne of Nkokonoko Small Monje have already been given to Kevin Beckongncho."

"Who? What?"

Ngobefuo repeated himself.

As though in ordinary conversation, the Governor successfully extracted all that he needed to know about the man called Beckongncho from the unsuspecting Ngobefuo.

Chapter Four

There's many a slip
between the cup and the lip.
(Anonymous)

NGOBEFUO, NDENWONTIO, and Ntongntong showed no signs of repentance for the outrages they had perpetrated. Even more than that, they completely refused to discuss anything on the Governor's declaration that he would make Anuse their chief. They made it very clear that there was no human force that could shake them from the decision they had taken in giving the crown, sceptre and bangles of the throne to Kevin Beckongncho. They even dared to add that they had sharpened their cutlasses back home, waiting for the new DO who will question the rightness of the action.

In the Governor's view, this was provocation of the highest order. Yet, he permitted them to return to Nkokonoko Small Monje unmolested, without being subjected to the kind of harsh interrogation that should have been necessary as a preliminary to any further action. That he would regret very much later as a tactical blunder. In his mind he was convinced that he was armed with all the facts of the situation and the one and only solution to the crisis. The three Paramount Chiefs, those three wise men, he thought, had been sent by God to help him out of the mess. There could never be any other source of information that would be more reliable. None. And see just how that villainous Ngobefuo had confirmed every single article of what they had disclosed to him. Utterly mindless of authority, intransigent in extremes. His every word was an insult, a threat to peace. It was indeed a security risk to have given him any position of authority in the tribe in a state that regarded peaceful co-existence as the ideal policy.

31

Anuse! What kind of logic was there to explain the exclusion of such a peace-loving and selfless citizen? Ready to abandon his very lucrative enterprise in Likume, ready to offer money to obtain his own birthright, not for its own sake, but just for the sake of peace. What else was the definition of a good citizen? Those so-called leaders of the so-called Council of Elders, they would be punished accordingly. Every single one of them. But first, Anuse must be installed as the new Chief. Those rebels still in hiding, especially that blood-thirsty Ngangabe! They would be lured back to the palace. And it is only the return of Ngobefuo and the others to Small Monje, unharmed, that would do the trick. That way, even though they still resisted the Government's decision, it should be easier to persuade them to yield. Only thus could the Government deceive them into believing that it sympathized with them. Only thus would they accept Anuse.

Soldiers would lead them back to Small Monje. A pretext would be found to continue to keep them lingering there. It will be said that they were waiting for the installation of the new DO. Without doubt, Ngangabe and his other cohorts would come out to join Ngobefuo. With Anuse then firmly in power they would all be arrested, tried for subversion and summarily executed. That was what was to be done.

Without even investigating the situation further, an error for which he would pay very dearly, the Governor thought that the more pressing issue now was the crown and the other things which the old men claimed they had given to their agent Beckongncho in Sowa. Those things must first be seized and left in the keeping of the Government.

As the old men were leaving for Small Monje the Governor sent a radio message to the DO of Sowa:

The pieces of the puzzle behind the bloody crisis in Nkokonoko Small Monje are finally falling into place. All that remains now is for us to lay hands on the man who is likely to provoke further trouble. Send word to the Government Primary School in Ngeung-ale for the headmaster, a certain Kevin Beckongncho to be led here at once, under police escort. At once.

That's the man we want.

Part Two

Chapter Five

Quem oderint dii, hunc pedagogem fecerunt.
(Anonymous)

*T*HE SOWA Government Primary School in Ngeung-
ale of which Kevin Bekongncho was a co-
headmaster ran a two shift system. Every other week one
headmaster, a set of teachers and pupils attended classes from 7.30
am to 12 noon. Another headmaster took over with another set of
teachers and pupils thereafter. Beckongncho had been on duty in
the afternoons of the previous week. It was now Wednesday and
he had had his afternoons free since Monday. On that sunny
Wednesday he lay resting in his bedroom. It must have been around
2 pm when he heard the noise of a vehicle drive up to his compound
and halt. He had not quite fallen asleep. He heard his dog bark
several times round the house and as he sat up in bed he heard his
small son tell his mother:

"Mammy, soja de cam plenty for has."

Mrs. Beckongncho was dressed simply in a loin cloth which she
wrapped over her breasts. Sowa could get very hot in the privacy
of their homes. The woman went through the narrow corridor to
meet the visitors in front of the house. They were not soldiers but
policemen, three policemen. When she called the yelling dog and
held it by the strap round its neck, the three men climbed down
from the deep blue Jeep.

"You go tie the dog-eh, madam," one shouted carelessly.

"Okey sa," the woman answered.

One of the windows of Beckongncho's room overlooked the
main road, so that when he pulled the curtain slightly he saw the
visitors. At first he had thought the vehicle might belong to the
parents of one of his pupils who visited him from time to time.
When his wife, answering to the demand went to tie the dog behind
the house, he noticed the three men walk assertively to the veranda.
They were all carrying guns.

"Welcome sir," Mrs Beckongncho said as soon as she came back. The man did not care about the greeting.

"Where is Mr. Kevin Beckongncho?" he barked. His face remained cast in a mould of anger.

"Come in sir. Sit down," she implored.

Two of the men walked through the veranda and stood at the open door. The woman went into one of the rooms presumably, according to them, to fetch her husband. That permitted them to look into the house. What they saw awed and impressed them. The roads in Hausa Quarters where Beckongncho lived were untarred and could become very dusty during the dry season. There was nothing anybody could ever do to keep out the dust from entering cupboards, bookshelves, wardrobes and even boxes. It was even said, though by way of an exaggeration, that a man once opened a tin of sardine in that quarter but could not eat it because of the amount of dust that had found its way into it.

Yet, dusty as the whole environment was wont to be, there was not a single visible speck of dust either on the brown Formica top of the tables or the armchairs. There was a brown plastic carpet that ran from wall to wall. In the centre of the room was laid a large multi-coloured rug, probably purchased from Northern Nigeria, or from some Muslim who may have brought it back from a pilgrimage to Mecca. The portion of the carpet that was not covered by the rug and which showed between the armchairs in the centre and under the dining table at the far corner looked polished, as though someone had been hired to clean it every five minutes. Flowers hung from pots at various corners of the ceiling.

The policemen lifted their eyes to the walls. The polished brownness of the wood around a massive wall-clock bespoke the same commitment to neatness. Above the clock in very bold lettering was carved the adage:

CLEANLINESS IS NEXT TO GODLINESS

And indeed it was really next to godliness because on the wall opposite the clock hung two pictures of Christ, one with Him on the cross and the other with Him tending his flock.

***

Beckongncho was a God-fearing man, who no longer went to church. This needs to be explained because it was a blemish in his life which he knew and which he himself publicly admitted. The decision not to attend holy mass was reached some three years ago. He had been invited along with his wife to attend the wedding of a former pupil of his at the Nenkom parish, not too far from the cathedral where he regularly attended mass.

All went well. He was especially impressed by a certain Father Malikintan, a dark thick-set man of medium height, in just about his late thirties or early forties, who was to bless the wedding. The priest was a born orator with a wooing tongue and perhaps some hypnotic powers by which he was able to convince everybody present to offer something substantial to the church. As the alms were given he castigated all evil, advised the couple to adhere to their marriage vows, to love their neighbours as themselves and things of the sort.

The priest left immediately he finished saying the mass. The congregation was gradually walking out for pictures to be taken with the newly-weds when Beckongncho sensed that he might have to go to stool. He did not know anybody in the neighbourhood, so he ran into the Parish Secretariat to seek help.

"Ass Father," one of the wardens said, when he explained his problem. He walked up to Father Malikintan, greeted and said:

"Father, I am dying. I think I have a running stomach. I need to go to toilet right away. Please help me."

Malikintan had been receiving money from some people and recording it at the same time. When Beckongncho spoke he looked up at him and returned to his writing without saying anything.

"Please, Father, I am really dying," Beckongncho begged like a child, actually clasping the seat of his trousers as if to hold back the pressure.

"We have no public toilet here," Malikintan said, and turned to the next person for his fees. By this time Beckongncho's sphincters were on the verge of explosion. One of the women in the group offered to save Beckongncho. She searched her purse for a key which she gave him.

"That is the house opposite," she said. "There is a toilet to the right as you enter the parlour." She pointed to a house just outside the Parish gates.

Beckongncho grabbed the keys, thanked the woman and hurried out. Malikintan might have felt a little guilty because he seemed to try to clear himself:

If it is a running stomach that he has, and he goes to toilet here once, how is that going to stop it?"

Some people found it funny. Just a few. The rest stood silent, scandalised, many of whom knew Beckongncho well as a man of integrity. When Beckongncho returned he thanked the woman again, went up to his wife and told the story. He decided he would not stay on for the rest of the ceremony. She too decided to leave with him. It was she who told their hosts that her husband was not feeling well, and that they needed to go home at once to try to help him.

Beckongncho generally kept his feelings and problems to himself. But Father Malikintan's conduct bothered him so much that he told his wife he would write to him.

"I want to give him a piece of my mind," he said "What do you want to say to him?" she asked.

"Condemn his behaviour and demand an immediate apology," he said.

She did not dissuade him, but she asked:

"If he does not reply?"

"He had to," Beckongncho told her. "If he doesn't I will consider something else."

That night too he spoke to a lawyer friend of his, a certain Lekechacha Luke, and the other head master of the school. Both men condemned Malikintan's conduct and agreed that the should write to him. But, again, they wondered whether the letter would change such a man. They even went on to disclose several other atrocities perpetrated by the Reverend Father. They told him how the man made passes at people's wives, and how he divulged secrets he got from people during confessions. Beckongncho sat down and drafted the letter:

Dear Father Malikintan;

The writer of this letter is Kevin Beckongncho, co-headmaster of Government Primary School, Ngeung-ale. I am writing to totally deplore your behaviour towards me yesterday during a marriage ceremony at your Parish. I entered your office in all politeness to explain that I had suddenly developed a stomach complication which made it necessary for me to use a toilet. Without even raising your head you declared that your toilets were not for the public.

A black man, Father, talking to another black man like that! Then after some Good Samaritan had offered to give me the chance to ease myself you wondered aloud how I could solve a running stomach just by going to stool once. Such callousness, Father, I find to my thinking totally incompatible with the basic tenets of your calling which should be to help the needy. And I dare say you turned a deaf ear to my dire request while at the same time collecting monies from faithful Christians like myself.

If you were under the impression that my using your toilet facility would violate the sanctity of the Parish, or cause the spread of cholera, then I can only remind the holy Father that even the Good Lord, whose example on earth you are supposed to emulate, dined with sinners of all categories.

I would also like to remind you that even if it was an automatic toilet you have in there, it was purchased off the generous donations of Christians like my humble self.

Dear Father Malikintan, I intend to take this issue a step further, should you think this act is not of such gravity as to warrant an immediate apology.

Sincerely Yours,
Kevin Beckongncho.

To give the matter the seriousness that it deserved he took the letter to the mission himself. Malikintan read it and told him to go to hell.

"The Archbishop will hear this matter," Beckongncho told the man.

"You can write to the Pope, if you think this Parish is a clinic for cholera patients," the priest retorted.

Determined to hurt the man, Beckongncho returned and wrote a very strongly worded letter to the Archbishop on the issue. When he mentioned to his lawyer friend the new line of action he had taken the man simply told him:

"I don't see how the Archbishop will react to such a case. That Malikintan man is from his tribe."

That did not discourage him. He did not take the letter there himself. He sent somebody else. One whole week later, he read from His Grace. the reply was a quotation from the Holy Bible. Behind a card bearing the picture of Christ talking to his disciples, the Holy One wrote:

Dear Mr. Beckongncho;
Your letter was received.
Thanks. But remember the Good Lord:
JUDGE NOT, THAT YE BE NOT JUDGED. FOR WITH
WHAT JUDGMENT YE JUDGE, YE SHALL BE JUDGED;
AND WITH WHAT MEASURE YE METE, IT SHALL BE
MEASURED TO YOU AGAIN.
May God Bless you.

Prior to that event Beckongncho went to church regularly and donated generously. He may not have taken the best decision in life, but thereafter, if he went to church at all it was mainly because his wife had persuaded him to see that staying at home on Sundays would be setting a bad example for their children.

"Let them also go to church," she said. "And if they later have reason for not going, that will be their problem, not ours. Let them not begin by staying away like you."

These facts were family secrets, and you needed to be very close to the Beckongncho family to know them. The policeman was a stranger to the family and so had every reason to look overwhelmed by the Godliness in the house

***

To the right as you entered the house stood a huge mahogany cupboard that must have been a metre and one half high and about three metres long. On it stood a record player, a radio cassette and a record holder on which the very first records read: *HANDEL: The Messiah, MOZART and BEETHOVEN - Petite Musique de nuit*, and GREAT MOMENTS IN OPERA. There were some Ghanaian and Nigerian High Life records by E.T. Mensah, Victor Olaya, and Bobby Benson. There were a few Miriam Makeba records, a few Christmas Carols by Harry Belafonte. At the extreme end of the cupboard was a set of *ENCYCLOPEDIA BRITANNICA* beside which lay three books. THE THIRD REICH, T.E. Lawrence's SEVEN PILLARS OF WISDOM and PEATE'S COMMENTARY ON THE BIBLE. Above the cupboard stood a board bearing some writings which compelled one of the officers to step in and read the contents which seemed to fascinate him. It read:

```
   MONEY
MONEY NO DOUBT, IS A POWER"
BUT A POWER OF WELL-DEFINED AND
      NARROW LIMITS.
IT WILL PURCHASE PLENTY, BUT NOT PEACE: IT WILL
FURNISH YOUR TABLE
      WITH LUXURIES,
BUT NOT YOU WITH AN APPETITE TO ENJOY THEM, IT
WILL SURROUND YOUR SICK-BED
      WITH PHYSICIANS,
BUT NOT RESTORE HEALTH TO YOUR
      SICKLY FRAME,
IT WILL ENCOMPASS YOU WITH A CLOUD OF
FLATTERERS.
BUT NEVER PROCURE YOU ONE TRUE
      FRIEND;
IT WILL BRIBE INTO SILENCE THE TONGUES
      OF ACCUSING MEN,
BUT NOT AN ACCUSING CONSCIENCE;
      IT WILL PAY SOME DEBTS,
BUT NOT THE LEAST ONE OF ALL YOUR DEBTS TO
THE LAW OF GOD; IT WILL RELIEVE MANY FEARS,
      BUT NOT THOSE OF GUILT
THE TERRORS THAT CROWN THE BROWS
      DEATH.
            (ANONYMOUS)
```

Over the dining table section hung another board which compelled the inquisitive policeman to go further in. It read:

12 THINGS TO REMEMBER

1. THE VALUE OF TIME
2. THE SUCCESS OF PERSEVERANCE
3. THE PLEASURE OF WORKING
4. THE DIGNITY OF SIMPLICITY
5. THE WORTH OF CHARACTER
6. THE POWER OF KINDNESS

7. THE INFLUENCE OF EXAMPLE
8. THE WISDOM OF ECONOMY
9. THE VIRTUE OF PATIENCE
10. THE IMPROVEMENT OF TALENT
11. THE OBLIGATION TO DUTY
12. THE JOY OF ORIGINATING
(Marshall Field)

The skin of an enormous python spanned the length of the wall over the cupboard. The officers, now oblivious of their mission, might have spent much more time marvelling at the orderly arrangement of things in the house had not Mrs. Beckongncho's return from the room interrupted them. She came out this time wearing a blouse of the same make as the loin cloth she had on when they first arrived. That seemed a more reasonable attire in which to receive guests.

"Where is he?" the officer repeated.

"I said he is sleeping," the woman insisted.

"Na lie mammy," the small boy interrupted. "Yi just dey for bed."

"But we say you wake him up!"

"When he is sleeping nobody is allowed to wake him up."

"What kind of law is that?"

The woman shrugged.

"Is he a Reverend Father? Show us where he is sleeping."

The woman did not move. Even the five-year old boy refused to lead them, indicating that the entire family knew Beckongncho's orders could not be contravened.

One of the men glanced at his watch and said:

"Madam, if in one minute you don't show us where your husband is sleeping you will answer for it, you hear? We no come here for play."

Beckongncho himself had heard them and change into a T-Shirt and a pair of trousers. When he emerged from the room the officer said immediately:

"Good afternoon, Mr. Kevin Beckongncho,"

"Good afternoon," he responded with a slight tinge of uneasy suspicion at the sheer formality of the address. Beckongncho was not a man to insist on being called by his title, but it had become his name to call him. H.M, which was the colloquial abbreviation for his official title of Head Master. Everybody called him that, even children. Very few people knew his real name. That was the way all the policemen he had so far met called him. And those who had come in knew him well enough to avoid any undue formality. But they had chosen to call his two names. This made him wonder.

"Anything, officers?" He too decided to be more formal. "Sit down for Christ's sake," he entreated them courteously.

The two men hesitated for sometimes as people do when they have to give bad news to somebody they respect or fear. One stepped forward and said:

"This is for you." Beckongncho rose and came toward him and showed his hand. He placed an envelope in it and asked him to open it and read.

Beckongncho tore it open and took out a curt note:

CONVOCATION:

To Mr. Kevin Beckongncho.

MESSAGE:

Your presence is urgently wanted at the District Office.

Signed.

The District Officer

Sowa.

"Thank you very much," he said to the officers. "Tell him I am on my way coming," he added, placing the note on the table to go in and change clothes.

The man hesitated for a while.

"The District Officer says we should return with you," one of them said.

"**WITH** me?"

"That was his order. It is written there, sir."

Beckongncho sensed that there was something wrong, even if he could not tell what it was. His brows drew together into a knot of amazement. His wife had gone back to the kitchen behind the house. When she overheard the sharp exchanges she came to ask him what the matter was.

"The District Officer of Sowa has sent these officers to come and bring me to his office."

"In their lorry?"

"They say those are the orders. Go back and take care of the children," he told her and went in to dress up. He had put on his trousers, shirt, coat and was just about to knot his neck tie when one officer announced impatiently:

"The District Officer said we should bring you back at once."

"But what if you did not meet me in? It's just by coincidence that I am at home now."

"But we met you."

He abandoned the tie, laced his shoes and came out to join them, taking his wallet with him. They asked him to move ahead of them. He did and they followed him out of the house into the waiting Jeep.

***

Talk of best integrated men alive, Beckongncho was one of them. In an age of widespread duplicity, an age where morality had become a vice, an age when headmasters used their offices to line their own pockets and make wives of their pupils and members of staff, Kevin Beckongncho conducted himself with scrupulous discipline and respect. He never trifled with the virtues (if it is possible to use such a word to describe them these days) of his pupils or female members of staff. He treated everybody with loved and respect, without fear or favour, accepted no bribes, and yet was ready to render anybody any service that lay within his reach without expectations of a reward of any kind. His records were clean. He was very aware of this fact, and liked to keep them so.

As he was being marched into the Jeep, neighbours and some passers-by who happened to have seen the vehicle stood watching and what they all saw contradicted anything they knew of Beckongncho. No doubt, rumour-mongers amongst them were ready to make anything out of the situation — bribery, misappropriation of public funds, or impregnation of school girls. Anything. One woman in particular said:

"I be dong talk say one day one day tha money go comot some man for nose."

A lesser man would have protested against this indignity, if only to let the on-lookers see that he was innocent.

But Beckongncho yielded with a resigned dignity that made it impossible for the officers to raise either their voices or hands at him.

44

Chapter Six

The bigger they come, the harder they fall.
(James Corbett)

*T*HE SUN continued to pour its unrelenting rays on Sowa when the blue Jeep carrying Beckongncho wheeled into the premises of the District Officer. A police officer jumped down first, asked Beckongncho to get down, and as soon as he jumped down the second officer dramatized the whole situation by jumping immediately after him, making it look like they were guarding him from escape. They all walked up to the door, knocked and without waiting for an answer from within entered.

The DO, a man in his fifties had turned and was sitting with his right shoulder to the door, his left hand clasping the telephone receiver. In front of him was a blank sheet of paper on which he was scribbling meaningless letters and criss-crossing lines as he spoke. They all remained standing until he pushed the receiver aside and swung half to the right, facing the visitors. He then ran his hand over his well-polished forehead several times, looked straight at Beckongncho and in a tone that is customary in addressing condemned criminals, he said: "Mr. Kevin Beckongncho, you are wanted without no delay forthwith by the Provincial Governor in Tetseale."

The spittle dried from Beckongncho's mouth instantly. Metropolitan Sowa had only three Government Primary Schools. By virtue of his position as co-head of one of these institutions he had always figured among the special guests invited to parties in the DO's residence or the Cultural Centre on many important occasions. Besides, the DO had come to his office twice within the last school year to discuss the progress of his two children there with him.

This did not, however, imply that any particular bond of friendship existed between the two men. But Beckongncho was painfully convinced that the man was sufficiently acquainted with him and the position he held in that community to treat him with greater respect than he had shown.

He did not, of course, expect the DO to greet him, or to smile to him. But he could even have sent a telephone message and he would come. It did not need a whole contingent to make him come.

Again, he did not, of course, expect the DO to stop talking in the phone and welcome him. But it was no impossibility to use one's hand to indicate a welcome or show somebody a set while at the same time conversing over the phone. He, Beckongncho, had done that on numerous occasions, had seen the DO do it before, and was confident he could still have done so. But the DO had chosen not to. He had chosen to leave him standing between the officers as though he were some much- wanted, some notorious criminal! The DO had even denied him the opportunity to greet him.

What hurt Beckongncho like a physical pain was the sheer banality of the conversation which left him standing as though he had come to ask for some special favour from a god. The DO, probably was talking to a girl when they came in, for as soon as they entered the office he swung his easy chair first to the right and half-way to the left. He was saying:

"Aaaha, you know the man wey you di joke with am? My own thing nodi hard. When I hold you I go nakam, nakam."

Later he was heard saying:

"You craze tin, hole be hole. You no know so? all water de quench fire. Cow de old liver de old?" The note on which he ended the conversation was:

"A promise is a debt. So before you promise, think thrice because, you know my engine saw how i de cut."

"Does the District Officer know by any chance why I am being wanted at Tetseale with such urgency?" he inquired with subdued anxiety, but with the politeness that was second nature to him.

The DO eyed him malevolently, insolently, suspiciously. It only remained for him to say "you stupid idiot, you know exactly what you are. Why pretend?" He twisted his lips obscenely and asked:

"You are from Small Monje right?"

Beckongncho cocked his ears as if straining to catch a distant sound. His eyes moved round the office. Was anybody else listening? His heart beat faster, he held his hands behind and stretched a bit, then he ground the knuckles of both hands against each other. He seemed to bend and straighten the toes in the shoes. He looked at the DO again, the man was still looking at him with fixed intensity, expecting an answer. Beckongncho bit his lower lip, and with his eyes blinking or rather twitching at the corners he untied his hands behind his back and said calmly:

"I am, Sir." The SIR came as an after thought, as though its inclusion might soften the matter.

"Your coming here has to do with Small Monje. You know fully well what you have done there." The DO turned away immediately, implying that he was in no mood to continue any dialogue with a confirmed scoundrel.

Beckongncho felt a very rare flutter in his veins which he immediately fought hard to conceal. He smacked his lips and shook his head briskly. He was wanted in Tetseale by the Provincial Governor in connection with the disturbances in Nkokonoko Small Monje! That gave the clue, the vital clue to the DO's contemptuous attitude towards him.

It may now not matter how much the people of Ngeung-ale in particular and Sowa in general loved and respected him. It may now not matter how efficiently he had discharged his duty over the years. He came from Nkokonoko Small Monje, to which he was still bound like a tree to its roots, like the umbilical cord bound the child to the mother's womb. Small Monje had just gone through a series of bloody events, and he, Kevin Beckongncho knew he had been directly involved in the crisis at every crucial stage. He reviewed his involvement in his mind. He could feel each thought pressing down on him until it seemed to suffocate him. There was something he wanted to know: just how much did the Government know about his involvement in the crisis?

"When am I wanted in Tetseale?" he inquired. His voice sounded as though his vocal chords had been compressed.

"Now." The DO gestured to the Jeep outside. "That vehicle is ready to take you there, right away."

"In that case I go back and inform my wife, Sir?" His voice was weirdly hoarse. He had to clear his throat twice before talking again.

"There is not that much time, I am afraid," the DO said.

"That I can't even inform my wife?"

"You have to go right away. Your wife will be informed."

"Am I under arrest then, Sir?"

"You would have been told. Please they are waiting for you outside."

The DO gave orders for him to be led away.

Chapter Seven

He who is circumcised outside his house stead
does not face the enemy bravely.
(Ngumbu Njururi: *Gikuyu Proverb*)

THE SAME Jeep that brought Beckongncho from
his house to the DO's office took him to Tetseale, a
distance of some four hundred kilometres. They left at about
5 pm, had four breakdowns and arrived at about the same time the
following day.

Two policemen had escorted him and they had stopped short of
putting handcuffs on him. Beckongncho had refused to eat or drink
anything in two of the police stations where they had halted. He
had hardly even closed his eyes by way of sleeping.

His mind was gnawed by an unrelieved apprehension of the
consequences that awaited him in Tetseale. He was dying to know
how much the Government knew already concerning his
involvement in the uprising. The DO of Sowa had told him that he
was not under arrest.

Whom was he fooling? He was just being ridiculous. Force a
man out of his house and secret him at gun-point to Tetseale without
allowing him to say a word to his wife and children. What else is
arrest? He would not attempt to deny his involvement in the affairs
of Small Monje. He would accept it, but he would give them the
facts of the situation as he knew them. The whole truth. If they
were ever to allow him to defend himself, and if they were ever
able to listen, he would make them reason with him.

***

Beckongncho may ultimately have been detained. But from the
Governor's standpoint, whether he would be locked up or not would
depend on how he would respond to the interrogation as soon as

49

he arrived. The Governor usually stopped receiving visitors at 4.30 pm. After several breakdowns the Jeep bringing Beckongncho from Sowa arrived at 6 pm The policemen knew that they could not take Beckongncho to the Governor's residence. From the manner they had seen the DO for Sowa treat him, they felt that there was only one place to take him to: The Central Police Station.

There the driver climbed down first and shut his door immediately as if afraid that Beckongncho would storm his way out of the vehicle and perhaps escape. The man to Beckongncho's right jumped down and ordered him to climb down.

"Follow me," he shouted.

The second policeman stepped behind Beckongncho so that the two more or less hemmed him in signifying maximum security. The three mounted the steps and passed through a large veranda on which friends and relatives of detainees sat on benches on either side of the entrance, conversing in soft tones, eyeing one another each time a new convict arrived.

A large wall-to-wall counter occupied the left as they entered the building proper. It was so high that you could not see anybody sitting on the other side. The policemen stopped in front of the counter and drew the attention of the officer on duty. The man whose friends called him **"Django"** must have been about two metres tall, for when he rose, he leaned over the high counter as though it were a mere writing desk. He was without his cap and one could see a large bald head which seemed to have been made from two panel-beaten sections. The ridge separating the two parts ran from above one ear to the other, across the middle of his head.

"So, na how?" Django bellowed to the visitors.

"Governor will see him tomorrow," the first policeman said.

"O.K, okay," the man nodded and using his left index finger drew a right-to-left arc, indicating that Beckongncho should walk round into his office space. The two men who brought him conversed with each other for a while, walked away gradually and casually until they could neither be seen or heard.

Beckongncho surveyed the man's office from the door. Below, a large table stood close to the counter, with many files and thick ledgers on it. A small parcel of groundnuts lay on one of the files while the peelings lay in a dirty cement-bag paper near the right edge of the table. To the right of the porch stood a large cupboard without shutters, exposing three shelves stuffed with dirty clothing: socks, caps, shirts, shorts, trousers of different colours, shoes and the like, from which an uncomfortable odour issued.

"Insite," Django ordered Beckongncho belligerently.

He stepped in.

Django pulled his chair, sat down facing the visitor and with his elbow leaning on the table asked:

"Ya own na weti?"

Beckongncho was standing about two metres away, but he could smell *afofo* or some other kind of cheap alcohol in the man's breath.

"You mean-eh," he looked at Django, his mood having undergone a sudden revulsion mixed with obstinacy.

"I say your problem is what?"

"Nothing," Beckongncho said. "I don't know why I am here. I was supposed to come to see the Governor."

Django smiled gently at first before he burst out laughing, exposing a very complicated dental formula. One could see three teeth each struggling to get under the other, in the upper row and two in the lower once, one carrying the other. Perhaps there were more, but they must have been hidden far inside his jaws. He seemed to completely ignore the latter part of Beckongncho's answer.

"You don't know why you are here?" he asked.

"I don't know," Beckongncho repeated.

"Okay, undress na," Django said.

Beckongncho looked into the man's eyes. They were red, perhaps from drink, perhaps from birth, he could not tell. But they made him look like some untamed animal, a tiger or a venomous cobra staring at its prey. He made no movement. When the man repeated his order he said:

"I have not done anything to deserve this. Perhaps you are making a mistake. I have told you that I came here on the Governor's invitation."

"I gif you wan to fife," Django said with a fury in his voice.

"When Governor want see you I de send na police Jeep for bring you? If you no strip I go strip you. And I strip with my stick," he shouted, striking his baton on the files on the table, scattering both his groundnuts and the peeling across the table.

Beckongncho saw both the risk and the futility of arguing with the monster. He took off his coat, then the shirt. Django stared into his eyes and used his baton to point at the shirt. Django stared into his eyes and used his baton to point at his singlette.

Beckongncho took it off. He did not know where to put the things.

"Instite there," Django ordered him, pointing to one of the overstuffed shelves in the huge cupboard.

Beckongncho heaved a long sigh, folded the things carefully and placed on the clothes in the uppermost shelf.

"Remove the trousers too," Django said, in a freezing tone.

Beckongncho bit his lips and asked:

"Please, won't you tell me what I have done to be disgraced like this?"

Django took one long step and holding the waist band of the pair of trousers indicated that he would tear off his body.

"Let me do it myself," Beckongncho begged.

"When are committing crimes you are children," Django mumbled. "When you reach the Police Station you want to be treated like a **DO.**"

"I am no criminal," Beckongncho supplicated.

"Yes, Mr. No Criminal, welcome to this church." Django said. "You say you be Governor i classmate..."

"I did not say that," Beckongncho tried to correct him. "I said..."

"Whatever you said, go insite. There are many other Governor's brothers and friends like you insite." Django was talking and placing his itching baton on Beckongncho's back and pushing him gently towards a large black door of cast iron at the end of the wall along which stood the cupboard of clothes. But as he pushed Beckongncho forward a current seemed to pass through him as though he had touched the untouchable. He withdrew the stick, went back on his own and taking Beckongncho's pair of trousers gave him and asked him to put it on.

"Thank you," Beckongncho appreciated the favour. He put it on and walked towards the door.

Django reached for a bundle of keys from a nail at the window, put one into the key-hole and turned twice to the left. The hinges groaned and the door pulled apart just wide enough to admit Beckongncho's bulk.

***

It was as though a witch's cauldron had been thrown open. A thick current of foul air threatened to hold Beckongncho in check at the door.

"Insite," Django growled.

Beckongncho put his right foot in and as soon as his left heel disappeared the hinges groaned again, followed by a bang with which the door closed. He remained standing near the door. He did not know where to go because the room was dark, except for two shafts of light that stole in from two narrow windows virtually on the roof.

He thought he had heard noises from within when he was being bullied at the porch. But now there was no sign of anybody inside.

Just then he heard a voice:

"Let there be light."

Somebody switched on the light, a faint lone 25-watt bulb on the ceiling some five metres away. Beckongncho looked round.

Indeed there were people inside. He studied his new environment very fast, in spite of the bitterness. It was a large room about seven or eight metres long and about five metres wide. There were about twelve or more people inside, all naked save for their thin and messy stinking underpants.

Along the width opposite the entrance there was a closed door with the name **JOHANESBERG** written boldly in white chalk. Six people sat with their backs to the wall on both sides along the length of the room. One sat on a dais in the middle and two sat in front of him, one on either side of him. They stared at him in such a long stony silence that he was forced to say:

"Good evening."

They must have planned and rehearsed their reaction hundreds of times in the past because they all burst into uproarious laughter. When they stopped the man on the dais asked:

"You say what?"

"I just greeted," Beckongncho said.

"Your jaws do what?" the man on the dais inquired with unprovoked anger.

"I did not say jaws," Beckongncho said calmly. "I said just. I said I *just* greeted."

The inmates laughed again. When they stopped the man on the dais asked again:

"Did you go to school?"

"Today?" Beckongncho looked over at the man. The question was as absurd as it was vague.

"You be dong ever go school?" another inmate asked bit more seriously.

"I think so," Beckongncho said, gently casting glances from one face to the other.

"Turn and read the notice," the man pointed to the door behind him on which was carved the command:

KNOCK BEFORE YOU ENTER.

Beckongncho's lips formed an embarrassed smile. A smile in difficulty.

"Did you knock?" the man on the dais inquired.

Beckongncho threw his hands in the air helplessly and said:

"But the command is inside, and I was coming from outside..." While he was yet talking there was a knock at the door.

"Yess, comin," they all shouted. You would think it was a scene they were reenacting, for presently the door opened and a new inmate joined them.

Beckongncho would learn in the not-too-distant future that when a man knocked it was a sign that he had been in there before, and so must be treated with special respect.

"**Protocol**," the man on the dais shouted.

"Your Excellency," one of the men sitting to his right jumped up.

"Give Ambassador a seat."

The new arrival was taken to a corner and shown where to sit. Beckongncho tried to follow him.

"Stand there, you lackofhomtraining," **Excellency** shouted. Beckongncho froze in his track.

"Where are you from," **Excellency** asked.

"I am from Sowa," Beckongncho told him. He did not know for how long he would live among these people, so he instinctively fell in line with them. But not quite so.

Excellency did not look satisfied with Beckongncho's answer. He turned to the young man who had just been pushed in and repeated his question.

"From Cameroon," the young man said.

"Where are you how?" **Excellency** inquired.

"**ZZ-ZAAN-ZZIB-BAARRR,**" the man said, the others joining in as soon as he pronounced the first syllable.

Excellency looked across at Beckongncho as if to inquire whether he got the message.

"You are a visitor to Zanzibar, you hear?" The man pointed to the name over the door.

"Yes," Beckongncho said, looking above the door again.

"Say, **Yes Your Excellency,** Protocol corrected him.

"Yes Your Excellency," Beckongncho said with suppressed amusement. He could as well play the fool. after all what could be worse.? as his people would say:

"A man who has fallen into a latrine
should not fear to fart inside."

"**Information!**"

"Your Excellency," somebody answered.

"Over to you!"

The second man walked up to Beckongncho who was still standing up and asked him to kneel down.

He hesitated for a while but went down. The man began; "Take this paper in your right hand and repeat after me." Beckongncho took and repeated after him:

"The evidence that I shall give, shall be the truth, the whole truth, and nothing but the truth."

The man then went on to inquire about Beckongncho's name, tribe, profession in Cameroon and the like. It was when Beckongncho responded to the question as to why he was in there that they found something amusing. After a long laugh Information asked him:

"At the emigration outside there, what did they write on your entry visa?"

Beckongncho moved his knees, they had begun to ache.

"Nothing," he said when the man repeated the question.

"Ya work is what?"

"HM. Headmaster," he said.

The man thought for a while.

"You pregnant school pikin?"

Beckongncho shook his head in denial.

"You climb man i woman?"

"No," he said.

"You chop School fee?"

Beckongncho shook his head in denial again.

"Maybe you wanted to go to **JOHNESBERG** instead," Information said, pointing to the door at the far corner. Again Beckongncho would learn that **JOHNESBERG** was the toilet where they locked up recalcitrant inmates.

"Finance!"

"Excellency."

"Over to you!"

Excellency tapped one of the men nearest to him. the man went up to Beckongncho and ordered:

"Declare ya assest."

"What?" Beckongncho asked. How could he declare his assets in jail? Somebody told him that they wanted to know how much money he had in his pocket. **Excellency** then went on to explain the reasons for the exercise. The money would be used to buy food for those who do not have relatives to feed them. He was further told that when food was brought nobody refused, even if he did not have the appetite. When they were sure that lunch was no longer expected, they would all sit down and have the food shared out amongst them.

"Nobody starves in ZANZIBAR," **Excellency** ended up.

"Justice,"

"Excellency."

"Over to you," **Excellency** said.

The man to the right of **Excellency** rose and came up to question Beckongncho further on the reasons for his detention.

Beckongncho stood firm on the declaration that he did not know why he had been brought there. But the inmates were used to hearing people swear and retract. They persuaded him to tell them what he suspected even remotely as the possible cause of his arrest and detention. One of them, a jailbird, told him that the trial he would undergo in **ZANZIBAR** would be the same as the one he would eventually undergo in the court in Cameroon.

"The mind of the Lawyer and Magistrate work exactly like we own in here," he said. "Thas why they call them to ass we question." They only difference, the man added, was that a Lawyer and a Magistrate could easily declare a man guilty and send him to jail.

"Tell we what you tink" the man went on," and we sha tell you wha they will ass you, and how you wi hanswer them."

***

Beckongncho did not think he was incapable of defending himself before anybody. But at the same time he thought it would be wrong to ignore any counsel that may make it easier for him to confront the authorities. Besides, these were hardened criminals. He therefore decided to tell them all he knew about the Small Monje crisis: how he had read and interpreted a letter to the Elders which had caused the rejection of Nkoaleck as the new Chief, how he had brought the news of the missing statue to the Elders which had led to the arrest and execution of Nchindia and the others, how on the night of the discovery of the theft by the Elders, Ngobefuo had taken him to show him where he hid some important items belonging to the throne of Small Monje.

The people listened very carefully and in the end told him to tell the court or his interrogators only what he knew they knew already.

"If you know someting they don know, keep it unti they press it out of you," They warned him not so say he read a letter and interpreted to the Elders which sparked off so much trouble; that he should not even mention that he knew that part of it since nobody could prove that he did; that he should never say his personal investigations led to the discovery of the theft of the statue. Finally, that he should not mention the hidden articles. Somebody even said he was being wanted to produce the things.

"But what if they prove that I knew more than I have told them?" Beckongncho inquired.

"They cannot proof. Ya head is not cupboard they wi open to see what you refused to remove. Anytime they say someting true wish you did not want to say, say you had said it. If they argue, tell them you tought yu have said so. Tell them you forgot. Who does not forget?"

Beckongncho remained silent.

"But member," the man continued. "Dont't over hanswer. Sometimes people go to prison jus because they hanswer question whish they no ass them."

Beckongncho would remember this all his life.

***

The morning after their arrival in Tetseale Central Police Station the Governor was informed that Beckongncho had been brought and that he spent the night in the cell. He did not query anybody as to why Beckongncho had been kept there. He did not ask to talk to Beckongncho. He merely told the officer who brought the message that he must not be beaten or tortured until he had interrogated him. His word was done at and the closing hours of that day he ordered Beckongncho into his presence.

It was the Governor who greeted first.

"Good evening, sirr! he said.

"Good evening, Your Excellency," Beckongncho answered. He knew the sir in the Governor's greeting was a mere mockery.

The Governor studied him as he walked towards his desk.

Beckongncho had a large skull with rapidly receding hair. You could tell he was not naturally bald, for there was a tuft of hair that stuck stubbornly just above his fore-head, indicating where probably not too long ago, the hair ended in front. There was then a gap that rose in an arch which curved into the middle of his head. The gap, as shiny as a calabash in the sun, ended in scanty hair that gave way immediately to a baldness that moved in from the occiput. His forehead was creased, his eyebrows thick, his eyes sleepy but clear as spring water, his nose broad with wide open nostrils, and his mouth rather small. You would guess that although his face looked bushy he shaved regularly because there were two fairly distinct layers of hair. First you could see a layer of thick hair from jaw to jaw passing under a much thicker and greying layer of hair on the chin. Then on both sides towards the ears and towards the eyes, nose and mouth, there were strands of hair that had grown within the last week, blurring the boundary line between the two layers.

He had a thick moustache that stretched from one end to the other over the upper lip. Below his lower lip a line of hair ran from the centre of the lower edge to the beard on his chin giving that area a W shape with hair forming the outer portion. He wore a much rumpled black coat and trousers. The shirt underneath was dirty and equally rumpled. But the clothes did not look old, which implied that they might have been clean and well-ironed before his detention.

When he spoke his voice was soft, but there was something prepossessing about his entire appearance which commanded instant respect. With every nerve militating against composure and calm he moved with faltering steps to where he was shown to sit, but, by an eerie coincidence, he chose not to sit down. He knew he was too dirty to sit down. The Governor did not insist. He instead made mental note of it and recalled that Ngobefuo his arch-accomplice had refused to sit down when he had been brought before him.

"You are Kevin Beckongncho, right eh?"

"I am, Your Excellency," the man replied.

"Do you have your National Identity Card?"

"I do, Your Excellency," he replied nervously searching his rumpled coat pocket and pulling it out, together with his professional card. He gave both to the man who looked at them for a tense minute.

"Are you from Nkokonoko Small Monje?" He asked.

Beckongncho could not answer at once. From where he stood he could not tell where the Governor was looking. The black of his eyes looked hidden below his upper eye lid. All Beckongncho saw was a furious cadaverous whiteness that stool frightfully still.

Did the Governor mean to know whether he was coming directly from Small Monje, or that Nkokonoko Small Monje was his home? He indicated with a wry contortion of the face that he had not understood the question properly.

The Governor apparently did not notice the ambiguity in the question, or the doubt on his face. Perhaps he decided the question was clear enough.

"I am from Sowa now, Your Excellency," Beckongncho said.

"But Small Monje is home. I was born there."

"How long ago is it since you were last thee in Small Monje?"

"Not up to one month, Your Excellency."

"Am I therefore right in believing that you know what has happened in Samll Monje?"

Beckongncho was silent for a nerve-racking moment. He wished with all his soul that the Governor would save him the agony in his heart by asking him a direct question so that he could say what was on his mind.

"Up to a point, Your Excellency," he stammered.

"Up to what point?"

Silence.

"Don over hanswer," Beckongncho heard the warning ring in his ears.

"What do you know about what has happened in Nkokonoko Small Monje?"

"I know that the DO has been killed, Your Excellency. I know too that the Chief and Reverend Father have been killed, together with some Elders too."

"How do you know?"

"I have read it from the newspapers, Your Excellency."

"Which papers?" the Governor queried.

"**GOOD AND EVIL,** your Excellency."

In spite of his determination to conceal the truth, the Governor would be told later the private press, **GOOD AND EVIL,** had not only published the true version of what actually took place but also gruesome pictures of some of the murders.

"They were killed by who?"

"I do not know, Your Excellency."

The Governor grinned, placed his hands on the desk in front of him and leaning forward said:

"They were killed by Ngobefuo. And you know that very well-eh."

"I did not know that, Your Excellency."

"Know it now then-eh."

"Yes, Your Excellency."

***

While the Governor noted something in his file Beckongncho reflected. He knew, or rather believed that these were mere preliminaries. His belly rumbled over and over like some muffled growl of a hungry bulldog. He knew he stood accused, that he would be condemned. The sheer fright of that impending accusation and its attendant consequences made him nauseous.

"Are you Kevin Beckongncho, a prince of the royal line of the tribe of Nkokonoko Small Monje?" the Governor seemed to ask from a tangent.

"I am not, Your Excellency." Beckongncho felt slight relief.

The Governor nodded several times, noted down something in the file before him.

"I have asked for you to be brought here so as to tell you to surrender the crown, the sceptre and bangles of the throne of Nkokonoko Small Monje which Ngobefuo gave to you," he said. His tone was extremely severe.

Beckongncho adjusted himself in his standing position with a start and looked at the Governor with unseeing eyes, and unhearing ears, speechless with the feeling of a man who has just been shaken out of a nightmare.

Was that why he had been brought to Tetseale? Had his whole instinct been at fault? He swallowed hard to gulp down the thought that he was after all not what his fears had made him think was why he had been brought to Tetseale, then he would like to know something else. The question highest up in his mind was: "Your Excellency, who said I was keeping the things?"

That would be silly to ask. The Governor certainly must have contacted Ngobefuo. They were the only two at the time the things were hidden. And Ngobefuo had extracted from him the mighty oath of **Ku-ngang** to keep their whereabouts from him on the pain of death. And Ngobefuo himself was under the same oath.

Could he have broken his word? That corresponded to nothing he had ever known about Ngobefuo. He was not the kind of man to break an article of the tradition. Not even when it meant death. But, given that under the most exceptional circumstances Ngobefuo had been forced to break his word. Why had he not told the Governor directly where the things were hidden? Why had he to refer the Governor again to him.

"Do you understand me?" the Governor interrupted his reflections.

"I do, Your Excellency."

Beckongncho dismissed his initial fears and inquired very politely: "Your Excellency, may I know who said I am keeping the things?"

"The people who gave them to you. o How else could I have known.?"

Beckongncho looked first at the man's face before he looked away.

"There was only one person present, Your Excellency," he managed to point out.

"And that one person was Ngobefuo right?"

"Right, Your Excellency."

The Governor bit his lips and nodded with self-evident satisfaction. He had now had the final confirmation of the stories of the atrocities of the villainous Ngobefuo. He had claimed that the tribe gave Beckongncho the things. Beckongncho had contradicted that lie. Marcus Anuse and the three wise Chiefs had been perfectly right in saying that if there was ever to be any peace at all in Small Monje, Ngobefuo must be eliminated.

"The state needs those things Now," the Governor declared. "Without any further delay. A lorry will be placed at your disposal immediately and you will go back to Small Monje or Sowa or wherever you have kept those things and bring them back here. Am I clear?"

"You are clear, Your Excellency."

The Governor rubbed his hands together. He was just about to call in an officer to take him where the necessary arrangements would be made for the journey, when Beckongncho recalled the predictions of his inmates. Seeing that he was in no serious danger he said:

"But, Your Excellency, I am under an oath not to release any information on the whereabouts of the things."

"I am not interested in any shit. You have the audacity, the effrontery, the cheek to tell the Governor that you are under an oath not to release information that would lead to the solution of a bloody crisis."

The Governor looked furious, his eyes bulging from the sockets, and his voice rising higher and higher in indignation as he spat out the words.

Beckongncho had gradually but surely come to perceive that he was not being held responsible for the crisis. And with this realization he became aware for the first time that there was an air conditioner in the Governor's office. He felt for the first time the pressure of fresh air against his lungs and he could sense that his breathing had once again become regular. He found himself able to think again, to weigh one statement against the other. Despite the uncertainty and apprehension in his mind, it did not take much ratiocination for Beckongncho to grasp the full implications of the Governor's statement. He pointed out:

"I beg Your Excellency not to misunderstand me. I do not mean to disobey or to show disrespect. To break this oath is to bring destruction on me personally and on the entire tribe of Small Monje." He had wanted to add "I had been made to take the oath they knew I knew that I am not a man to violate it. Because they knew I knew the consequences." But he remembered his lawyer's advice in prison:

"No over hanswer."

Besides, had he attempted to do so it would not have been possible because the Governor cut in with:

"That is as silly as anything imaginable. I call that **shit,**" he cursed.

The two men seemed that brief minute to personify that perennial conflict and mutual incompatibility between the Coastal people and the tribes far inland. The people of the interior tribes which Beckongncho now represented had always blamed those at the Coast where the Governor came from, for defiling the traditions of the black man by yielding too willingly to the white man's doctrine. The white man taught that it was primitive and heathen to worship idols and to offer sacrifices to them, to believe in witchcraft, visit native doctors and the like. The people of the Coast who first came into contact with these teachings embraced them with both hands. They therefore looked on the tribes that still practised them as enemies to progress in the state. Beckongncho was one of those who, in spite of his education, still believed that it would be wrong to throw away those things which represented their own civilization. He believed in Chieftaincy, the tribe and its traditions in the same way that the Governor believed in politics, the National Assembly and the National Constitution, and the One Party System.

With a sudden intuition, Beckongncho began to sense some spontaneous conspiracy toward the throne that fired rebellion in every muscle and every nerve in his body. Was Chieftaincy about to be abolished? Did its continuous existence depend on the secret thought. and he thought deeply, but again bearing in mind his lawyer's advice in prison **'don let them know what you are tinking about."**

He had never let Ngobefuo down . He could not do it. It was not for nothing that Ngobefuo had made him the only witness when hiding those things of the throne. And he was not really of the royal line. It was because Ngobefuo loved and trusted him.

Ngobefuo had brought him closer to the throne and its secrets than any of the princes of the royal line could possibly come. He, Beckongncho, liked it. He was impressed by it. Not that he was ambitious in the sense of wanting or wishing or hoping to be in a power position in the tribe. To rule Small Monje was never his goal. If he ever thought of the throne as often as he did, if he did, if he ever felt any embarrassment at the degradation it was being subjected to, it was always through the medium of some other emotion - an irrepressible passion to protect the culture that it stood for.

"I wouldn't mind giving up the eighty thousand francs I earn every month as headmaster" he once said at a cultural meeting, "to become a messenger of the Chief, if only that will give it back its prestige." It was heart-rending, all that was happening to the crown of Small Monje. The DO should never have changed the succession from Nkoaleck to Nchinda. And having done that, he should never have encouraged Nchindia to steal and sell their god.

Did the survival of Chieftaincy lie in what he had to say about those things? But what exactly had happened in Nkokonoko Small Monje, he wondered. Why had he become so important as to be arrested and brought to the Governor in Tetseale to be thus interrogated? If he were being accused of the involvement he had feared, that would have been understandable. It would have been believable. But he had not been brought for that. Why should the Governor want to know whether he was of the royal line or not? Why had Ngobefuo even decided in the very first place to make him see where he was hiding the things after telling him that the chief had been condemned? Why was the Governor asking him questions about the throne? Was there not something wrong with the accusations?

"I have asked you to be brought here so as to ask you to surrender the crown, the sceptre and bangles of the throne of Nkokonoko Small Monje."

That Ngobefuo gave the things to him. That they were in his keeping. Why had the Governor not said that he Beckongncho knew where the things were? Why did he insist that he should go and bring them rather than that he should tell him where they were?

He was being ordered to go to Sowa and bring the things! This order was an absurdity in the context of the tradition. It assumed that the crown, sceptre and bangles of the throne were some common chattel to be carried about at will outside the tribe. That was very wrong. the bangles and sceptre, as far as he knew, could only leave the palace as part of the Chief's royal accoutrement. The Chief wore the bangles and carried the sceptre. But for the crown itself! At no time within living memory had it ever left the palace. Even when the Chief attended an important meeting somewhere outside the palace, in a tribe within his kingdom, he did not wear it. He wore only a coronet. Therefore, either the Governor had been misinformed or he had misunderstood Ngobefuo, wherever it was that they had met.

There was one likely possibility. The Biongong rendering of the English expression "We have chosen him as the Chief' is: *"We have given him the things of the throne - the crown, sceptre and bangles."*

Yes. That was what Ngobefuo most probably had said. And the Governor certainly had taken him literally.

Although Beckongncho had no ambition to rule Small Monje, it did not mean that he could not rule. He was capable of ruling that tribe and giving it something it had not seen for decades. Ngobefuo was not incapable of convincing the rest of the Elders to make him the new Chief. After all things had reached a stage in the tribe where only a man of his calibre could restore it to its former pre-eminence.

He tightened his lips, screwed his courage to breaking point and with wistful persistence asked a question, the answer to which, he computed, should be the answer to everything puzzling him; the answer to which should give physical form to his tormenting thoughts.

"Your Excellency, I beg to know whether a new Chief has been chosen already for Small Monje..."

"Shit," the Governor sputtered. "That is a silly question. It's no concern of your eh. Let me have those things at once."

Beckongncho blinked for a few seconds. He had been careful to have his eyes on the Governor. He had therefore been watching from the corners of his eyes to see his reaction to the question. He had noticed the man's breasts rise and fall rapidly before he blasted his answer. More importantly, there was in the voice in which he had framed the utterance, a quavering streak of anger. In Beckongncho's perceptive mind, this concealed nervous agitation could only be interpreted as a unsuccessful attempt to suppress a truth too bitter to be confronted.

That was as he had feared. A new Chief, he concluded, had been chosen. Perhaps it was he himself. Perhaps the Governor was about to violate their tradition again by reversing their new choice. He would not release any information on those things, unless one condition were fulfilled. He told the Governor:

"Your Excellency, I beg to go to Small Monje first before I give up the things."

"Why?"

"I want to speak to Ngobefuo, Your Excellency. He gave the things to me, as you yourself said."

"You are not seeing any shit."

Silence.

"Let me know in one short syllable, are you ready, unconditionally, to give up the things right now or not?"

Beckongncho licked his lips and wiped his mouth with the back of his left hand. But he did not talk back.

Chapter Eight

Non stillant omnes quas cernis in aeres nubes.
(John Withals)

BECKONGNCHO WAS led back to the same cell with instructions that he should be treated with the merciless severity. The Governor would not talk to him soon, until he had worked out such a definitive line of action as would convince Beckongncho that it would be fatal to hesitate to surrender the said articles of the throne. To this effect he dispatched another set of soldiers to small Monje for a very special assignment. The soldiers returned four days afterwards. But the Governor did not ask to talk to Beckongncho until the seventh day.

***

When Beckongncho returned to the cell he noticed some changes. Not in the physical structure, but in the inmates. Apart from **Justice, Excellency, Protocol** and three other men, many strange faces had appeared replacing the ones he had known.

"**Cabinet Reshuffle,**" he was told when he asked what had happened in his absence. This simply meant that some of the inmates had either been released on bail or had been discharged, or even taken to prison. However, **Excellency** was still thee, so was **Protocol** and **Justice**. Uncertain as his future was, Beckongncho had come to enjoy the company of his inmates Beckongncho recalled to mind the Biongong saying that:

"When rain drives you to take shelter under a tree, you do not choose those to stand with you."

On the fifth day when **Excellency, Protocol** and **Justice** fell victim to another "**Cabinet Reshuffle,**" he felt the weight of his detention much more than ever before. But upon his return from meeting the Governor, on the very first occasion **Information** had

67

summoned **"a Press Conference"** during which Beckongncho had been called upon to tell them all as honestly as possible what had transpired.

"You like to be Chief of Small Monje?" somebody asked him.

"I don't hate the idea," Beckongncho said.

"Thas means what?" somebody asked him. "If you like it say so. Don begin to talk round and round like a lawyer who has not been given all his money."

"I like it," Beckongncho admitted.

"Then don tell them where the tings are. No way to way," somebody said.

***

Once or twice Beckongncho had been slapped and made to lie on the wet stinking floor. And the fact that he bore all these without letting out the secret endeared him all the more to his inmates who continued to give him encouragement and advice. As the number of inmates reduced food supply also reduced. So when eventually Beckongncho was left alone he had fed entirely on the remains which a kind policeman on duty threw at him after his meals.

At first he decided he would not eat, that he would starve himself to death. But he thought it unnecessary to take away his own life. The pressure soon became unbearable. The tap in the latrine functioned only sporadically, and the water that was held to him in the darkened cell tasted like the fermented dregs of palm wine in an unwashed calabash. His breath stank foully, and his whole physique had completely crumbled. But he bore it with calm obstinacy and resolve, especially after his wife visited him.

"This is your last chance, my young man, to surrender those things," the Governor said when he came in.

Beckongncho did not know how to answer him. The Governor showed no uneasiness as of old, at the stubbornness. He even seemed to like the insult which now justified the line of action he had already taken.

He repeated his words.

Beckongncho stood silent.

The emblem of Nkokonoko Small Monje was the eagle, and it stood as much for pride as for strength of character, a peculiar hardness of heart. A typical Small Monjean had a fanatical reverence for his traditional values, and a streak of inbred intransigence lay deep in his being which could not be easily destroyed, even under very exasperating conditions. Beckongncho was a true representative of his tribe.

But something else had turned his heart into stone. In the set of his underpants he carried a letter which was virtually the key to all his suffering. Two days after his miraculous disappearance from Sowa his wife arrived in Tetseale Police Station. She had gone up to the D.O's office in Sowa to inquire why her husband had not returned. There she had been told that the man had already been imprisoned in Tetseale for subversion. She had decided she would take the night train the following day to Tetseale and see him.

But the same night that Beckongncho was taken away, two men arrived in Sowa from Nkokonoko Small Monje. They had come to see him. They had brought a letter from the Council of Elders in Small Monje. It had been meant to be a secret communication between that Council and Beckongncho. But because of the circumstances that had arisen, they permitted his wife to read it and see if she could be of any help. She tore it open and saw the message:

> *Council of Elders,*
> *Palace of the Paramount Chief,*
> *Nkokonoko Small Monje.*
> *8th May, 1967.*

Our Dear Son Beckongncho:
We the undersigned members of the Council of Elders that rules the eleven tribes of this tribe have written to wholeheartedly ask you to hurry back home here and help in the great duty of cleansing the throne of your father that has been twice soiled.

We are all waiting for you. Affairs in the tribe have come to a standstill, pending your arrival. That is how important your coming is to us and the tribe...

Once of the two men bringing the letter had carefully explained to her the atmosphere both in Small Monje and Likume. He had said:

"We passed through Likume on our way here. There, people have already sewn uniforms with Anuse's picture on them. They say he will be the Chief. They say he had bought the office of Paramount Chief of Small Monje from the Governor with 500,000 francs. They say they are just waiting for the day of his coronation to dance with the uniforms. They say Anuse had already picked his successor and his own Council.

"But before we left Small Monje, Ngobefuo, Ntongntong and Ndenwontio had returned there. They had been arrested and taken to Tetseale. They were saying that the Governor had tried to force them to accept Anuse as the new Chief, but they had all refused. They had already chosen Beckongncho, and so could not change it. The tribe cannot accept Anuse as the Chief." Beckongncho's wife had made the journey as she had planned, taking along with her the letter and the information communicated to her. The two men had decided they would wait for her to return before they left for Small Monje.

In Tetseale she had looked for and found the Police Station where her husband was said to have been locked up. She had come in tears, carrying with her a sickly child who wept every second. she had spoken most imploringly about the need to see her husband and talk to him about the condition of the child.

The officer on duty that morning, a flagrant inebriate, had come to work dead drunk. This had added levity to his distorted sense of duty and he had permitted the woman to see her husband "for hap minute". She had told Beckongncho exactly what she had heard. With the greatest cunning she had succeeded in smuggling the letter into his hands. After she had gone away he had managed by the light in the ceiling, to read its contents, which he disclosed to his inmates.

Beckongncho had hoped that at the very last minute he would show the letter to the Governor to explain his insistence.

"Your Excellency," he pleaded after a very long pause, "I beg you very much to understand and sympathize with me. I have told you why I cannot surrender the things. And in addition, I have evidence..."

"What was the condition you gave for releasing the things?" the Governor interrupted him with a surprising sense of understanding.

"Your Excellency, I requested to see Ngobefuo who gave the things to me. I requested to see the members of the Council of Elders of Small Monje. I said that I had taken an oath..."

He was just about to mention that letter when the Governor pressed the bell on his table and an officer came in.

"This man wants to see Ngobefuo," he said theatrically. "Show him Ngobefuo, and whoever else he wants to see. Then bring him back, eh."

***

Confused, dispirited and unable to take the Governor's instructions in jest or in earnest, Beckongncho rose and was led out. From the way the people took him out it seemed as though the Governor had long foreseen that he would not yield and so had

since decided on what to do next. A Land Rover was already waiting for them outside the office. And when he climbed in he noticed that the driver drove away with two officers without even talking with one of the men who had brought him out of the Governor's office.

They drove not to the Police Station but to the Military Hospital. There they were received in silence by some three officers who must have been expecting them for quite sometime. They were two Lieutenants and a Sub - Lieutenant. The driver of the police vehicle that brought him spoke to the lieutenants for a fraction of a second. They nodded.

"Forrow us," said.

They passed through a complicated network of corridors with sunlight and shadows taking turns in flirting on the uniforms of the officers in front of him as they moved from one corridor to the other. The corridors became very short. They were nearing the rear of the hospital where shafts of the mid-day sunlight speckled with the soot from the laboratories and kitchens and filtered downward from openings on either side.

They crossed gutters reeking and stinking with the stench of army hospital waste and finally came to a halt in front of the Casualty Ward. The officers that had led him there handed him the house that stood apart from the rest of the hospital buildings. There they stopped.

The windows of that house were shut, a detail which drove the mercury of Beckongncho's fears soaring into the skies. All along, he had decided that he would not ask anybody anything.

Thoughts he could never have imagine crossed and re-crossed his mind with the magic speed of dreams. At one time he imagined that Ngobefuo might also have been arrested and locked up somewhere in the Police Station. This was when they were driving away from the Governor's office. But he had dismissed this thought when he found that they were going elsewhere.

As he climbed down at the hospital he had begun to imagine that Ngobefuo might have fallen sick, or must have been wounded during the crisis in Small Monje, and was being treated there. Then as they approached the Casualty Ward his heart began to pump erratically. There, vague terrors began to assail his mind, and his instinct stirred apprehensively. He had begun to imagine that Ngobefuo must have attempted to escape from captivity, and that he might have been wounded in the process.

These were very frightening thoughts indeed. But there was one thing he refused to consider - that Ngobefuo may not be alive. Another officer came down to them with a bunch of keys as they stood in front of the isolated house. He sorted one key, fitted into the key-hole and turned the lock open. Another officer pushed the door with his knee. The hinges yielded with a mournful and articulate groan which left a frozen echo inside Beckongncho's flesh that trembled over his bones like a mass of jelly.

The man stepped in and switched on the light. Then in a rather ordinary manner he beckoned to Beckongncho and said:

"Here they are. Ngobefuo is one of these." Beckongncho lifted his foot, now heavy as if tied to a boulder, and stepped in, hoping against hope that it should be a prison where the men had been put, fearing and shivering that it could be worse.

When he raised his reluctant head and followed with unwilling eyes the direction the officer's finger was still pointing, he gave a gasp of horror and turned away his face. Nothing that he had imagined or even feared could touch the grim and bloodcurdling reality of the gory sight that met his eyes. There, strewn on the bare floor and in something like a line, were the bodies of seven people. He tightened his lips, clasped his hands over his head and moved towards the spectacle.

72

They were lying on their backs, motionless and still in death, cold. A bloody gash seemed to cross each forehead. Their faces were all patched and nearly totally disfigured with coagulated blood, as though they had been bludgeoned to death before being slashed with bayonets. some pieces of paper were tagged to their frozen feet. The air was stifling. With a super human effort Beckongncho moved closer and bent over the feet and read. Ngobefuo, Ndenwontio, Ntongntong, Kwindie....

He lifted his head, struck by the terror of a brute, trying in vain to rise above the shock. He had participated several times in the compulsory military service that the state had instituted. There, during the training sessions, they had often been shown films of torture and horror, of bloody accidents and murders. They were often taken to hospitals and shown corpses and the wounded and dying, in all conditions of agony. By so doing they were being familiarized with suffering so as to test their strength of character. He had come out of those exercises with distinction in composure. But the sight of the battered corpses of people he personally knew, personally respected, personally loved, his own parents so to speak! It broke his manhood.

Beckongncho tried to speak but terror seemed to glue his lips. He closed his eyes tight, to restrain a threatening flood of tears. He swallowed loudly, convulsively. His face become wet instantly. He felt as if he had physically received the kind of death blows which had struck the life out of the Elders.

***

When they reentered the Governor's office the man looked into Beckongncho's eyes and asked:

"Did you see what you wanted to see?"

Beckongncho's lips trembled in his silence.

"That should tell you that I need those things more than I need anybody else. More than I need **you!**"

Beckongncho did not think he was talking to a human being any more. Anybody who would order the murder of helpless old men of that nature has long crossed the boundary between man and beast, between madness and sanity.

73

"Are, you therefore, ready to release them, or not?"

Beckongncho heard a voice growl again with appalling indifference as to the enormity of the dead. He seemed to count the words.

For once in his very austere life, Beckongncho felt the urge to kill a human being. What could he do? What could he say? He had not yet overcome the shock of the deaths. What guarantee was there that he would be saved if those things were given? And even if they were given, even if he lived, what would life be worth? How was he ever going to live with the consciousness that he had been responsible for the death of the whole Council of Elders? What could be worse than the sight of the corpses to which he had been exposed? What was the throne worth, what was the tradition worth without those old men who knew all the stones with which to cross all the rivers of their culture and tradition? Nothing. Nothing.

He tried to speak, to tell the Governor to destroy him the way he had destroyed his fathers. But bitterness made him dumb. His mind instantly filled with pounding blood, a current of thick bile, bitter as vinegar, rose in his throat, threatening to explode through his nostrils, his eyes or his ears. He bit his lips until they bled and he sensed blood trickle through the spaces between his teeth and descend to mix with the bile in his throat and sink with a rumble.

***

Whatever might have happened to Beckongncho thereafter will forever remain a matter for conjecture, for, the minute that he stood with his life in a balance a telephone rang on the Governor's table that was to change not only the man's fate but also the course of history in Nkokonoko Small Monje.

The Governor picked it up and said:

"Abraham-Isaac speaking."

"The Minister of Territorial Administration speaking." The voice from the other end said. Apparently somebody had informed the Minister of the secret execution of the Elders. It will be recalled that the Governor had not actually ordered the immediate killing of the old men. He had merely told the guards to tie them up so that Beckongncho would see that he was serious. But the men had gone ahead to kill them. The Minister, however, had not shown any remorse at their death. There was tension in the air during the few seconds following the introduction from the other end of the phone. Then the Governor said:

"Yes Sir."

"I still haven't received any word from you about the crisis in Small Monje. What is happening? What is the situation?"

The Governor looked across at the petrified Beckongncho. He then pressed a bell on his table. Somebody came in.

"Take him to wait outside," he said.

Beckongncho was led out. The Governor then resumed:

"Can I come over and talk it over with you, Sir?"

"I would be much obliged," the Minister said. His voice sounded dry. "Right away," he added. "I'm waiting."

The Governor took the file for the Small Monje crisis which he put into his brief case and, asking an officer to remain with Beckongncho at the porch into the office, he rose and went to see his boss. Of all the Provincial Governors, only the Governor of the Lower-Middle-Belt Province had his headquarters in Tetseale. All the others settled their problems in their administrative headquarters in the Provinces. It did not therefore take much for Abraham - Isaac to travel to see his boss.

***

"Affairs in Small Monje are not yet really solved Sir," the Governor began when he sat down in the Minister's office.

The Minister pulled down the sides of his mouth, folded his hands and sat up. He was a man in his early sixties who took his responsibilities extremely seriously. He was not glad to hear what the Governor had said, and was even more disturbed that he had to call for the Governor to hear that. Disappointment could be seen sinking like a carving knife into the age lines of his face.

"How do you mean?" he asked the Governor. "I asked you to order a full scale investigation into the affair and bring the rebels to justice."

"I did, Honourable Minister," the Governor told him.

"What then?"

As if reading from some internal memorandum the Governor began:

"On the seventh of May I dispatched Captain Abongo immediately to being peace to the area. I communicated this to the Minister..."

"I remember," the Minister nodded.

"Then because communication lines had been completely destroyed by the rebels I did not get in touch with him until an officer returned two days afterwards. He said there was no rebellion and that after the killing the murderers ran into hiding. I told the Minister this too..."

"I remember."

"The outrages were said to have been committed by a certain Ngobefuo and Ngangabe. Both men committed suicide while being brought here to answer their charges."

"I never heard that, the Minister said. "That is news to me. Perhaps it's because I have not heard from you since."

The Governor sensed the barest trace of reproach in what the man had said. He paused.

"By their suicide," he went on, "they had meant to make it impossible for me to get at the truth of the matter. But as soon as I received news from Captain Abongo I asked for the major Paramount Chiefs of Biongong to be sent to me.."

The Minister nodded. The Governor no doubt was making up much of it on the spot.

"I guessed that they would be in the best position, if not of telling us the precise cause, of suggesting a solution..."

"They came?"

"They came, Sir. The Paramount Chief of Nonudji, Moneki and Djungo."

The Minister gave an impressive nod.

"What did they say?" he inquired.

"They gave me both the cause and the solution. They assured me that the root cause of all the trouble was a man named Ngobefuo, a tyrannical slave who seized power as a caretaker of the tribe when the father of the late Chief lay on his death bed. They said the right person to rule was a certain Anuse who had been forced by Ngobefuo to flee to Likume and take up trading.

76

"They said since Ngobefuo knew that as a slave he would never be accepted as a Chief, he decided by devilish means to block all avenues to legitimate succession to the throne. They said the whole tribe wanted this Anuse man, and that it was in a bid to try to convince the people whom Ngobefuo had confused that the DO met his untimely death. I gathered that the late Chief was included in the massacre because he openly expressed the desire and willingness to surrender the throne to the rightful ruler, Anuse. I had no reason to doubt their word."

"Where is the man in question?"

"Anuse?"

"Anuse?"

"He is in Likume, Sir."

"Have you spoken to him?"

"I have Sir. I sent for him too when the Chiefs told me about it."

"What are his views on the matter?"

"The same Sir. He confirms that he has been constantly cheated of his right.

"Is he the centre of the unrest then?"

"Not him, Honourable Minister. Just that he cannot be the Chief because of Ngobefuo. And he seems to be the only man capable of acting as a vital link between the Government and the recalcitrant people."

"But what stops you from sending a delegation there to declare him the new Chief?"

"That is exactly what I was contemplating on doing, Sir, when you spoke to me. I learnt that Ngobefuo had placed another impediment in the way. He had again disregarded the cry of the people and had chosen another illegitimate Chief to whom he had secretly given the crown to hide."

"Are you saying that there is another illegitimate ruler on the throne of Small Monje?"

"That is what could have happened, Sir. But I acted rather swiftly. In fact, if not of this impediment I would have come to see you ever since, Sir. The gentleman in question doesn't even live in Small Monje. So, Sir, you see that even with my best efforts, order cannot be restored because this man would not release the things he is keeping illegally."

"Have you met him personally?"

"I sent for him the very day I learnt of his involvement in the crisis. For the past week I have trying to appeal to his reason, to persuade him to understand the threat to national peace that his detention of the crown was posing. He just would not yield."

The Minister allowed the thoughts to sift through his mind. Then he asked:

"Do you say you have asked him to release the crown and he has refused?:

"A million times, Minister. I have only resisted the temptation to subject him to torture. Sir, I was just about to inform you about it when you rang."

After reflecting for a whole minute he inquired:

"Where is he?"

"In my office Sir. His is there. I was talking to him when you rang."

"Bring him here. Let me speak to him."

Chapter Nine

If there's a lid that does not fit,
there's a lid that does.

        (Gabriel Buchanan: *Japanese Proverb*)

*A*BOUT HALF an hour after the Minister gave instructions for Beckongncho to be brought to see him, a tallish man was led into his office. His beard was tangled and unkempt and he wore a twisted, dirty black suit. His hands and nails were black and somewhat grimy, and to the Minister who had an acute sense of smell, his whole body gave off an unpleasant odour. There was in his sunken eyes the look of a man encumbered with nameless fears and doubts, a man completely dispirited. But through this a certain aura of authority or nobility of spirit seemed to radiate in compelling waves. He greeted the Minister but the man did not respond.

"Who are you please?" the Minister inquired.

"I am Kevin Beckongncho, You Excellency."

" What do you do for a living?"

"I am the co-headmaster of the Government Primary School Ngeung-Ale in Sowa, Your Excellency."

The Minister looked surprised. He did not know much about Beckongncho. Then searching his mind he said:

"I guess that Mr. Kevin Beckongncho, as headmaster, is aware, of a Governmental Circular of the Eleventh February 1955 which forbade all persons in the employ of the Civil Service of this Republic to mingle in local politics."

That was something Beckongncho had long forgotten of.

"Are you aware of it?"

"I am, Your Excellency," Beckongncho lied. He feared to give the Minister the impression that he had acted in ignorance. The very fact that he had been brought to the Minister instantly suggested to his mind that there might be some other solution to the problem than

79

just killing him and throwing away. He must give answers which would permit him to explain himself, and maybe, convince the Minister.

"Are you, Kevin Beckongncho, aware of how necessary peace is in this country?"

"I am Your Excellency." There was silence.

"The Government of this country has got a lot to tell you.

But first, you are being called upon to make available to the state the crown and whatever else in your keeping that pertains to the throne of Small Monje."

***

Aliou Ndam Garga, the Minister of Territorial Administration, was one of the very few of the Cabinet Of Ministers who had established a reputation for fair-dealing among the educated citizens of the republic. He was the only man who was still being believed to know what democracy was and practise it. He was known to believe firmly in dialogue, even with outrageous criminals. The story even went that the only reason the government had not been toppled by a **coup d'état** was because he was still an active member of it.

Beckongncho had heard of him years ago and liked what was said about him. He saw in the demand that he be brought to speak to the man, the working of the hand of God. He was now convinced that even if he was to die the very next minute, he would not die a criminal's death, that it will be possible for him to leave information which would make the image of Small Monje less dishonourable in the eyes of the Government. He knew about Small Monje, which a man like Aliou Garga would be glad to know.

"Do you understand me?" the Minister inquired.

"I do, Your Excellency. But I Beg to say that I am not keeping any of those things."

The Minister looked at the Governor in great astonishment.

The latter rose to his feet and asked in a voice charged with subdued fury:

"You want to deny your own words?"

The Minister did not give him time to defend himself. He asked:

"Do you know anything about the things at all?"

"I do, Your Excellency."

" What do you know about them?"

"I know where they were hidden, Your Excellency."

"Where they were hidden or where they are hidden?"

"Where they were hidden, Your Excellency. It is a long time ago, and they might not be there any more."

"Who hid them?"

"Ngobefuo, Your Excellency. The caretaker of the tribe. I was with him when he hid them."

The Governor threw open his hands, looking across at the Minister as if to say "Did I not tell you?"

The Minister, however, was more concerned with Beckongncho himself.

"Where did he hide them?"

"In the palace in Small Monje, Your Excellency. "

"Where exactly?"

"It is difficult to say from here, Your Excellency. The palace is very large and one has to pass through a complicated route to reach the exact spot. Unless I take somebody there he cannot find the place because it is a hole in the ground."

The Minister studied Beckongncho for along time.

"As I said before, you have to bring the things here. Immediately," he emphasized.

"Yes, Your Excellency."

"Go outside and wait. The vehicle to take you there will be brought at once. Go."

The Provincial Governor was sitting in an armchair slightly to the right of the Minister, so that Beckongncho was facing both men. A sharp penetration glance from him reached Beckongncho from the corner of his eyes as he turned his back. It was the kind of glance in which you saw a death threat. The kind of glance which said"

"I am just biding my time before I crush you."

He had detained Beckongncho for eight days. He had subjected him to torments that would have tried even the patience of a Job. The traitor had said nothing tangible. And he was now jeopardising his future political career by revealing information likely to make his boss think that he, the Governor, lacked the tactics of interrogation. Beckongncho was merely hastening his death, he swore to himself. He sank back where he sat until the nape of his neck was soon resting on the back of the seat.

On his part, Beckongncho did not go straight out as soon as he was ordered to leave. He took three steps toward the door and stood silent just long enough to make what he was about to say not look like he was defying the Minister's command. There, in a voice that could have melted the hardest heart he asked:

"Your Excellency, can I say something?"

"Mr. Beckongncho, whatever you have to say, you will do so only after you shall have brought back the things the state is asking for."

"Alright, Your Excellency," he said resignedly and turned to go out.

The Minister did not look happy at the turn of events.

But he seemed to find the deep feeling in the answer irresistible. He called Beckongncho back and asked:

"What did you want to say?"

"Your Excellency, I wanted to let you know that the killings in Small Monje were as embarrassing to us the elites of the tribe as they were to the Government."

"So what?" the Governor blasted.

His gloomy dignity, the weight of certainty and the calm assurance with which the words were uttered drove away any inclination in the Minister's mind to consider the answer as an insult.

"What do you mean? he inquired. His voice was grave but not loud, not as loud as the Governor's if he were asking the same question in the same frame of mind.

"Your Excellency, I mean that from my understanding of what has happened so far, when I hand over those things to the state, matters will only grow worse. It will solve nothing."

The Minister contemplated the full import of what Beckongncho had said very deeply."

"Let me have them first," he told him decidedly "If things get worse that will be no concern of yours.

"Okay, Your Excellency," he said in a manner which to the Minister's discerning mind implied that he had been denied the opportunity to offer a solution to the problem.

The Minister allowed him to go out. After meditating for a while he sent for him again.

"What makes you think that the surrender of the things will only worsen matters?" he asked when Beckongncho came in.

Beckongncho was still finding words in which to express his thoughts when the Minister repeated the question. He them said:

Your Excellency, although I went to school in the Coast and have worked there ever since, I have kept very close touch with the life of my people in Nkokonoko Small Monje. I know their hearts. I know how things happened, and how they are likely to happen again."

A feeling of security seemed to invade and systematically replace his previous fears, as he noticed that the man was willing to listen to him. The pitch of his voice had taken on a serene strain of maturity and an engaging confidence which seemed to throw a charm over the Minster.

"How have things happened? How are they likely to happen?"

Beckongncho once again began to search his mind in silence. Then, very solicitously he said:

"Your Excellency, I beg to speak to you alone."

The Minister looked from the Governor to Beckongncho. While he was still pondering in his mind whether to grant him the private audience the Governor rose with a smile of embarrassment on his lips. He took Beckongncho's request for a personal insult, which was not helped at all by thoughts of how he had revealed information to his boss which he had withheld from him for a whole week.

"I' II be right back, Sir," He said. His words sounded casual and even careless, as though he had noticed some conspiracy between the criminal and the Minister.

He was not really afraid that Beckongncho could say anything that would be worse than what he had already done to his reputation. He was only angry. He decided and walked out that Beckongncho would not survive another night in prison. He would be killed and a report of suicide submitted to the Minister or any other person who might be interested in knowing what had happened to him. Anuse would be asked to rule without the crown sceptre or bangles. After all those things were mere symbols. Something could always be devised to substitute for them. He would have nothing more to do with Beckongncho. Beckongncho would die and go and meet Ngobefuo and the other devils in hell. There he could wear his crown. Idiot.

83

***

As soon as the Governor went out the man pressed the button of a tape recorder that was fitted into his desk and asked Beckongncho what he wanted to say. Beckongncho saw him do it and knew that his words were to be recorded, a clear indication that he was about to be taken seriously, that he would not be killed at once. This, he believed was likely to be the only opportunity he would have before his own death, to say anything he was capable of saying about the crisis, Its causes or solution. He decided he would spare no detail especially where it touched on the Governor's involvement in it. He recalled his people's saying:

"Why fear to bite a man's nose because of
catarrh who will bite your anus without
fearing excrement?"

And since this was also an opportunity to defend himself he would make the Minister understand that he was not a criminal or a rebel, that he was not abetting crime, and that he was actually trying to avoid further blood-shed. The Minister must be made to understand that he was very well-versed in the politics of the tribe, that he had been chosen Chief, that it was no accident, that Ngobefuo was no rebel, and that his selection as Chief had been intended as a solution to the crisis and not a means of intensifying it.

The Minister must be made to understand that, he alone, was the solution to the problem, under the present circumstances. But he would say only what would save his life, what he knew the Minister would like to hear.

He remained silent.

"Your Excellency, I beg you to understand first of all that I am not talking to defend myself at all," he said. "I am not talking to save my life. As far as this affair is concerned, and as far as I have seen and heard, I know that I am absolutely incapable of saving my life..."

The Minister's brows drew together and he tilted his head as though he would contradict him on what he had just said. But he did not say anything.

"I am talking as somebody who know that he might never live to see the crisis resolved, But somebody who know how It can be resolved, and who will be glad to die if only he was sure that his death would bring peace." The Minister nodded.

"I will begin from the beginning, Your Excellency, with the ways of my people..."

The Minister glanced at his watch and seemed to gnaw at his lower lip as if he felt uncomfortable with the roundabout manner in which Beckongncho was going about his answer.

Beckongncho noticed the uneasiness and hastened to explain:

"Your Excellency, what I have to say cannot be abbreviated without distortion. For you to really understand all or it, you need to hear all. It is boring, but very delicate at the same time."

"Go on," the Minister waved to him. He went on:

"The root cause lies in the ways of my people. They are a highly conservative people. By they, here I mean myself too, Your Excellency. This I know is no compliment. The late DO could have ruled over them for as long as he wanted if he had just a little more foresight than he possessed, and if he had been just a little more cautious.

"He interfered in the tradition of the people to very dangerous extents, without caring to understand or trying to find out the risks involved so as to arm himself against any eventuality. Your Excellency, I am not by any means saying that he should have allowed the people to behave the way they pleased. That would only breed anarchy."

"I was about to say," the Minister put in.

"Go on," he told Beckongncho.

"After all, there are hundreds of customs in hundreds of places that simply have no place in this modern world." he said. "You are the boss of all administrators in this country and you know how human beings react to change. You know how people who have lived for centuries in a particular way of life would react if that way of life is to be modified. They resist, even if the change is for their own good. Therefore, it is not the mark of good administration to effect a change as though it were a caterpillar bull-dozing a path through a forest. Even the best of men in any country in the world would rebel. This was precisely the approach the late DO had taken.

"He should have know even from readings in the history of the tribes of this country- not only in Small Monje- that on points of a breach of their tradition they can be very uncompromising. I am sure the **Tombo Trouble** in which the natives killed all strangers and marched to give themselves up to the police is still fresh in Your Excellency's mind."

The Minister nodded with a faint smile. He was very impressed with what he had heard so far, even though it had not touched the main point.

"The real person to rule Nkokonoko Small Monje after Chief Fuo-Ndee was Antony Nkoaleck, a young man that had just returned from the university. One would have thought that with his education the DO would understand that it would be a great advantage for the government to have him as Chief, because he would be more pliable. but on the eve of the ceremony that was to make him Chief, the DO came to the palace and forced the Elders to change the succession from him to Nchindia, the chief who has just been killed. Nchindia had from childhood been literally an outcast, with nothing in his past life that was a preparation for the office of Paramount chief, which was the highest institution in Small Monje. I mean after the Government.

"If the DO took his responsibilities seriously he would not have needed a second party to tell him that the whole tribe felt insulted by the act. It had never happened before. I was at home then. I saw how the people were feeling. When the people yielded and bore the injury calmly, that did not make him any more prudent. As though he has never done anything to anger them, he went on to practise one evil after the other. He slept with people's wives as if it was a rule. And when the husbands dared to protest he ordered their arrest and detention without any trial.

"As everybody had foreseen before protesting the choice of Nchindia, He proved to be a failure, a total failure as Paramount Chief. Far from seeking ways and means to console the people on whom he had imposed the much detested Chief, the DO proceeded to use Nchindia's failings to insult the traditions of the people. He created an unbridgeable distance between him and the local population, and bought a pack of bull-dogs with which he chased off visitors from the villages. So even those who could have advised him to be wary, were denied access to his unwilling ear. A rebellion was brewing up.

"The worst of these outrages was the tricking of the Chief into cutting off and selling the statue which the tribe worshipped as their supreme god. This he personally carried in his Land-Rover to the coast where he sold to a white man. In the minds of our people, nothing could be conceivably worse. But they directed their anger first against their Chief and marched to the DO's house, demanding Nchindia's dethronement. It was during the holidays and I was home then too.

"The DO told them in the most insulting terms that they could not do so because it was the Government who had chosen him as Chief. What was more, he took the Chief from the palace into his house and told the people that the Chief would rule them from there. The following day I left to return to Sowa. After a week I learnt of the uprising. Your Excellency, I think it was at this point that they lost their heads."

"By this time the Minister had already formed an opinion about Beckongncho which ruled out the possibility that he could be a rabble rouser. If anything, he believed that he had been made the scape-goat of the crisis. At any rate, he did not betray any emotion that he was being won over by Beckongncho's eloquence and logical unfolding of the events

There seemed to be some unexplained twist in the narrative.

" How do you enter the scene then?" the Minister queried.

Beckongncho hesitated. He then searched the seat of his underpants for the letter which he had received from his wife, stretched it out and said:

"I would like Your Excellency to read through this. I apologise that I should be taking it from where I did. If I did not put it there I would have been destroyed in the same way that the men who wrote it have been destroyed."

He had wanted to respond to Beckongncho's allegation of destruction, but he decided to read the letter first. He took the letter, opened it and read it over twice, scrutinizing the fingerprints appended to the names that followed it.

"Are you a prince of the royal line of Small Monje?' he asked.

"I am not Your Excellency. But I have a very slight claim.

"My father was of the same father as Nchindia's father.

But I could never have insisted on such a claim."

" Do you imagine that the tribe can never accept you as their Chief with such a slight claim"

Your Excellency, that letter is the decision of the whole tribe."

"How did you get this letter?"

"My wife brought it to me when I was in prison, Your Excellency. She said it was..."

"You have not been in prison Mr. Beckongncho. No citizen of this republic can be imprisoned without trial. You have not been accused. You have not been tried. So you cannot talk of prison."

"I am sorry Your Excellency. I meant when I was being detained for questioning..."

"That's better," the Minister said. "Are you saying that you were not chosen by Ngobefuo?"

"Ngobefuo cannot choose a Chief on his own, Your Excellency."

"He hid the things with you in any case."

"He hid them with me, Your Excellency."

"When was that?"

"On the night of the day that the Chief was discovered to be implicated in the theft of the statue, Your Excellency."

The Minister was silent. He did not doubt the genuineness of the letter of anything that Beckongncho had yet said. But he felt it necessary to squeeze the last drop of truth out of him. He said with calm decision:

"I put it to you therefore that Ngobefuo on his own chose you..."

"Your Excellency..."

"I am still talking Mr. Beckongncho."

"I am very sorry Your Excellency."

"Ngobefuo chose you on his own," he resumed soberly. "The proof is that long before you were made Chief, he had already given you the crown, or rather he had made you alone see where he hid it, which was the same as giving it to you. We have been rightly informed that Ngobefuo had always acted in this treacherous way. That he is the centre of unrest in Small Monje. That you connived with him to keep the legitimate ruler of the throne out. The rightful ruler should have been Anuse. Not you." Beckongncho's agony began to return in full force. When he was certain that the Minister had finished talking he said:

"Ngobefuo could never have made me the Chief on his own, Your Excellency. The tradition does not allow him to do so. He is the care-taker of the tribe, and it was through his respect for the tradition that he was made that. If he hid those things with me, and I am now being invited to come and be Chief, it is not that he

88

decided to do so on his own. Your Excellency, it can only mean that before he hid them with me they had already decided it. There was a very long meeting of the Council of Elders prior to the hiding of the things. And as for saying that Mr. Anuse was the rightful person to rule, Your Excellency, even Mr. Anuse himself knows that he could never rule..."

"Why?"

"He has never done anything to merit the title. He knows that his conduct has offended every member of the tribe. That was why he needed to bribe the Governor to kill me and make him the Chief. That was why he needed to ask the Governor to kill the Elders of the Council from which alone the truth of my selection as Chief could have been obtained. He knew that with any of those people alive, he would never be permitted to set foot..."

"Nobody killed them," the Minister said, trying to cover up what he knew could very well be the truth. "You have to watch your words. Those are very dangerous allegations," the Minister cautioned.

"The Elders of the so-called Council committed suicide when they heard that they were being brought here to answer their charges."

"Nobody committed suicide, Your Excellency. The old men only died when I told the Governor that I must speak to them before releasing the things of the throne. It was then that they led me to the army hospital this morning and showed me their battered bodies. Anybody with eyes could tell you they were killed."

The Minister drew his ash tray towards him, pulled out a cigarette from a packet, lighted and stuck it to his lips. Beckongncho was watching him, waiting for him to settle down again.

"I am listening," the Minister said. "I don't listen with my mouth," he added without a smile. Beckongncho went on:

"The Governor, having taken so much from Mr. Anuse, found that old men stood in his way. They therefore had to die. I learned that after the death of Nchindia the Governor sent for Anuse as the Chief. They refused."

The Minister pulled at the cigarette for a while. He then withdrew it from his lips, changed the position of his legs and leaned back in his seat.

Beckongncho went on:

"Your Excellency, you know that the House of Chiefs had long been abolished. The office of Chief does not carry with it more money than I earn as Headmaster. The only reason I cling to the offer is because it is the best solution, it is the only thing to bring lasting peace in Small Monje. And I would like to add that the Elders back home are still waiting for me as well as for the Elders whom we know have already been killed, and thrown away.

"No Elder of the Council of the tribe has ever been buried outside the tribe. Should I therefore lose my life too as it seems now, knowing my people, I do not know what kind of force will stop them from doing even worse things. Your Excellency, that is why I said that it will only worsen matters if I give the things back to the state."

Chapter Ten

Every duty which we omit, obscures
some truth which we should have known
(Ruskin)

THE **GOVERNOR** had already returned to his office by the time the Minister finished talking with, or rather, listening to Beckongncho. He had, however, left word with the Minister's body guard at the porch into his office that he should be contacted in his office whenever he was wanted. Thus when the Minister needed him he rang the man and said he would like to speak to him again. When the Governor came he said:

"Let's give that man Beckongncho a chance."

The Governor took in a loud long breath.

Beckongncho had been asked to wait with two policemen outside the office. The Governor looked at the Minister, surprised and uncertain about the meaning of what the man had said.

"I don't get you, Honourable Minister."

"Where has the man been all this while?"

"At the Central Police Station," the Governor said.

"Doing what?" the Minister inquired.

"I interrogated him everyday, Honourable Minister. I kept him there because he was intransigent, as you yourself must have noticed. I wanted a way of making him cooperate with the administration in resolving the crisis," the Governor explained.

The Minister leaned toward him.

"Mr. Kevin Beckongncho is a senior civil servant in his own right," he said with calculated solemnity. "He is the Head Master of an institution, just like any of us is in his own domain. He has been locked up with hardened criminals for a fortnight..."

"Not up to a fortnight, Honourable Minister," the Governor corrected, as if that made the deed less humiliating.

91

"Even for a day, Mr. Governor, that should not have happened without ascertaining that he was guilty. We should be happy that this is happening only here. In a developed country, if he sued you, your budget for five years would not be enough to pay for the damage."

The Governor did not say another word.

"Can he go to Moki?" the Minister asked. Without waiting for an answer he added:

"I would like him to be sent there."

The Governor took in a very long breath. There was incomprehension in the eyes with which he looked at his boss. Finally he said beside himself:

"As the Honourable Minister says."

***

The man felt betrayed and shamed. To ask for Beckongncho to be sent to Moki did not suggest that he should be set free because it was a detention camp. But it implied several things to the Governor. First it implied, as the Minister's condemnation had indicated, that Beckongncho had so far not been accorded the kind of treatment he deserved. It even seemed to imply that he did not deserve all the torture that had already been meted out to him. Did the Minister understand the complicated nature of the crisis he was dealing with? He would be informed in due course that Beckongncho was not just a suspect but an accused. Moki was a detention camp for very important Government personalities from the rank of District Officers upward to Governors and even Ministers, who are suspected of some major default that was yet to be proved. They were kept there while investigations were carried out to clear or incriminate them.

Moki was a maximum security camp run entirely by army officers. Every detainee had a room and a parlour with a modicum of the luxuries of a home. There were books to read and a canteen where all sorts of drinks were available. The barman was an officer who was careful not to oversell to any particular customer. Each room was provided with a servant, an officer who did all household chores. Detainees who had wives were allowed to be visited by their wives in the secrecy of their rooms, for as long as five hours during the day.

The Governor could not by an stretch of his imagination guess what Beckongncho must have told the Minister that so completely changed his status. He was still contemplating this when the Minister said:

"Also, can I get the file on Nkokonoko Small Monje?"

"It is in my vehicle outside, Honourable Minister. You need it immediately?"

"Yes."

The man rose and hurriedly went out. He soon returned and presented it to the Minister. The Minister took it, went through the pages very carefully for a very long time without saying a word to the Governor. When he had finished he said:

"And, please, leave the matter entirely in my hands."

"I beg your pardon, Honourable Minister."

"Pursue the case of Nkokonoko Small Monje no further. Leave it in my hands. Entirely," he emphasized.

The Minister grew progressively indignants as he spoke until when the Governor bade him good-bye he answered only with a silent nod.

***

It is not that the Minister believed everything Beckongncho said as the Gospel Truth. But he was sure that all of it could not be false. There were certain points Beckongncho mentioned which did not differ radically from what the Minister knew the Governor was capable of doing. Beckongncho, however, had raised certain questions that required further investigation.

The Minister sent out a team of private investigators to probe the Governor's recent activities, especially the death of the old men and Anuse's alleged bribery. The results were as he had suspected, and except in a few unimportant details, the findings had corroborated with what Beckongncho had said. On the case of the death of the Elders who were buried in a mass grave soon after Beckongncho saw them, it was proved that the men had actually been killed in the army barracks on the instructions of the Governor. Their corpses were exhumed and a fingerprint specialist examined them and proved that seven of the fingerprints on the letter from Beckongncho matched those of the seven corpses.

Further investigation also proved that the Governor had been visited by Anuse soon after the killings in Small Monje. But what complicated the issue here slightly was that Anuse was said to have come with three Paramount Chiefs. Although this somehow contradicted what Beckongncho had said, it was, however, proved that they had not come on the Governor's invitation. It was also Elders whom he had tried very unsuccessfully to intimidate to accept Anuse as the new Chief. Lastly, a cheque of two hundred thousand drawn by Anuse. It took three days to assemble these results.

On the afternoon of the fourth day the Minister summoned an emergency meeting of the Top Executive Committee on Internal Affairs. The meeting was attended by six of the seven Provincial Governors, and the Chief of National Security. Also present was the Minister of Mines and Power, the Minister of Economic Planning and the Minister of Works and Transport. The Vice-Minister of Territorial Administration was present, so was the Secretary of State in the Office of the Prime Minister and the Secretary General in Governor Abraham-Isaac's office. Governor Abraham-Isaac himself was not invited to attend.

The Minister of Territorial Administration, as chairman of the meeting, spoke first. He thanked them for responding to his invitation at short notice, especially the Provincial Governors who had to travel long distances.

"We have on our hand," he went on, "an emergency and I am sorry that I should be summoning a meeting which should have been convened by Governor Abraham-Isaac who is absent for reasons which should be obvious by the end of the day."

He was wearing a sky-blue **agbada.** At this point the 1.79 meter tall Minister pulled first at the right sleeve which he threw over his shoulder. He did the same thing to the left sleeve. Placing both hands on the table and bowing slightly towards the participants said:

"The emergency is that in the principality of Nkokonoko Small Monje the natives have taken the law into their hands and, in very cold blood, have murdered their Chief, some eight Elders of their traditional council, a Reverend Father, and, for Christ's sake, the District Officer!"

"Oh nnoohh! the Minister of Transport shouted.

94

"Iyess!" the Chairman said. "They've murdered the District Officer and his wife, and his children."

"But," the Minister of Economic Planning cut in. "I thought it was said that there was only a Chieftaincy problem to which they had appealed to the D.O? That was what **STARLIGHT** said."

"It was," the Chairman admitted. "That was for public consumption," he said with a mischievous smile flickering at the corners of his mouth before disappearing under the seriousness of the moment. "This is an election year. You must be careful with the facts you throw at the public."

He looked at the Chief of Internal Security. The man was nodding.

"The extremely bitter truth in the matter is that DO Martin Ezeatebong is no more. All said and done, he fell victim to his own tactlessness as well as that of his immediate boss. Yet, his place has to be filled. It has to be filled by somebody whose safety we have to and are here today to guarantee. It would seem to me that the people of Small Monje are not yet satisfied with the outrage, guilty as they are."

"What?" the Chief of Internal Security shouted.

"Yes. I spoke with somebody who knows the absurd intricate nature of the ways of those people. He thinks they can do worse things."

"What exactly is their problem?" the Governor of the Extreme-South Province inquired worriedly.

"Chieftaincy. The idea of Chieftaincy takes on a strange dimension in Small Monje."

"With the House of Chiefs long closed?"

"Sure," the Minister said. "The closure of the House of Chiefs did not mean that chiefs should no longer exist."

"But why not wipe it out completely and forget about them?"

The Chairman was silent for a while.

"Nnoh!" he said. "We are here today to work out a strategy..."

"But Mr. Minister," the Extreme-South Governor went on: "There may be something in this matter which I don't know. Why should a small problem in Small Monje engage the attention of all these personalities? A place I cannot even place on the map!"

"Thank you for mentioning it," the Chairman said. "I began by saying I was summoning a meeting which should have been convened by Governor Abraham-Isaac. He did not do that. And the consequences of that neglect are grave. I don't quite agree with the Governor that the crisis in Small Monje is small. Don't be deceived by the appellation. Even if three quarters of the population of this country were made up only of DOs, the murder of any one of them cannot be described as a small thing. "The murder of six policemen, eight Elders and a Paramount Chief can never be considered small..."

"Honourable Minister," the Governor interrupted him, apologetically: "I didn't mean to minimize the death of all those people. What I meant to say was that the decision on the matter could quite conveniently have been taken without consulting this entire body."

"That much I know." The Minister was getting impatient. "But there's so much more which we all needed to know about Small Monje, only when we come together this way. Even if we cannot place Small Monje on the map, its strategic and economic importance cannot be overlooked."

There was a long silence. Then the Chairman said: "I don't know whether the Minister of Mines can give us a word on the economic value of Small Monje."

He then sat down.

The Minister of Mines rose. Probably in his late fifties, he had served the Government in various Ministerial posts for over a decade. But the was new in this particular ministry, hardly a year old. Clean - shaven and tall and dressed in a well-stitched black three-piece suit, he was a naturally inarticulate speaker. He had to undergo several years of speech therapy to help him overcome his stammering disability, a setback which many thought should have been enough to disqualify him from any ministerial office. But he was a brother-in-law to the Head of State, and that was enough to keep him in there. At any rate, he stammered his way through the explanation:

"I-I-I-j-j-j-jus-jus-t-t-te-te-too-too-took over th-th- this...of-of-of-office...B-b-b-but-th-th-the-r-r-r-re-ecord shows...th-th-that Es-es-es-esseHanyang an-an-anand Es-es-esseNkap con-con-t-tain la-

la-la-larged deposits o-o-o-of d-deposits o-o-o-of d-d-diamond, box-box-box-bauxite an-an-andcopper d-d-d-deposssits."

The chairman stepped in.

"So you see that we cannot ignore a place of that nature. Esse Hanyang and Esse Nkap have mineral deposits which when exploited should change the face of this economy."

The Minister of Economic Planning nodded. The Chairman went on:

"If I may add, there's above all, rich oil reserves. It looks like the Minister of Agriculture has something to add."

The man rose, thanked the Chairman and said:

"The entire Biongong area produces-quarters of the palm oil, half the cocoa and about half the coffee we export."

"And let me add here,: the Chairman cut in. Small Monje is the gateway into Biongong."

"Thanks for that. I was just going to say that myself," the Minister of Agriculture said, even though he had virtually finished talking. Economically, therefore, Biongong is an important nerve centre to this system."

"Security wise," the Chairman resumed his position. "Does Small Monje mean anything to the State?" he turned to the Chief of Internal Security.

"A lot," the man said, rising. "Very much. I'll go back to the point the Minister of Mines may have omitted." The Minister of Mines seemed to instantly take offence, even without actually hearing what it was that he must have omitted.

"I-I-I-d-d-d-did nnn-not s-s-s-say ev-ev-everything th-th-th-tha-tha-that I-I-I wa-wa-a-wanted to say," the man interjected.

"I did not say you did, Mr. Minister. Excuse me. It was no criticism of what you said."

The Chairman had to intervene.

"Excuse me, Honourable gentlemen. We have a problem in hand and I want to believe we all know that whatever is said here is an attempt to find a solution and not to offend. We must not misunderstand motives for comments."

He sat back down and beckoned to the Police Chief to continue.

"I am sorry if my observation hurt the Honourable Minister," the man said.

"But I still have to say that the oil we are boasting of exists in what geologists describe technically as synclines. If you write the letter U," he actually traced a large U on a piece of paper which he held up to the listeners. "The beginning and end of the U are mouths of the oil wells." He then ran a line between the two arms of the U. "This intersection line indicates the territorial boundary between Nigeria and us. One of the wells opens in Nigeria and the other opens in the Bevet area in Biongong. Nigeria has long started tapping their oil. The boundary does not cut across the oil syncline," he said with a sly touch of humour which the group did not miss.

Somebody chuckled loudly, then the Chairman rubbed it in: "We wish it did!"

There was a general laugh. The Police Chief went on:

"All the boundary disputes between Nigeria and us in the Biongong area have been as a result of the Nigerians trying to annex the Bevet people. Lives have been lost and many more will be lost in future. Many of the people in this border area speak both the Nigerian language and ours. Whatever Small Monje is asking for, therefore, we must be careful not to say a loud NO. Let us not give the Nigerians the opportunity to say they ae reclaiming their people."

When he sat down the chairman thanked them all for their very enlightening contributions which he said now placed the problem of Nkokonoko Small Monje in proper perspective. He closed one file, opened another and said:

"But the main reason I have invited all the Governors is not so much because of the economic and strategic importance of Small Monje, as the Governor for Extreme South had wondered earlier on. It is because of Governor Abraham-Isaac. and I am constrained to dwell on it a bit longer than might be expected, because he has fallen into a trap that could have been laid anywhere."

Here he poured himself a drink of imported mineral water. He had known Governor Abraham-Isaac for a very long time. Their first official encounter was some four years ago, over the very same deceased DO of Small Monje. At that time the deceased was DO of Ndungbeko in the Northwest of the country. He had been implicated in a case of fraud - having misappropriated one million francs Government funds given to him to construct a bridge. The Minister had been in office for only once year. A Top Executive

Committee meeting had been summoned and there he had decided that the DO be asked to retire immediately from Government service. He was already past retiring age.

Governor A braham-Isaac had not seen eye- to eye- with him. In a marathon speech that has lasted seventy five minutes he had defended the accursed DO - no learned lawyer could have done better. He was the Governor of the region he still ruled at the moment. His arguments has been purely on humanitarian grounds, or so it had seemed. He had suggested that the punishment be commuted to a transfer to the Middle-Lower Belt Province to work under his "watchful eye". Defending the man further he had pleaded:

"We stand for justice. But as human nature is what it is, the cause of justice should not be pursued so absolutely as to make us forget what human frailty is. Man is born weak." Abraham-Isaac had equated the request for a man's retirement coming after a scandal in which his name was mixed up, with **ignominious dismissal.** This too he had called "an act of ingratitude on the part of the Governor for a man who has put in the best years of his life to the selfless service of his native land."

The Minister and the rest of the Committee had found it hard to resist Abraham-Isaac' request. He had made his first and last concession - the DO had been transferred to the Lower Middle-Belt Province where he had now perished under the **watchful eye** of the Governor.

The Minister was to learn afterwards that Abraham- Isaac's plea for clemency had not been based on genuine humanitarian grounds as he had given people to believe. He was told that the DO was not only from the same tribe but was also a distant cousin of the Governor to solicit his intervention on his behalf, in the event of a disciplinary committee being summoned.

***

Thereafter the Minister's opinion of the Governor had changed. On this particular occasion the Minister talked briefly about his past knowledge of the Governor. He went on to narrate the story of what had taken place in Small Monje. He mentioned the details which his investigations had turned up.

These he said were not failings common to man in the Governor's oft-quoted theory of "to err is human, and to forgive divine." He regarded them as "glaring symptoms of a depraved personality, inimical to the kind of political system we have adopted and are aspiring towards." Then he went on vehemently:

"Governor-Abraham-Isaac is no stranger to me. He is no stranger to the administration of this country. He knows what I want, and he knows that it is what the state wants...How is it possible for a Provincial Governor to stoop so low as to receive petty bribes, thereby intensifying tension in the teeth of an as yet unresolved crisis that has already resulted in so much loss of life? This is a deliberate affront on the very core of my own personal authority and on that of the Head of State."

The depressing situation, he argued, could never have arisen if the Governor had agreed with him when he first suggested that the DO be retired. He made it clear that the Governor had not attempted at all to solve the problem posed by the uprising in Small Monje.

"The people have just learnt nothing from their mistakes," he said.

Drawing attention to the murder of the Elders in the army barracks he said: "The punishment must always be related to the crime. The killing of those old men, when and how it happened, and, guilty as they were of the uprising, had very little or nothing to so with their killing of the District Officer, their own Chief and the other Elders of the council. My Governor would have ordered a full scale investigation into the cause. He would have organized an open trial for the people to be openly proved guilty. He should then have ordered them to be openly executed, following the evidence of the trial.

"That way, the people of Small Monje and any other people anywhere else, would have seen the dangers of contemplation any such acts in the future... But to declare that you had pardoned the criminals, or to have even given them to believe themselves pardoned, only to go back again and smuggle them from the villages to come and kill them and bury them secretly, thereby obstructing the justice of knowing the precise cause of the problems

Here he shook his head and, like an attorney rounding off or imputing sinister motives into a charge he lowered his voice and said:

"Gentlemen, I am afraid, this kind of solution borders on the lunatic fringe of civil administration."

There was a long pause. Then he resumed, and throwing his open hands at the listeners said with a fall in his voice:

"Our brother the Governor has completely forgotten that a Reverend Father was one of the victims, that the Catholic Mission had threatened to close down its Health Centre, close its schools, cancel plans to open a college, to pull out altogether from Small Monje, unless the appropriate action is taken against the culprits."

"Let me even go further," he raised his voice a bit. "when news reached us that the DO and the others had been murdered, we were under the impression that Small Monje was in a state of war. Accordingly a contingent was sent there to impose a state of emergency until peace had been completely restored. The war, no armed resistance of any sort. One would have expected the Governor to reduce the number of soldiers in order not to alarm the civilians unduly.

"Rather than do this, Governor Adraham-Isaac caused the Company Commander to ask for more troops. This created a problem on two fronts: first of all it gave the impression that there was indeed war, secondly it gave the impression that the people of Small Monje were dangerous, that it was unsafe to venture there.

"From more reliable reports on the precise nature of what actually transpired, it would appear that Do Martin overstepped his bounds. Had he not done what he did, there would have been no trouble of any sort. From an initial force of one hundred soldiers, the number grew within a week to five hundred. And you know the liberties which soldiers can take in an atmosphere of tension. Stories of unnecessary harassment, rape and looting were reported. That was not all. Under a state of emergency like the one Governor Abraham-Isaac created, it costs at least 7,000 francs to feed a soldier per day. That means 400 soldiers would cost 2,800,000 francs per day. The soldiers were there for three weeks, so the Government spent the sum of 58,800,000francs. Had the soldiers been fed exactly as they ought to, I would not be speaking with so much vinegar on my tongue. But Governor Abraham-Isaac personally undertook to supply food to the soldiers through his agents.

"Information reaching us indicated that the soldiers ate less than 7000francs per soldier per day. That means our good friend made a profit of about 17,6400,000francs in a week. That doesn't sound like administration, it sounds like business."

"Business Administration, it sounds like business." humouredly.

Besides himself, the Minister smiled.

"Business Administration indeed," he said to himself.

His last words on the topic were heavy with the final condemnatory tone:

"Governor Abraham-Isaac may succeed in business," he said without the slightest touch of irony. "But he has failed as administrator.

Before the meeting finally broke off several resolutions were drawn up to be submitted to a higher council for study and implementation.

Chapter Eleven

Wise men learn by others' harms
fools by their own
                    (Anonymous)

Don't hang up a sheep's head at the frontshop
and sell dog meat.
                    (Daniel Crump Buchanan:
                    Japanese Proverb)

LATER IN the evening of the day of the Top Executive meeting, the phone rang in the study of the Provincial Governor. He was sitting in a chair with his head held down in very deep thought. He had already got wind of the extraordinary meeting from which he had been excluded. And this, coupled with the Minister's decision a few days before that Beckongncho be moved to Moki had left him an emotionally shattered creature of a man. For the past three days he had expected the Minister to give him some explanation for the decision, something that might give him a clue to what Beckongncho had said that had so completely turned the tables against him. But the Minister had said nothing.

When the phone rang he picked it up and said:

"Abraham-Isaac speaking."

"Aliou Ndam Garga speaking," said the voice at the other end or the line. This was followed immediately by an order:

"Please arrange for the release of Mr. Beckongncho tomorrow morning. Also ensure his very safe return back to his home."

As soon as he said so he hung up without allowing the listener one second to say anything.

***

103

The Minister's words did not mean that the Governor should personally go and release Beckongncho. It only permitted him to give orders to the Chief of Security concerned for the man to be allowed to go away. But rather than do this he chose to go down to the camp himself.

At 9 o'clock the following morning Beckongncho heard a knock on his door. When he rose and turned it open all the hopes and confidence of eventual survival, which his miraculous transfer to Moki and generated in him, evaporated in the instance. The very first man his eyes fell on was the Provincial Governor. immediately behind him came his body-guard and two senior army officers, all dressed in uniform.

The officers had no reason to greet Beckongncho. The Governor's mind was ridden with a burden of guilt at what he had done against Beckongncho. Besides, he was also very frightened by something he could not explain, but which upset him all the same. The Minister's opinion of Beckongncho seemed to be growing everyday. The previous night, for example, he had called him "Mr. Beckongncho." If he the Governor was to lose his job as he now feared in is heart, was it Beckongncho that would replace him? Whatever the case, it would be safest to be on the best terms with the ex-convict now, if only to make him less anxious to take his revenge at some later date.

As if suffering from some intense physical exertion, the man let his thick lips pull apart in what might have been meant for a smile. The effort did not succeed, and he entered with his face twitching in a manner which only deepened Beckongncho's fears. Perhaps there was much he had wanted to say to Beckongcho and speech. He took two hesitant steps towards Beckongncho and said:

"You will make an excellent Chief. You have stood the test of time. All that has happened to you has been designed by me to test your power of endurance. A troublesome spot like Small Monje needs a man of great patience and an iron will to rule it. You have proved yourself worthy of the title of Paramount Chief. Congratulations." As he said the last word he lowered his hand for a shake.

Beckongncho was flabbergasted. Was the Governor just mocking his end? Was that the last word before his execution? Or was he really about to be released? He held out a reluctant and trembling hand to the Governor and allowed him to shake it almost out of its socket. Then relaxing the grip the Governor said:

"You will now go back to your people eh. And remember to call on me in case of any difficulties in the discharge of your duties."

Beckongncho stood dumb. Surely that must be a dream, he thought. His eyes were wide open. He closed and opened them several times. It was no dream. the man standing in front of him and talking was no figment of the imagination. He was His Excellency Abraham-Isaac, Provincial Governor of the Lower-Middle Belt. He was declaring him free! He cleared his throat several times to get out his voice that had been drowned in fear. Then he stammered with a tingling exhilaration:

"Your Excellency, thank you very much."

But that did not make him any more relieved. He had lived in fear for two weeks, and no doubt, it had become part of his system. His, now, was not a state of mind that could be altered by a single declaration.

However, he was gradually coming back to himself. He was gradually beginning to assemble his thoughts realistically. He knew that he was not just being flattered by being told that he was a man of iron will, that he was a man of very great patience. He was certainly that, and more. And if it was no hoax that he had been released, if he had actually been released, then it was through the force of his own personality. He had not just been tempted. He had narrowly escaped death. Miraculously escaped.

For the Governor to say he had just been tempting him, it was next to saying he had merely been tempting those Elders who had been killed and buried. If he had been released, then it was not unconnected with what he had said to the Minister the day he was brought before him. He remembered that the Minister had listened to him with greatest concern and sympathy.

"There is a vehicle waiting for you outside eh," the Governor said with a fatiguing effort. "It will take you safely back to Small Monje-eh."

Beckongncho lifted his eyes and looked into the Governor's face. Only then did he notice that he had undergone a complete transformation. He had shrunken incredibly within the interval of just a few days. It now looked as though he too had served a prison term! His chubby cheeks which had glistened and bubbled with health and vitality the last time he saw them, had crumbled like a deflated balloon. The fleshiness around his eyes had turned to wrinkles that had developed and multiplied, adding many years to his age. The eyes themselves had become dull and pale, and his lips so dry that he licked them every second to make his words comprehensible.

This strengthened Beckongncho's thoughts that he was in fact, being released, and that this was very likely not the Governor's own decision. Still intensely suspicious of the Governor's motives, he said very politely:

"I am very grateful, Your Excellency. If I have really been released..."

"You have been released," the Governor said with a mechanical smile.

Beckongncho rubbed his hands on his thighs. Then he said again:

"If this is so, then, Your Excellency, I will not go to Small Monje now. I want to go to Sowa first. My family is still there,"

"But your people are waiting for you," the Governor said rather earnestly.

Beckongncho sighed and remained silent again. There was only one thing on his lips - that the people who should have been worried about his delay had by his wicked orders been killed and thrown away. He did not say so. Instead he told him:

"Your Excellency, they will wait for me still."

"The driver will take you to Sowa then?" the Governor said.

The offer was really genuine, or might have been so. But, in Biongong, there was a saying that

"A man who has just been bitten by a snake, will
not stand at the sight of a millipede."

And this was not just a millipede! It was the very serpent itself . He ignored the deep feeling of begging lurking behind the offer and objected with all courtesy:

"No, Your Excellency. Thank you very much for your kindness. I would want to go alone. I would like to go on my own." He found it hard, even under the auspicious circumstances, to under estimate the influence the Governor had over the army.

He did not wish to be the victim of a planned "accident".

"You have transport money?" the Governor asked.

Beckongncho had no money. He had emptied his purse in **ZANZIBAR**, and had been too excited with his promotion to Moki to try to get anything. Besides, those who took the money must have been released or imprisoned.

"I don't have anything, Your Excellency," he confessed.

The Governor put his hand in his left breast pocket and took out a bundle of notes. He withdrew a five thousand franc note and gave to Beckongncho. That one Beckongncho did not refuse.

"Thanks a million, Your Excellency," he said, folded the money and put it in his own breast pocket.

Chapter Twelve

The block of granite which was an obstacle
in the pathway of the weak, becomes a stepping-stone
in the pathway of the strong.

(Thomas Carlyle)

*T*HE **RELEASE** of Beckongncho was only the beginning of his troubles. There was first the trauma of the arrest, detention and psyche would not be easily eradicated. The Governor's eventual decision to allow him to go as he wanted, did not ease the burden of fear and doubt on his mind. Once out of the Moki grounds he decided to give himself a moment's respite. He stood at the street corner, dazed with desperate confusion, like the only survivor in a plane crash in which he had lost his entire family. All his strength of concentration had been scattered in endless fits of anxiety, despondency and fear for the past weeks.

He was anxious to quit Tetseale, and do so within the shortest possible time, before the administration changed its mind and began looking for him again. He knew in his mind that he was heading for the lorry station where he would take a vehicle for Sowa. There was a taxi station just at the entrance into the Moki camp. It was easy for one to find a taxi which would drive him for a small fee to the Sowa lorry station. But in the welter, jumble and turmoil of his mind he passed it without a thought. And for nearly two hours he wandered about from one street to another. What brought him back to his senses and made him remember that he was supposed to be in his way to Sowa, was exhaustion from trekking. He sought a taxi cab which took him to the Sowa bus station where he bought a ticket and took a seat in the bus bound for Sowa.

Only after travelling some two hundred kilometres out of Tetseale did he remember that his half-brother Ephraim Njikem lived in Tetseale, and that he should have tried to send a message to him during the weeks of his imprisonment. It was amazing how the Governor had attempted to so completely destroy his mind.

Already in his mind he had started thinking very seriously of his future and that of Small Monje, in the light of what had just taken place in the tribe. Whatever way the Governor regarded the act, the murder of the Elders of the Council in Tetseale would never be accepted in Small Monje as a justified action. He knew that as far as Small Monje was concerned, the killing of the DO had been undertaken as punishment for a crime he and those who had died with him had committed against the tribe. They certainly still expected an apology from the Government for sending such a man to rule over them who paid no respect to their traditions. The death of those old men and their secret burial was bound to be received as a brand new outrage perpetrated by the Government against the tribe, even surpassing the theft of the statue in magnitude. And for that Beckongncho, knew that the tribe would be ready to fight to the last atom of its strength.

As Beckongncho, and as their Chief, he could not choose but side with them. One thing was immediately obvious: a new DO would be chosen as soon as possible to take the place of the deceased. He would definitely be the target for the grievances of the tribe against the Government .What was also obvious was that the Government would now have its eyes skinned on Nkokonoko Small Monje. If they were going to take their revenge against the Government for the death of Ngobefuo and the others, if he was to be involved in it, then it must be thoroughly planned. It must be approached with maximum caution and foresight. The slightest flaw in handling the situation on his own part, was likely to result in an up uprising even more bloody than the last. And the results could be guessed at: the Government would send troops to massacre them all, raze the palace to the ground and put an end to Chieftaincy.

That was no mere pessimism. It was a possibility. It was an inevitability unless he acted with greatest prudence. Was that his intention in submitting to that gruelling torture for weeks? Certainly not. The aim had been to restore and not destroy the throne. Otherwise, what stopped him from releasing all the information the Governor required and returning quietly to Sowa the very day he was summoned?

Every available device must be employed to obtained the singular objective of defending the glory of the throne. There was no gain in immediate and blind vindictiveness. He knew well what his people said about caution in vengeance that:

> "If you will take your revenge on a man
> who has used your wife, wait until the
> sweat cools off from his body."

A far-ranging plan of revenge was to be worked out. Exactly what form it would take he was yet unsure. What he was sure about was the fact that his people would never forget or forgive the Government.

But in the meantime, maltreated as he was, he must pretend to be on the best terms with the Government. That was what the Government implied in exposing him to the luxuries of Moki Camp. The Government must be made to look very innocent in that really inflammable problem of the death of the Elders.

For his own imprisonment, it was never to be mentioned at all to anybody who did not know about it already. It was unfair to communicate it to somebody he loved and whom he knew would be more disturbed by his plight than he himself. Now that he had already survived, and now that he was coming back to himself, he would choose a moment distant in place and time to release any information on the matter to anybody. Thank God he had not seen Njikem. Thank God he had told his wife not to let anybody know what had happened to him

Chapter Thirteen

Those who live at the base of the tree
know what the tree-ants eat.
(Ngumbu Njururi: *Gikuyu Proverb*)

*T*O RULE Nkokonoko Small Monje without Ngobefuo or any of those old men who had perished with him in Tetseale meant starting from scratch. Nobody was more aware of this than Beckongncho himself. He took the challenge with rare determination.

He was in Sowa just long enough to hand over his responsibilities to a new headmaster. Before he came back the Governor had already contacted the DO of Sowa to whom he had explained that the arrest had been an error, and that Beckongncho should be treated with very great respect.

On his part, Beckongncho did not think it necessary to grudge the DO, or, if he did, to show it. He went to see him on his returned, and in his address at the party that had been held to send him off, he thanked the DO heartily for the co-operation and love he showed towards him throughout his stay in Sowa.

The following day he bade goodbye to Sowa and left for Small Monje leaving behind his wife and two children. The two men who had brought the letter from the Council of Elders were still waiting for him, and he left with them. He had already worked out a tentative plan of action..

As a first important step, the vacuum created by the death of the councillors was to be filled immediately. He would not go straight to the palace. He was still strong enough to walk about. He would visit the Sub-Chiefs whose villages made up the tribe, his kingdom, and seek their views and advice on the formation of a new Council of Elders.

The name he had in mind when he was thinking of a man on whom he could count for sound fatherly advice was Sub-Chief Mbe Bejaah of Kamba. Mbe Bejaah was a man of very great stature in the politics of the tribe. If Ngobefuo had been preferred to him, as the care-taker, it was only because, as the saying went,

"If two men drink from the same calabash,
one must drink before the other."

And although everybody had wondered how he was going to react to the choice of Ngobefuo, which implied his own defeat, he had taken it in very good faith. He had promised Ngobefuo and all the tribe his co-operation in anything that demanded his attention.

But he never got on very well with Ngobefuo. Ngobefuo found him too conciliatory to be consulted in matters that called for ruthless and immediate action. To avoid continuous conflict with Ngobeuo he had told him that he would withdraw from active participation in their affairs and only play an advisory role.

Ngobefuo had never directly spoken to Beckongncho about Mbe Bejaah in a particularly serious context. But Beckongncho's was conversant with the way things were being run in the tribe, so he inevitably came to know about the man. His desire to withdraw from active participation did not taint Beckongncho's opinion of him. He held him in very high esteem. If he were still alive, and if he saw him, Bejaah would be the man he would suggest as care-taker of the tribe or the man to help him choose one.

But when he reached Kamba, he was told that Bejaah had deserted his palace at the approach of the Government forces and had never returned. Nobody knew where he had gone, or whether he was still alive or not. This was very sad news for Bechongncho, and a new crisis of bad humour set in. But he bore it all patiently. He had ten other Sub-Chiefs and Quarter-Heads to count on.

His next stop was Shega. The newly dug motorable road did not reach the hills over which a good number of the Chiefs settled, and so it took him two days to cover that distance of only twenty-five kilometres, using horses acquired at Kamba. The terrain was very difficult, and there was virtually no means of communication between one village and another. The Chief of Shega was Komia. He was in his palace when the three men entered.

It was here that Beckongncho first sensed that he had already become a Paramount Chief. In Kamba he had met only a few women and children, none of whom really knew who he was. So he had not been received in any respectable manner. But at the sight of the three men, Chief Komia ran out with great excitement and came as if to embrace him. When Beckongncho opened his hands to receive him, the man halted a meter off, clapped his hands three times, each saying 'mmmmmmmmooohhhh,' and bowing until his head almost touched his knees. Then rising from the third bow said:

"Son-of-Man, my mouth cannot say how glad we are to see you come."

Son-of-Man was the local title for Chief-Designate Beckongncho warned himself not to look too surprised or excited, an attitude which he knew was the mark of mature authority. He smiled from that respectable distance and thanked Komia.

The old man went on at once to the inevitable. He inquired about the Elders:

"Son-of-Man, where is your voice, shadow and ear?"

This was the moment he dreaded above all. How long, he wondered, could he withhold such very bad news without being held or thought truly responsible?

"They were taken to come and bring you back. Have they gone ahead to prepare for your coming or what?"

Beckongncho did not answer. He asked for a cup of water. And when he had sat down and drunk, he supported his chin with his left hand.

"My father, our tribe is going through strange things," he said. "None of them has returned. None of them will ever return. They have added their names to this legend of the dead that has become the story of our people. They all perished in an accident in a river when they were still going to Tetseale to meet me." The lie came without effort, as though he was used to telling lies.

Mbe Komia's face fell and his eyes closed and opened a million times. He sat mute with stupefaction for a whole minute.

Then he inquired:

"That they all died Son-of-Man?"

"Every single one. Soldiers and all," he said in a desolate voice. He wished with all his soul that he could tell the truth.

"Where are their bodies, son of man?"

"It was impossible to see even the lorry. It sank with them. Father," Beckongncho went on," do me a favour."

"And what favour will Son-of-Man ask of me that I will not do for him?"

"Let us not talk about it," Beckongncho said. "Let us not dwell on the issue of the dead again. We mourn for them and then we try to see how we can get the tribe going again. There are far too many banana peelings on the road."

There was no more talk on the topic. The old man believed every word of Beckongcho's. All the Quarter-Heads and Sub-Chiefs had secretly vowed to give him all their support in everything. It was the only way of restoring the throne to the prestige it had lost under the intractable Nchindia. When Beckongncho told him about the problem that faced the throne at that critical moment, that of choosing a new Council, Komia did not even allow him to explain in any great detail. Intoxicated by the prospects of becoming the new care-taker, he simply threw himself into Beckongncho's service, promising him the co-operation of the ten other Chiefs. He begged Beckongncho to do him the honour of waiting in his palace while he and his men personally went round and contacted the rest of the Chiefs for him. Komia and thirteen people set out on horseback.

In two days, the mission that was to have taken Beckongncho weeks to accomplish ended with very great promise. All the Sub-Chiefs whose services he desperately needed convoked in Shega and the day after they proceeded to the palace in Small Monje. It was on this occasion too that he was told (though he doubted at first) that Mbe Bejaah was not missing. He was told that the man had long gone to the palace on a mission which was to be explained to the Chief in the palace.

***

Beckongncho had not even been consecrated Chief. He had not been crowned. But he entered the palace of Nkokonoko Small Monje on a palanquin flanked by six prominent Chiefs of the tribe, all sworn to the one indomitable purpose of giving the throne back its respect. Such was the love and honour the people had for him, and such was the force of the unflinching support they wanted him to expect to get from them. And in the consciousness that he was indeed the kind of man they really wanted, he found the chief consolation for all the indignities and tortures suffered in Tetseale. Half the problem was solved.

Chapter Fourteen

There is no failure except in no longer trying
There is no defeat except from within
No really insurmountable barrier
Save our own inherent weakness of purpose.
(Kin Hubbard)

M ***BE BEJAAH*** had indeed gone to the palace in Small Monje. The story that he had disappeared had been invented and left behind by himself to conceal his whereabouts, should the soldiers want to seize him too as they had seized the other old men. He had not imagined that Beckongncho would take the trouble of passing through his palace, so he had not made exception to the person to whom the story would be told.

When the soldiers from Tetseale had come for Ngobefuo the second time he Ngobefuo had sensed something amiss and had sent for Bejaah. They had never been enemies. They had merely agreed to disagree, without letting their disagreement affect the smooth running of the tribe. Bejaah had come, and in the presence of the other Quarter-Heads Ngobefuo had said:

"We are no longer master of our tomorrow. They have come for me again. They say I should go and bring our Chief back. My blood shakes me. Should I not return, I give the reins of the tribe as temporary care-taker to Bejaah, if you agree, He will be care-taker until I return. Or care-taker forever if I do not return, and if you my brothers think it so."

This was the decision which Komia had hoped to reverse with his obsequiousness. Ngobefuo never returned. The onus of narrating the sad event of the death of the remnants of their council in Tetseale fell on Komia. A supreme actor and sycophant. He told the story to the shocked assembly as though he had actually seen it all happen. A bridge, he said, the height of a palm tree, had broken with their lorry in the middle of it. They had then fallen to their death in a river from which not even a piece of the lorry had been seen.

This Backongncho had confirmed as true. Bejaah declined from questioning Beckongncho any further on the death. They all accepted it as the will of God.

Later that night, to Backongncho's greatest delight, he was informed that Bejaah had been named the new care-taker. Beckongncho thanked God that his judgment of the man's worth had not been at fault. That night too Bejaah told Beckongncho that there was not going to be any "catching ceremony," because he was already universally known as the Chief-Designate. He said there would only be a crowning ceremony. As to the whereabouts of the crown, sceptre and bangles he said:

"I know where they are. Ngobefuo showed me. He did not know whether he would come back." Beckongncho could not conceal a broad smile. As his people would say, that night, Beckongncho 1 of Nkokonoko Small Monje. As his first move he immediately declared fourteen days of mourning for all the Elders who had died as a result of the uprising and its aftermath.

***

He was crowned on Saturday. On Monday evening, barely two days after that, while he sat relaxing in the palace listening to his National Broadcasting Service two momentous news items were made. The first announced a drastic reorganization in the Provincial Governorship. The Governor of the Northern Province was transferred to the South, while the Governor of the South became the Governor of the Coastal Province. The Governor of the East-Central Province became the Governor of the South-West, while the latter took the place of the former. It was not said that Governor Abraham-Isaac had been relieved of his duties. It was simply announced that the new Governor of the Lower-Middle-Belt Province was Abdu Karimu, a new entrant. The population was left to fill in the blanks:

"Justice has had its reward," Beckongncho told himself.

The second announcement would be remembered for decades because it drove waves of confusion down the spine of the entire tribe of Nkokonoko Small Monje. It said:

According to Presidential Decree no. 25/816/423 of 29th June signed in Tetseale today, Mr. Kevin Beckongncho, presently Paramount Chief of Nkokonoko Small Monje, has been named the new Senior District Officer for that District and Bimobio. He takes over from Martin Ezeatebong, deceased.

Beckongncho felt sick. Somebody in the radio house must be playing pranks on his life. In the first instance, Bimobio and Small Monje has from time immemorial been separate people, falling under two different administrative regions. To now call them as belonging under the same SDO was as ridiculous as to imagine that being a headmaster was the best qualification for an SDO. Were they now about to make him an agent of a system he had always ridiculed?

He had found much to laugh at each time there had been a cabinet reshuffle. On one occasion, the University Librarian had been taken straight from his office and made the Minister of Health. He was still holding that office. The man who was then the Minister of Education had been appointed immediately after his return from a three-year course in photography in Sweden. And the Chairman of the Chamber of Commerce, a former butcher, was at that time the Chancellor of the University.

Now he had been made the SDO, with hundreds of people wandering jobless, on whom the Government had spent millions to train for such administrative jobs. He would go to Tetseale immediately after the mourning period was over, to know exactly what the announcement meant. In the meantime, he would accept the office. It was presidential decree, and therefore it would be suicidal for him to say no. Not in the light of what was known about Small Monje already.

In his discerning mind he could see in that nomination, a reason for arresting him (should he refuse) on charges of subversion and abolishing Chieftaincy. So when Bejaah asked him what he thought about the decree, he told him:

"If I am to remain Chief, and if this tribe is ever to have a Chief after me, I should not refuse."

This point he would ignore to his cost in future.

"I say yes," he reaffirmed. "What I want to know," he said, "is the idea of Bimobio. That is what I will want to know from the Government in Tetseale."

Everybody immediately saw, or was made to see something really advantageous for the tribe in the Chief's acceptance.

***

Two days before he was to leave for Tetseale to inquire about his responsibilities as SDO, Ephraim Njikem, Beckongncho's cousin visited him. He was a Chief of Service in the Ministry of Mines, Power and Fisheries, in Tetseale. In the morning of the very day that Njikem came Beakongncho had received a letter of congratulations from the former on his coronation as the new Paramount Chief. The letter had delayed a long time in reaching Beckongncho.

In that letter Njikem had made no mention of the impending visit he had now undertaken. He had reached Small Monje late in the evening and in the palace he told the Elders who received him that he had some very important information for the Chief and that he would be going back the following day. He asked to speak to the Chief alone. The Chief was in council with his Elders but he sent for Njikem who insisted on talking to him alone.

"You cannot ask the Chief to come out and meet you alone. You do not expect the Elders to go out so that you talk to the Chief's, an elder told him at the door. For some reason Njikem did not take the man seriously. When he insisted and was allowed into the Chief's presence he made the same request.

"These men are my mouths and ears,' Beckongncho told him.

"Meaning?" Njikem inquired with some embarrassment.

"Meaning that between them and me there is no secret.

Whatever is said to me in their presence will forever remain a secret, if I so will."

Beckongncho knew so early in his reign that the best way of using his advisers was never to give them the impression that they were in anyway unreliable. And even if he was to doubt their ability to keep secrets, it should not come so early. Thumbs up.

***

Beckongncho's judgment of the man may be very inaccurate or even harsh. But one thing was clear: He had never credited Njikem with much foresight, close as they were. He was, therefore, not anxious to lose the respect of his Elders by attending to the call of a man whose sense of judgment he held in doubt. Although Beckongncho and Njikem grew up together, calling themselves brothers they never seemed to agree on very many things.

They would disagree, for example, on the strength of local football teams whose records were clear. If Beckongncho declared that although a particular team had been promoted to the First Division, it wouldn't last more than a year, Njikem would take the contrary view. He would even argue very earnestly that the very team might win the championship.

Because Beckongncho's judgment was usually based on a careful study of the team's strengths and weaknesses, his predictions usually turned out to be true, or at least nearly always closer to the truth. That, however, did not make Njikem change his mind on many points of their disagreement.

Beckongncho expected that having heard what the Elders had said Njikem would say whatever he had to say in their presence. But Njikem felt insulted and withdrew without saying anything. The following day he returned to Tetseale.

It was just as well he returned without saying what he had in mind. He had come to tell Beckongncho not to accept the appointment as SDO because he believed that it might be part of the Government's plan to crush the strength of Small Monje by making its most powerful defender an Administrative Officer, an office which would make it impossible for Beckongncho to oppose the Government's decisions regarding that area.

Had Njikem succeeded in getting the argument across to Beckongncho, he would have been told that the trip was a wasted one because his mind had long been made up on the issue. The following day when Beckongncho learned that Njikem had gone away he wrote to him:

Dear Brother;
I was surprised to hear this morning that you had returned to your Tetseale station. I have the feeling that your sudden departure back implied you may

not have been particularly happy that you could not speak to me personally and alone.

I can only say I am sorry. It hurts, I know, but I could not have behaved differently. If you absolutely needed to talk to me privately, the best way would have been for you to write to me. Or seek a moment when I would be alone, Or even ask me to find time to talk to you alone.

To come down and demand on the spot that I go out and talk to you is a little out of the usual custom which we are trying to restore to its former glory. I had just been crowned and I did not want to be the first person to exhibit ignorance of the tradition of our people.

There is this second part of my appointment as SDO for the District: I know how critical you have always been of Dos and other politicians. That too I know will disturb you. It took me completely by surprise, and I had to think it over for a whole week before saying yes. To say no would endanger my position as Chief here, considering how much the former SDO interfered in affairs of the tribe. I thought it would be better to work from within to change things. I know I am no man's fool. We should only pray to God to help us all in making something good out of it. Give your family my love. And, please, do well to write soon.

Part Three

Chapter Fifteen

All deception in the course of life
is indeed nothing else but a lie reduced
to practice, and falsehood passing from
words into things.

                                    (Robert Southey)

BECKONGNCHO EVENTUALLY made the trip
to Tetseale. He would learn that there had been no
error in any of the announcements made either concerning
his nomination or the idea of the union of Small Monje and Bimobio.
His consternation at being chosen SDO had long been anticipated.
The new Governor explained matter-of-factly:

"We know that you did not go to any school of Administration.
But it shouldn't make much difference because as headmaster you
have been a kind of administrator. The Government preserves the
records of its civil servants, and your nomination should tell you
that we have been satisfied with your work. All you will require for
now is one month orientation here in Tetseale, say next month or
so. After that, the rest will come with time. You follow me?"

"Your Excellency," Beckongncho answered. Something else
required explaining. He began:

"But, Your Excellency, one thing I did not quite understand
was the range of my jurisdiction. The decree seemed to suggest
that Small Monje and Bimobio are no longer two different Sub-
Districts. And as far as I know there has been no move to make the
two one...."

"Yes the records show that there has," the Governor told him
confidently.

Beckongncho looked perplexed.

"A culmination of years and years of negotiation on the part of
the two peoples. It was decided at a referendum."

"Referendum!"

"Referendum. Or plebiscite, if you like," the Governor told him.

He asked for the file on the Small Monje Referendum. When it was brought he opened to the relevant section and gave it to Beckongncho to study.

A Referendum had been held six months earlier. At least, that was what the documents indicated. The decision reached for the union of the two tribes had been unanimous, and the letter containing results also bore the signatures of the two Chiefs of the tribes - Nchindia, for Small Monje and Zemto for Bimobio. It also bore the signature of the deceased DO and that of the Administrative Assistant of Bimobio. It was therefore a genuine and authentic document.

"I never heard of this, Your Excellency," Beckongcho confessed.

" Well, it will all be explained to you back in Small Monje by those who voted." Beckongncho had one last question to ask.:

"Your Excellency, how is this idea of SDO and DO worked out?" he asked.

The man explained:

"When the representative of the Head of State rules over a population of 7.000-15,000 he is called an Administrative Assistant or District Head. When the population is 15-24,000 he is called simply a DO, and the administrative unit is called Sub-District. Over 25000 he is the SDO, and the unit, Division. A full District is more complex, requiring more budgetary provisions than the Sub-District, to cater for colleges, hospitals and the like.

Then there is the bona fide promotion where a D.O is promoted to SDO while still in the same unit. This is when Districts with a total population of over 25,000 agree among themselves to come together and form a full Division, in order to enjoy the benefits of full Divisions. The D.O becomes SDO by *bona fide* because he happens to be on the spot when the union occurs. This is why you are SDO. The negotiations were made during the reign of your predecessor."

Beckongncho's return to Small Monje did not bring him nearer to the truth than he had been in Tetseale. His entire Council of Elders confessed that they had never taken part in any plebiscite. Mbe Bejaah and Fuo-Akeumbin very faintly recalled a certain rumour in which Nchindia had once talked to Ngobefuo about bringing the two tribes together under the tutelage of the Chief of Small Monje. They recalled that Ngobefuo had spoken to the Chief so bitterly that he had never raised the point again.

Fuo-Nchumbe mentioned that very many months ago he had heard of a meeting of the people of Bimobio in the market to decide whether they would join Small Monje. But the same man had added that nothing had happened because Ngobefuo had forbidden his people to go to the market that day.

There was a deeper truth, however, and it lay with the DO and Nchindia who were already dead. The DO had always been a shrewd contriver. To become an SDO had always been one of his foremost ambitions in life. His main attraction here was the huge budgets which the Government usually allocated to them for the development of the areas under their jurisdictions. It would be an excellent opportunity for him to manipulate the funds to his personal advantage.

But he could not achieve that ambition by ruling over Small Monje alone because its population was only nineteen thousand. He decided to effect a union with Bimobio which had a population of eleven thousand.

First he approached the Administrative Assistant of Bimobio whom he very easily convinced. If the man would co-operate with him and convince his subjects to join Small Monje, he would suggest his name to the Provincial Governor as his immediate assistant, when he became the SDO.

The man agreed. The two men then worked to convince the Chief of Bimobio.

Here they had practically no problem because the Chief saw that if they allowed things to follow their natural course, they would never have a college for their children, a hospital for their sick, or good roads, all of which were facilities enjoyed by full Districts only.

The main problem lay with the people of Small Monje. But he easily won Nchindia over to his side. He explained to Nchindia that in the yearly elections of the president of the National House of Chiefs, he held the casting vote. If, therefore, Nchindia succeeded in getting his people to unite with Bimobio, he would make him the president of the National House of Chiefs. There was, beside, the other facilities which would flow as soon as the area because a full District - pipe-borne water, Trunk A roads, cathedrals, colleges and the like.

Ngobefuo would listen to none of these. The Bimobio were a conquered people and virtually lived under the bondage of the people of Small Monje To agree to unite with them would imply an acceptance of equality of status, something which struck deep at the roots of their native pride. He warned Nchindia never to mention it again.

But the D.O was not discouraged. He succeeded in obtaining Nchindia's signature on the relevant documents, along with that of the Chief of Bimobio and the Administrative Assistant. He then went ahead to announce that there was going to be a plebiscite. The Chiefs were to discuss the matter in the market place. On that day Ngobefuo forbade his people from going to market.

Some thirteen people who had not heard of the order went. Eighty one people came from Bimobio. The chiefs spoke and the matter was put to the vote. A total of 75 people voted in favour of a union, and all were from Bimobio. It was the ridiculous scene which went down in the Government records Beckongncho had seen in Tetseale as *a unanimous decision*, of the two tribes. And it was the uninformed opinion of these 75 people that had decided the fate of the 30.000 people who constituted the two tribes.

When Ngobefuo heard that something of the sort had transpired at the market, he merely laughed at them all. By this time the relationship between him and the Chief had already broken down completely, and they were both waiting only for a miracle to save the situation. The result of the plebiscite had already been submitted to Tetseale where the Government was studying it. Only the murder of the DO and the Chief had delayed the release of facts submitted, and which Beckongncho had seen in Tetseale.

Chapter Sixteen

It was the best of times, it was the worst of times,
and it was the age of wisdom , it was the age of
foolishness,
it was the epoch of belief, it was the age of
incredulity,
it was the season of Light, it was the winter of despair,
we had everything before us, we had nothing before us,
we were all going direct to Heaven,
we were all going direct the other way.
(Charles Dickens: *A Tale of Two Cities*)

BECKONGNCHO **RETURNED** to Tetseale
for his orientation course two weeks after he had
come back to Small Monje. He was in Tetseale for five
weeks, during which time he was given a Jeep and a team of eighteen
policemen to aid him in his official duties. During this time too he
learned that as SDO he would not stay in the palace in Small Monje.
He would stay in the residence of the Administrative Assistant of
Bimobio, pending the construction of a new house for him. He
was also informed that a fine of twenty-one million francs had
been imposed on the people of Small Monje for damages done to
Government property and personnel. This fine was to be paid in
five years. He, however, succeeded in making the Governor extend
the length of time within which the debt was to be paid. There was
also going to be a police post and a resident Commissioner.

***

On his return to Small Monje four of his Elders came to him
that same evening. They were Mbe Bejaah, Fuo-Akendong, Fuo-
Akeumbin and Fuolebe.

"There is a fly in our soup in Likume," Bejaah began.

Beckongncho stretched himself for a while, sat up and asked: "What have my fathers heard?"

"News has reached us here that the cut-throat, Marcus Anuse, is throwing dust into people's eyes so that they should not see the glory which you are bringing this throne."

"What has he said, my fathers?" Beckongncho inquired anxiously.

"To repeat what we hear he said is to think that there is anything other than evil in it," Fuolebe told the chief. "The decision we have arrived at is that His Highness will go down and meet the people…".

"His Highness would still have had to go down, as tradition requires," Fuo-Akeumbin pointed out.

"Do not remove talk from my mouth," Fuolebe said to Fuo-Akeumbin. "I thought that was long agreed upon." He then turned to Beckongncho and said: "We hope that His highness is with us."

"Why should I disagree with you without even knowing the heart of the matter?" Beckongncho asked. "As for going down to Likume, it is part of the tradition. We don't even have to discuss it. We only have to set a date and arrange for the travel. The problem is that since this particular journey is further made necessary by something else, I need to know what that is and how we are going to counteract it. I know Anuse very well, there is nothing he cannot do on this earth. Anytime you want me to know what he said, do so. But know that we are together."

Beckongcho was eventually told that from stories spread by Anuse, he was being blamed for the death of the Elders, the fraudulent union of the two tribesmen and many other happenings in the tribe. His council met and discussed strategies and left the execution of the matter in the hands of the Chief who said he was equal to any task that would be set for him. On a more personal level, he wrote to Angelina Nchindia, the widow of the late Chief, inviting her to find time to meet him during his visit.

***

The visit of the Chief was announced one month in advance to give his subjects in Likume enough time to receive him. And a week before he was due to arrive a special envoy was sent to his colleague, the SDO of Likume to tell him of the impending visit, and also to ask for permission to use one of the big halls in town.

Before they finally got to Likume accommodation had already been arranged for him at the Government Rest House. There he was at liberty to exercise his full rights as chief in whatever way his tradition required. There he lodged with his whole entourage of four Elders and three of his wives, it was here too that his loyal subjects came to see him and pay their respects the very night he arrived.

But not everybody who came to see him came only to greet. There were people with grievances. One of these was a woman, Betong's wife. She came to tell the chief that her husband had been killed and that she suspected Anuse. Her son had met Anuse and her late husband quarrelling vehemently about a written commitment being demanded from Anuse concerning something he had promised Betong before a trip they had made to Tetseale. The day after that quarrel Betong had left for work and had not returned. His decomposing body had only been seen three days afterwards under a bridge far away form his office. The police had been told about what had happened prior to his death. The police had visited Anuse twice, and after that nobody seemed anxious any more to track down the man's killers.

She was pleading with the Chief to use his good office as SDO to ask his colleague the SDO of Likume to personally take up the investigation of her husband's death. Beckongncho felt sincerely touched by the news. But he asked her to exercise a little more patience until he had laid his hands on the real facts of the situation. The last person he spoke to was Angelina Nchindia, the widow of the late Chief.

"I have asked you to come, madam," he began, "as the wife of the throne. Tomorrow I intend to invite ALL the wives of the throne, past and present, to return to the palace. Yours is a special case and so I did not want to mention your name in the market place. What do you think?"

The women looked overwhelmed by emotion. She would not return to the palace. The palace brought too much bitterness to her

133

mind. She would never set foot on the soil of Small Monje, not just because she was pregnant with Nchindia's baby but because the place terrified her, she sobbed as she spoke.

"Then, very exceptionally," Beckongncho said with great compassion, "the throne will settle you in Sowa. The throne will give you a little capital to help you in a small trade to take care of your children.

***

Before Beckongcho went to bed that night the programme of the activities of the following day had been carefully described to him. The meeting was to take place in the Presbyterian Youth Centre auditorium that could hold over five hundred people. The meeting time was going to be 12 noon, but people were supposed to start going there immediately after the third mass at 10 o'clock, to avoid a last minute rush. After the meeting there was going to be some traditional dancing up at the Rest House for the entertainment of the Chief and his colleagues. That was going to be at 4pm. Then later that night, at 8 o'clock a select number of the Chief's subjects was to return to the Youth Centre again for a cocktail party on his behalf.

By half past eleven on that Sunday morning everybody had already come and was seated in the hall, waiting for the Chief. The people numbered about three hundred, and included not only people from Likume but also tribesmen from the neighbouring districts. The men were in the majority.

At exactly 12 noon a Land Rover drove into the premises of the Youth Centre. Two policemen jumped out and ran round, one pulled open a door and raised his hand briskly in salute. He was greeting the SDO. As the man emerged, the officer retreated, leaving the rest of the formalities in the hands of the Chiefs servants.

Two minutes afterwards, Chief Beckongncho entered the hall in full traditional regalia. Standing exactly 1.91 metres, he had never before looked more a Chief than he did on this particular occasion. He was wearing a long down-reaching gown, a mixture of blue and red laced together with bright yellow thread and intricate embroidered in front, along the sides and behind. A portion of the gown extended far behind him where it was borne by a servant. On his head was a cap that extended in two flaps that fell and rested one on each shoulder. Round his neck were two rows of blue beads and a row of cowries. He carried the staff of his rank in his right hand, his kingly bangles rolling back and forth in his left arm. He wore slippers of brown leather, coated with tiger skin, and he walked with such majestic slowness that one would think he was afraid he would step out of the slippers. Two women accompanied him, his first wife and the woman he slept with the first night after he had been crowned chief.

The hall rose as soon as he appeared at the door a compliment he acknowledge with a silent nod as he climbed on to the throne that had been erected for him then as soon as he stretched his feet over the broad tiger skin in front of him, he waved to the people to sit down.

The hall sank silently.

When everybody had sat down the president of the Likume Elements of Small Monje rose to the ground in front of the Chief, clapped his hands three times and bowed until his head nearly touched his clasped hands over his knees. Then he rose and very respectfully withdraw to a corner from which he partly faced the rest of the people. There he made his introductory address to the Chief:

"His Highness, the Paramount Chief and His Excellency the Senior District Officer of Nkokonoko Small Monje. We the Small Monje elements in Likume and its environs, have gathered here this morning with a heart full of inexpressible gladness to say welcome to you. Those of us, and I mean all of us who have been following the troubled history of our people very closely, know how long ago it is since we last came together to sit down as one people to receive our Chief with the pride that is in us this day. It is not one month ago. It is not one year ago not even ten years ago. It is full eleven years. Eleven years."

He was nodding himself as he spoke. "But today we are proud. We are proud because despite all the pressing duties of State and the tribe, our Chief has been able to find his minute to come down on his own and breathe the same air with us his children. We are glad and thankful again to the gods of our fathers and forefathers that we cried for a Chief that will deliver us from shame and, after all that we have known and seen they have given us a Chief." Here he bowed towards Beckongncho as a special compliment. The latter smiled. A very loud applause followed until the president raised his hand for the first time in the history of any people, the offices of traditional ruler and SDO have been entrusted into the hands of one single person our Chief." There was another applause, spontaneous, long . He went on:

"Whether this is an advantage or a disadvantage, we do not think that it lies in our power to tell. At least not at this early moment. But for those who have gone home amongst us during the last months, we think that there is reason to doubt that it is a disadvantage. The palace that was once on its knees is now standing on its feet again. And the dew has not even dried from our Chief's feet on the throne! This is something to make us fell proud.

"We shall not talk much. We shall not talk very much because this visit was our Chief's idea, not ours. And since it was his idea we know that his Highness has something to tell us first."

He folded his hands and looked directly at the Chief while pointing to his people.

"We have our problems quite all right. And there has been much unpleasant talk in the air especially on the point of the union of the two tribes back home, which we think his Highness must have got wind of. There has been much unpleasant talk too about the death of the Elders of the Council of Small Monje. We do not know anything about these things. So we shall only raise the point if they are not among the things his Highness had to tell us. His Highness the paramount chief and Senior District Officer of Nkokonoko Small Monje, your subjects say welcome to you."

There was an applause which lasted for several minutes. Then a silence.

The chief was going to talk. He did not rise from where he sat, Tradition did not allow him to stand when addressing his subjects. He merely sat up, holding a piece of paper bearing broad outlines of what he had to say to them. His reply was a series of thanks. He thanked them first for the massive attendance which he said had made him exceedingly proud of his decision to visit them. He said he was particularly happy in that such an attendance was an example of something he had come down to emphasize - unity. He thanked the president for his short and very meaningful address which he said he had completely understood and taken to heart.

On the point of the traditional ruler being at the same time the SDO, he told them that he shared with them the doubts whether it was an advantage or a disadvantage because it was new to him. But he gave them all the assurance that whatever it was meant to be, he would use it to the fullest advantage for the tribe because:

"This Kevin Beckongncho whom they have made SDO is of pure Biongong blood. He was Paramount Chief of Nkokonoko Small Monje before being made anything else. So he has to think first as one of you before anything else."

A thunderous applause greeted him. Nobody knew better than himself that it was an affair that called for very great prudence. He hated what had happened. But as SDO himself, he would be very careful not to talk too senselessly against the Government, which he now represented. He would be no Chief of Small Monje, if not SDO of that district too. There would be no more chief in Small Monje if he ceased to be the SDO. He would give the people the facts, as they could easily be easily verified and defended by him, without sounding emotional about anything. Then he would sit back and let their reactions determine his. If they looked sad, it meant they expected him to be sad. If they looked angry he would show anger too. But he would carry nothing to excess. Knowing that nobody, not even his worst enemy could ever have access to the truth, or accuse him of dishonesty.

"I would want to confirm with a very heavy heart that the union you have heard of in rumour has become a fact. It is a very unfortunate thing. And I call it so with a meaning - it is irrevocable. Nothing can be done about it because it has already become law. And it became law long before I became chief and the SDO of the district.

"Our people once asked why they could not have good roads, why they could not have a college, and why they could not have a hospital. None of these things could have been given to them since Small Monje was still a Sub-district. The late DO - God bless that he has already paid the price – had the intention of becoming the SDO. To be SDO you needed to have over twenty-five thousand people under you. Small Monje was Nineteen thousand, and Bimobio was eleven thousand. The details of how he did it are too shocking for me to be recounting here. But the sad truth about it all is that they deceived our Chief into signing an agreement uniting the two tribes, using the demands the people once made as the pretext. And he did this even without consulting the Elders of the Council. Without even consulting the responsible opinion of people like you down the Coast."

A hush fell over the hall.

"I know how it hurts the honour of our people. It grieves me because I should be the man to do something to save the situation. If there was a way. But I cannot. Not because l am weak but because l have been assured by the highest authority in this country that it is absolutely impossible for the situation to be changed. All I have to tell our people is to endure it. And in this respect I give you my word now that if you all agree with me that we should bear it, and co-operate with me in following the plan I have drawn out for the tribe, we shall turn that stroke of misfortune to the greatest advantage for the people of Small Monje – as far as it is humanly possible."

The president led the applause and they clapped until he raised his hand.

The storm was over, or so Beckongncho thought, he then proceeded:

"As your very able president has aptly put it, the palace that was once on its knees is now standing up. But that is not enough. A much greater challenge awaits us - to keep it standing. That I know is not easy."

He then went on to speak of the interdependence between the tree and its roots. He described the tribe of Small Monje as a tree. The people back home and the palace were the roots. The sons of the tribe down in Likume and other coastal towns were the branches of that tree. He pointed out that, if for some reason the branch broke from the mother tree, damage would be done both to the tree and that particular branch. Damage would be done to the branch in that it would be deprived of its source of livelihood. And the mother tree would be affected in that there was something in the leaves on the branches that sustained the tree too. The roots of the tree, he said, were fast decaying and needed nourishment from its branches, especially those that were in the sun, there in the Coast.

He spoke of the *Akeukeuor*, their god who was defiled. He told them that they would not answer an outrage with another outrage. They would not ask anybody to make another god for the tribe as he had overheard people wondering aloud. He said that after the purification of the tribe with the death of the culprits who were involved in the abomination, a shrine had been erected over the stump of the statue which was left. The feet of *Akeukeuor* are *Akeukeuor* still," he went on. "To that we shall continue to offer our sacrifices and prayers."

The debt of the tribe was the next important point. He told them that in the course of avenging the desecration of their god, their old fathers back home had made one or two mistakes, the consequences of which now devolved upon their children. The old men had destroyed a lot of Government property and as a result the Government had imposed the very heavy fine of 25 million francs on the tribe. It was to be paid within five years. But he, Beckongncho, had intervened. He had told the Government that such an amount of money could not be exacted from the people in so short a time without provoking another rebellion. He had made the Government see that the manhood of the tribe had drifted to the Coast. The Government had agreed and had extended the time. He explained:

"Let us forgive our fathers for that mistake and work for a better future. I have worked out a suggestion which I am bringing to you as people whom I know would not willingly allow the tribe to crumble, if they know that it lay in their power to save it.… By my own reckoning, there are 225 families down in this Likume and its neighbourhood. If each family gives just 1,000 francs every six months, let us say the family is just throwing that amount away in order to save us from shame, within a few years, that debt with which the Government had hoped to crush us to the ground, would have been paid. The Government extended the time to eight years."

There were silent nods, and then a slight murmur. He went on:

" I am not imposing it on you, I am not also asking you to do the impossible. I am asking you what I know you can afford. Imagine it as a demand for the donation of blood to save a brother or your own child who lies dying from lack of blood, and the doctor has told you that you belong to the same blood group. I am merely suggesting and begging and appealing to that blood which gave Nkokonoko Small Monje the nickname of *bundle,* to forget what has happened and see if this tribe on its sick bed can, through your help, be given another day to live. This is the truest test of our solidarity."

He spoke next of the Chief's wives, those who had been forced by the caprices and neglect of Nchindia to flee from the palace to become prostitutes in the Coast. He said he had built the palace back to at least one degree near what it once was before Fuo-ndee died.

"But what is a palace without people?" he inquired. "What is a chief's palace without his wives? Twenty seven women are out here, some in bars, others walking along the streets, day and night, looking for men, saying they are looking for money. And these are the same women who had once shared the same bed with the paramount chief of Nkokonoko Small Monje! The supreme being who represents everything your tribe could ever be proud of. I am not the one to say it is a big shame to the throne because that would only mean that you are blind. And you know very well that you have all your eyes with you."

He licked his lips, looked round and continued: "If you agree with me to help, if you see any sense in what I am saying, listen. Those women, all of them will be made to go back to the palace, washed in the river of forgetfulness, and restored as true wives of the throne. Thank God that I am still strong," he ended up with clenched fists.

There was first a slight chuckle in the back row, followed by a general laugh, ending in a very long applause. In the Biongong dialect, to talk of strength with clenched fists in relation to a man, was a sign of virility. He had already proved that he was as good as his word in taking eight new wives.

Beckongncho did not betray the slightest smile. He just brought the top and bottom edges of the sheet of paper he had been holding together and fingered it until he was sure that they were quite again.

"And how are you going to co-operate with me?" he went on to ask. "Our tribesmen exist everywhere in the Coast, and in groups, as you are here. They have meetings. If you will permit me, let us make a law. Let our law be that nobody should have anything to do with any of those women who should by right, custom and tradition have been staying in the Chief's palace - as his wives. Not even if that woman is his mother. Not even if that woman is his sister.

"If you agree with me, let us say that we shall punish by a heavy fine, a very heavy fine, or any other way we shall work out, any member of this our family who disregards these laws and assists any of such women to continue to live that very disgraceful life."

He assured the women or their relatives of perfect happiness and a responsible occupation. The throne had hundreds of acres of coffee farms, cocoa, banana and oil palm plantations. All these were decaying for want of proper husbandry. The presence of the women would go a very long way to the reclamation of those lost lands. The proceeds, he made them understand, would be used by the throne to give scholarships to the children of the needy.

He thanked them once again for coming out in such numbers to receive him and listen to him, and hoped that they would cooperate with him. Then he sank back. This time it was the important and elderly members of the assembly who led the applause. Everybody saw that he meant to take his responsibilities as paramount chief very seriously, in spite of the pressures from his duties as SDO.

The president of the meeting rose again and spoke. He said he did not even need to consult the views of his brothers before saying that they were all perfectly happy to hear what the chief had just said. This, he said was an indication of the monstrous efforts he was already making to redeem the throne from shame. He pointed out that all the proposals the chief had made were so much for the good of the tribe that there was not the slightest doubt that they would give him a hundred per cent support. In his conclusion he said:

"We cannot make our chief regret for contemplating such good for the tribe that delivered us all. We cannot make the chief regret for ever accepting the office… His Highness, when you go back home we will come to see you ourselves. We had come here uninformed about what services were going to be asked of us."

There was first of all a very long applause, then a silence, followed by conversation in soft tones among the people. After some five minutes of relaxation the chief threw the floor open. It would turn out to be a grave error! He told them that if there was anybody who had something to say, or any questions to ask he or she could do so. He had said nothing about the death of the Elders, nothing about the Rev. Father and the mission's threat. This was deliberate. If the Government had said nothing to him or Small Monje concerning compensation to the mission, he saw no reason why he should remind the Government when Small Monje could not handle the first fine. He had not said what the people expected to hear about the choice of the Chief as the SDO. This too was deliberate. His experience as headmaster and his twelve days of detention had taught him that it was embarrassing and even self-accusing to answer a question that had not been asked. He expected to answer definite questions on the subjects. If they did not ask him, he would remain silent over it and return to rule as he thought fit. If a general question were asked about it he would answer only in general terms. He knew he had not spoken on the points raised as the president had intimated. Yet, he counted very much on the frankness of his speech and the extent of his enthusiasm. He could see already that it had so completely disarmed them that it was not possible for any body to confront him, unless such a man bore a deep personal grudge against him.

***

There was such a man in the audience. He was Marcus Anuse, or simply Pa, as Beckongncho and a few others called him.

As soon as the chief declared the floor open he rose proudly to the floor with a grin that was definitely calculated to make the chief look mean and contemptible. Mid-way in the space between the chief's dais and the assembled subjects he stood, turned first to the people, and looked very briefly at the chief.

"I salute you, my people and the chief," he began. Everybody drew in their breath. Although he had untold problems pronouncing ch, fl, fr, thr and several other consonant clusters, Anuse could express himself well in English. But he had spoken in the local dialect, not English. Not a foreign tongue! Not the language in which the Church and Government had always insulted their fathers. The point, no doubt, was to show the people that the Chief had made a mistake.

142

But on his part, Beckongncho was not disturbed. He had deliberately and consciously chosen to speak in English. Although he had come down to speak to them as their chief, he knew that he was still the SDO, an agent of the State. He knew that there were security officers around to cover his visit, and that he had come down to talk on an extremely delicate issue. He did not want to be misquoted either in the papers or to the Government by a reporter who got his information at second hand.

This, however, did not interest the people who, just then, seemed to have been swayed by those first eight words. For a true Biongong, there had always been a dividing line between the tribe and the Government. Anuse had shown them where he belonged. He was on this side – with the people. The Chief who was supposed to lead that crusade against the alien infiltrator, was on the other side – with the enemy.

Anuse had an even more important reason. The Biongong dialect abounded in metaphors and logical ambiguities which a master of casuistry of his calibre found ideal for his purpose. With it he could poison minds, persuade, express scorn or anger far better than he could do in English. Arms folded he went on, having completely turned away from the Chief to whom he gave his back.

"The chief has thought so well of us as to come down and talk to us. We have all been quiet to hear him open his mouth and talk to us."

An uncomfortable silence crept in. In that very first sentence Anuse had employed a devastating metaphor. To open one's mouth and talk, for those who knew the Biongong dialect well, meant to speak insensibly. It amounted to gibbering, or saying what one had no conviction in, and does not even expect others to believe. In Biongong, people talk that way only to fools or to children to send them away or to make them stop crying.

The message Anuse wanted to pass across was understood: their chief held them all of so little esteem that he did not think it necessary to talk sense to them. The people rose to the edge of their seats and listened.

"We have all let our ears hear our Chief say how close to his heart the interest and well-being of the tribe's lies," he went on.

In Biongong dialect again, to let one's ears hear something was a direct insult to the speaker. It implied an unconscious and disinterested participation in a talk; it usually refers to noises made in a market place, not a consciously prepared and well-directed utterance. A man does not shut his ears when such noises are being made. He simply lets his ears hear them. According to Anuse, then, their ears could not help hearing the sort of rubbish the chief was saying.

"We have let our ears hear how he has sacrifices everything to protect the tribe; how he intends to use his position as SDO to the fullest advantage of the tribe, and how he will use the monies that the tribe will contribute and send to rebuild the tribe and give scholarships to children of the poor. I would like the chief, as a man who wants us to take his words seriously, to tell us first what he has done, as one who has the welfare of the tribe at heart, about the Elders of the Council of Nkokonoko Small Monje. I am talking about Ngobefuo, Ngangabe, Ndenwontio, Ntongong and Kwindie–eshuo. I am talking about all those who were seized and hanged with them by the orders of his Government, an institution that has converted our living history into a legend of the dead."

Nobody stirred a muscle. Not an eye blinked.

***

Anuse was the most important person who had not come to pay his respects to the Chief the previous night. But that did not tell the Chief the extent of his grievance. He had not discussed what he was going to say with the president in advance. The president was therefore taken completely unawares. So was everybody else. He could not even tell Anuse to sit down because he knew he would not, once he had risen to speak. And that was what the Chief expected the president to do. Unfortunately, in Likume, when Anuse spoke or rose to speak, nobody had the right to interrupt him.

The Chief too was silent, very uncomfortably silent. And in the people's minds his reaction seemed to imply an admission of guilt. Anuse went on mercilessly:

"Our Chief the SDO gave our poor ignorant people back home in Small Monje to believe, after his victorious return from Tetseale, that the Elders died in an accident along with some soldiers. This our chief and SDO knows was not true. He still knows, and would admit it here and now if he likes, that no soldier ever died. He knows that there was never any accident. They were simply killed. Those our Elders who died did not want their Chief to be made SDO because the havoc a mere DO had already wrought in their land was still fresh in their minds.

"But our Chief wanted to be SDO, so as to turn the office into fullest advantage for the tribe," he said with vicious sarcasm. "An office nobody wanted. An office nobody wished for. An office at the mention of which everybody's blood runs cold. An office which stands for everything any true son of Biongong should hate."

He looked round the hall and seemed to smile and shake his head contemptuously. There was silence.

"When our fathers the Elders protested they were sent for from Tetseale where our Chief was. There they were killed at the hands and by the instruction of the same man whom they had violated all tradition and blood relationship to honour with the title of Paramount Chief, and to which he has now added that of SDO."

He creased his brows and seemed to recollect from the dark recesses of his mind.

"Our Chief was imprisoned in Tetseale for eleven days, form Wednesday the 9th of May to Saturday the 20th because of the death of the Elders of the council. Yet on his triumphant return he told the old men at home that he was staying with Ephraim Njikem, his brother. There is nothing wrong with a man staying with his brother. But, by some grace of God Ephraim Njikem is here with us now and he is listening. Let him rise and contradict me if he ever saw our Chief's face for the two weeks that he was there in Tetseale."

He stopped talking and looked across in Ephraim Njikem's direction, eveybody's eye following his.

Ephraim Njikem was in the hall. When Beckongncho went to Teteseale for his orientation course he visited him twice. But on none of those occasions did Beckongncho ever make mention of the imprisonment. This was the first time he was hearing about it, it was by an accident that his visit to Likume had coincided with that of the Chief, and that he was in there at the time. He had no grudge against Becknogncho, and would honestly have risen to contradict Anuse if he believed that Beckongncho needed his defence. But he remained silent and confused. Perhaps his brother had actually been imprisoned. Anuse could not be completely wrong. Perhaps his brother had been involved in the death of the Elders. These revelations were new, as new to him as to the other tribesmen.

But the problem was not only Ephraim's. An atmosphere of silent outrage seemed to exude from every corner of the hall. There was not the slightest noise, except for heads that rose occasionally and looked in the direction where the Chief sat petrified, and then were allowed to fall and remain lowered. Lowered because they all feared there might be some truth in some of the things Anuse was saying. Lowered because they could not ignore the fact that in the power structure of all the Biongong tribes, Marcus Anuse was a cornerstone. Lowered because he virtually controlled Likume. And lowered still because they could all sense in this the inception of a major rift in the crumbling edified of the tribe which their Chief had already shown such signs of rebuilding. By saying that Becknogncho had sold the tribe to get the office he was suggesting that they used to be free, and would continue to be free if they made it possible for him to leave the office.

They knew that even if Anuse was speaking the truth, the Chief would not take it lying down. And in the ensuing combat, it was the tribe which would suffer. There were people, no doubt, who could have disagreed with Becknogncho on several points. But even these doubting Thomas's felt that Anuse had gone too far. What he had said and how he had said it was not an expression of the general feeling about the Chief. But he went on:

"Before our Elders were sent to their death in Tetseale, before our Chief became the SDO of Small Monje and Bimobio, Small Monje was Small Monje and Bimobio was Bimobio. Nkokonoko Small Monje is now an arm, a left arm of Bimobio. Slaves they drove away, to whom they gave land to settle on. Orders now come from Bimobio to rule Small Monje. Our Chief and SDO told us that he could not remedy it, what can be farther from the truth?"

He cleaned his eyes as if they were watering.

"If the Paramount Chief of those two places did not want to be the SDO of those two places, the two tribes would never, never, never have been made one at all… And our Chief and SDO tells us that he shares with us the doubts whether the holding of the offices was an advantage or a disadvantage. Of course he knows it is certainly to his own personal advantage. Otherwise, how could he have risked so many things to acquire an office whose advantage he doubted?"

Silence. He moved closer to the people in the front row.

"Those of us who still have our heads with us, and who have not allowed themselves to be misled by fine and sweet promises are amazed. We are amazed that a man so well-informed about the traditions of our people as to have been chosen Chief, would like to be satisfied that the death of the DO paid the price for the theft of our god. A cursed passer-by who had long forgotten where he was born. Our fathers will spin in their graves to hear this kind of thing. Our Chief will one day tell the gods what he did as compensation to the mission for the murder of the Reverend Father. Or he has forgotten that the Mission brought him up? Or that three-quarters of the people who now read and write in this country today were brought up by the mission?

"Our Chief strongly believes, and wants us to do same, that it will be a sign of cooperation, not madness, for us to pay money for what he chooses to call the *destruction of Government property*. Things raised by the labour of our hands, the sweat of our brows, and on the soil that was squeezed from the wounded palms of our old fathers!!! If a man is ever to contemplate taking from the mouth of labour the bread that it has earned, such a man ought never to be their chief. Such a man ought never to lead.

"What does our Chief want us to think about this his Government? By deliberately distorting facts which are the very seeds of our happiness, is it his private intention that we love the Government? And if he wants us to love the government does it mean that he is sincerely for or against us? And if his actions show that he is for the Government, is it not that he is against us? And if he is against us, what is wrong with telling us so that we know where we stand? Why treat us like children?

"None of these questions I shall attempt to answer. But better speak the truth and be damned than to mislead your people. Chief, you are welcome to see us," he ended up with a venomous snarl. Bowing insultingly, he resumed his seat in the front row.

There was silence, abrupt, long, dismal. The kind of very heavily charged silence which can be said to follow the blatant exposure of a villain who has always masqueraded as a saint.

Chapter Seventeen

Ai yori idete ai yori no koshi.
Homerareru yori soshirarenu.
(Daniel Crump Buchanan
Japanese Proverbs)

*A*NUSE'S ANSWER was more than Chief Beckongncho had bargained for. That was not the kind of definite accusation he had expected to respond to. It was a slap in the face. Yet he did not lose control of himself, and was determined not to do so. It was idle, he thought, to try to refute any of the accusations because that would only provoke violent exchanges.

He would do anything to avoid a scene. He did not start talking as soon as Anuse sat down. After all, they were not in any debate. He decided he would talk just because he felt such an attack could not be allowed to go unanswered. He gave himself a very long time to calm down and so make Anuse look stupid by keeping anger out of his voice.

Everybody expected he would speak, and sat with nervous expectancy. With nervous expectancy because there was also the vague fear that he might decline to speak, which would have left Anuse a hero in a spectacle of shame. Beckongncho versus Anuse. It was with the greatest relief that the people saw him sit up again in readiness to speak.

"My people," he broke the ice. "I feel I should speak to you again. I usually don't like talking long but I am afraid I have to break that rule and tell you all that is on my mind. All."

He spoke in English still, to the astonishment of everybody else. This again was done consciously. First, even if he had acted in error in speaking in English the first time, he did not want to make it look like Anuse had anything good to offer to the cultural heritage

149

of the people. Secondly, he knew that if he had anything of burning importance to say, the language of rendition would not be any hindrance to the people.

"I, Kevin Beckongncho, was born in 1928 in Nkokonoko Small Monje. My father was Junkem Alfons. He died in 1935. That same year too my mother died. From 1935 to 1948, thirteen years, I stayed with Mr. Marcus Anuse. He was my father then. I say WAS because he no longer honours that relationship. Mr. Marcus Anuse took full responsibility over me. He gave me food, clothes, and paid my school fees until I entered the Teacher's Training College. In short, this same Mr. Marcus Anuse, as I said was my own father then.

"In 1948 I passed the Entrance Exam into the Government Teachers' Training College in Obinikom. I was too big to enter a secondary grammar school. Mr. Marcus Anuse paid my deposit, 35,000francs. For the first year alone in Obinikom he spent over 75,000 francs on my school fees. He always gave me pocket money too.

"At the end of the second year I passed the Government Scholarship Exam. Since that exam was supposed to have been taken in the first year, all fees paid the previous year were refunded to all the successful candidates. That means 75, 000 francs came back to me. I could have done anything for myself with 75,000 francs. This is what my friends did and nobody ever knew. But I refused to do so. It did not lie in my nature to trick people.

"I bundled the money and took it home to Mr. Marcus Anuse. He thanked me and embraced me and confessed that he would never have known that the fees had been refunded. Still I did not abuse that confidence he had in me. That same day too that I brought the money to him I told him that the scholarship covered tuition, board and moderate sum of pocket money. I told him that since he had so many family involvements, he should ignore me as one of his financial problems. I said I would be able to manage with the little allowance to survive on my own in college."

There was a very long pause.

"I am not the kind of person who can easily forget a favour. And I have always kept this in mind not because I intended to use it against him some day. I always remember it because whatever I am today, I don't want to forget that I owe so much to him. It is very much, and I had never for once in my life imagined that I would be compelled to forget it all. But, there are injuries which cannot be pardoned, if inflicted even by one's own parents.

"You are all fathers and mothers sitting in here now. At least most of you. You were once children. But you like to be called grown-ups now. That means that when a child becomes a man the fact must be admitted. And now that I am what I am, if life is to have any meaning at all, if I am to have any meaning to you as your Chief, if I am to have any meaning to the Government as its supreme representative here, then all these things which my uncle has done for me, I must throw away.

"Because he himself has undone it all, now, today."

Here he took in a very long breath before going on:

"Children may make mistakes. They always make mistakes of course. But I sincerely cannot remember when, throughout my stay with him, I ever did anything even in hiding which made it necessary for him to take up the cane and beat me. I was careful never to do wrong. It was a habit with my other friends with whom we served him, that they just had to do something everyday which made them deserving of a very serious beating, at least three times a day…"

There was a long laugh from the back of the audience, which threatened to disrupt the solemnity and gravity of the speech. He looked up at them and they kept quiet.

"It is Mr. Marcus Anuse who looks for proofs and contradictions, and it will do him a lot of good for him to rise and deny any of the things I have just said."

Anuse did not stir. He even took what Beckongncho had so far said as a compliment. He did not know what Beckongncho was driving towards.

"The conclusion I drew from this was that I was not a bad boy. If my conclusion was hasty then, subsequent events in my life proved it perfectly right. It had never been my intention in life to go round blowing my own trumpet. But I have the misfortune that whenever a man has risen to blow it for me, he has always sounded the wrong note. Just as you have seen."

There was a slight chuckle at the rear again, Beckongncho had a mind that always wavered towards satirical or even sarcastic humour, even in the heat of a very serious issue. He remained silent until there was silence.

"I was chosen class prefect from the very first day that I entered college. I held that post every year through popular elections for four years. And even after that fourth year I had to give it up only because my services were needed for higher duties. I was to become the college senior prefect. When I started teaching I was elected, *in absentia*, secretary General of the Teachers' Association. I later became the president and held that post too for three years. That was the longest period of time for which it could ever be held. I founded the Biongong Cultural Association, and I headed that group until last year.

"As late as a few months ago I was headmaster of a Government school of two thousand pupils, and a staff of eighty-seven teachers. I would have risen to the highest echelon that honesty, professional consciousness and a good star could ever offer in the Civil Services of this country. There was that promise. There was that hope, because I worked without malice towards anybody. But I agreed to abandon that very bright and prosperous future, and all the pension benefits, which would have awaited me at the end. I abandoned them all to come and serve my tribe with an office for which I get no pay. I abandoned them all to come and redeem the throne of our tribe from shame and degradation. I thought I was righting a wrong. And what is my reward, from the very person who should have been the proudest to see me there?

"My uncle gives you to believe that I can only be a liar. That I can only be a murderer, a fool, an opportunist."

Here he sighed and shook his head sadly. Then he said. "My honest country men, if this story that I have told you about myself, about my past life, is a preparation for the picture of me which Mr. Marcus Anuse has just painted, I leave it to your own mature selves to judge."

He cleaned his mouth with the back of his hand, and look round for a few tense seconds. He told them:

Our people say the elephant has two sets of teeth. The one for eating and the other for show. I have both, and you will see them in due course I am very sorry that this is happening this way. I am very sorry that his is happening in this place."

He beckoned to an Elder behind him to pour him some water. Very respectfully the man did so and gave the cup to one of his wives who in turn gracefully handed it over to Beckongncho. He drank slowly, returned the cup, wiped his mouth and resumed.

" I did not come here to be tried."

Silence.

" I said I did not come here to be…"

He allowed the people to say, "TRIED", in order to get their fullest attention and thereby ease the tension that was mounting in them.

It worked. He gave them time to relax.

" I know it," he said. "You know it too. At least, I cannot be tried here, not now. I want you therefore to understand that I am not answering to any charge. I am the Paramount Chief of Nkokonoko Small Monje. I am also the SDO of that area. But I am no god. I am liable to error. But if I had made any mistake against my father, my years of respect towards him should have been an excuse for the error. If the Paramount Chief of Small Monje had done any of those things which only God alone knows he had never as much as thought of, and which Mr. Marcus Anuse finds joy in stabbing him with, the Presbyterian Youth Centre in Likume at 12 noon is not the right place and time to ask him about them.

"The Paramount Chief of Small Monje has a palace which all of us sitting in here now know, perhaps with the exception of Mr. Anuse. And according to the tradition under which we were born, it is there in the palace that a man can point at dirt lying on the Chief's face and ask him to remove, and he would do so without losing respect. These are facts which Mr. Anuse has refused to recognize.

"If things like this shall be said to me in such a place, in such a way and at such a time, how then am I your Chief? How then am I your SDO? How then can the President of the Republic be respected?"

He bit the left corner of his lower lip and shook his head in condemnation.

"As I said before, I am not answering to any charge. So I shall not attempt to deny or confirm anything he has said…"

"Of course you cannot deny any of tshem," Anuse interrupted him, forgetting in his ignominious anger to speak in the language of his people.

The President, a very nervous man by disposition rose and, bowing to the Chief turned to the people and said:

"If Mr. Marcus Anuse shall not listen to our Chief talk, he should go out of this hall, at once."

Anuse smiled.

"Have I held your tschiefs mouth?" he asked. The Chief waved to the president to leave him alone and sit down. Then he paused for a long time. When he next spoke it was as if he had just undergone a crisis of feeling too sudden and too severe for his mind to bear. A crisis that seemed to make his voice frailer than before. And he had to stop between sentences as if afraid to speak, or as if unsure of what to say.

There were three policemen standing at the door. They looked very agitated and one coughed slightly and fidgeted with his gun, implying that they wanted to discipline Anuse for his lack of respect for authority. Beckongncho by some kind of telepathy understood and discouraged them a calm waft of the hands. It took him a whole minute to say:

"I said I shall not attempt to deny anything." Then he paused to see if Anuse would risk another interruption for him to give his rage full vent. Anuse would not fall so easily into the trap. Beckongcho had originally decided he would not go beyond what he had already said. But now it seemed that Anuse still needed to be told much more than that. He told them:

" I have told you the story of my life. Now I shall only try to mention a few facts about my uncle which are certainly not new to any of you. It is only in this context that you, my honest subjects and citizens, will be able to tell from what motives Mr. Anuse has decided to drag the crown into the gutters. Perhaps Mr. Ansue does not know that there is no important secret about him which I do not know.

"Six years ago, when Chief Fuo-ndee died, Mr. Anuse refused to go home to attend the funeral and the catching ceremony. The reason was that his brother had not left out his own son, Nkoaleck – May he too rest in peace – to choose him as his successor. Such a thing has never crossed the mind of any sane human being anywhere. For some unfortunate reasons, Nkoaleck could not be made chief, and he had been dismissed from the services of the Government. He died later in Mr. Anuse's house. And how did he die?

"One day, long after his dismissal (they would say later that Bechongncho went too far in mentioning this) he received a letter addressed in Mr. Anuse's care. It came from the Ministry of Finance. Mr. Anuse interpreted the letter and the figures it bore as compensation for Nkoaleck for wrongful dismissal from the Government services. That night Nkoaleck died. And two days afterwards Mr. Anuse was sighted in the treasury with the letter.

"It turned out to be a document showing how much Nkoaleck would have paid as tax before going into retirement."

Eyeballs rolled from corner to corner.

"Our late Chief Nchindia - may he too rest in perfect peace – came down for his daughter's dowry. Mr. Anuse disgraced him in the market place, refused to release either the girl or the money. And when he died that disgraceful death, instead of hurrying home to help the Elders find a suitable solution to the problem of the succession, Mr. Anuse, together with a noble pillar of this tribe whom he knows what he has done to, led the Chiefs of the other tribes to Tetseale. There they confused the Governor with all sort of things so as to make him Chief."

He inevitably got carried away by his instinct for self-defence to the extent that he spoke as though he was not a Government authority. This bit of incautious pronouncement would be used to hurt him in the end.

"The Governor believed their lies. But when he sent for Ngobefuo and the Elders to try to convince them to make Anuse Chief, it would not work.. If the Elders of the council died in any other way than we honestly know, the reason certainly cannot be associated with the choice of Beckongncho as S.D.O. The Government does not seek the opinion of an individual if it is to make him an SDO. Much less that of the Elders of a tribe. It is no tribal affair. If they were killed by the Government as Anuse has been kind enough to disclose to us, the reason is clear. Having promised him the throne of Small Monje, the Governor found those plans blocked by the presence of the Council of Elders. For Anuse to be the new Chief of Nkokonoko Small Monje, therefore, those old men just had to die."

There were silence cautious nods from all sides as if the scales had fallen from their eyes.

"If I was imprisoned for one hundred years in Tetseale, it had nothing to do with the fact that I was to become the SDO. It was instead part of the plan to eliminate me and make Anuse the new chief. It is not necessary for me to mention that it was Anuse's greatest wish and desire that I too should be killed. How I survived can never be explained because I know he himself is surprised that his orders were never carried out. If I kept that secret to myself, it is not because I stood to gain by it. It was because I knew it was bad news. Nobody likes the bearer of bad news. The important thing was that I had been released and that the tribe had been given its rightful Chief."

He nodded to himself and looked across at the Elders. They were also nodding.

"The point I will want to make here is that it is not, and will never be in keeping with the tradition of our tribe, for a man to whom the welfare of the tribe might have been entrusted without fear, to ever attempt to offer cash for an office that had since time immemorial been handed down by blood relation…"

He was just about to add "and by consensus of opinion," when the piqued Anuse, now perspiring in every pore, humiliated beyond imagination, shot up and said:

"If it was a matter of blood and tradition you should not be talking to me Anuse sitting down. You are not a prince of the royal line of Fuo-ndee."

The sheer panic in his voice made the Chief smile a bit. He did not answer him.

" I shall take that title from you," Anuse moved to the centre of the floor and said to the Chief.

The Chief smiled again and shook his head.

Anuse moved closer, now desperate he held out a trembling hand and said: "If you doubt me strike here."

He was now standing just below the Chief's dais. The Chief remained silent. He knew he had carried the day. So did the Elders the wives and the entire entourage that had come down from Nkokonoko Small Monje. So also did many of those who had attended from Likume and other coastal towns.

But not all the important Likume Elements of Biongong saw the day's events in that optimistic light. At least, not the President of the group in Likume. In spite of the fact that Anuse had reduced his authority amongst his people to insignificance, and in spite of the fact that he would have liked to see somebody really humiliate Anuse, he greatly dreaded the consequences on the tribe as a whole, of the confrontation.

When he went up to the Chief to greet him after the speech, he did not offer any message of congratulations. And when one of the young men from the neighbouring city came to him and said:

"Finally Anuse has met somebody who can show him that he is still human," the president looked disappointed. He said.

" Stab wounds on the heart of the tribe. That is what it was, Anuse's wicked accusation and the chief's honest defence. This tribe will bleed from that for a long time. To death even. When elephants fight it is the grass that suffers."

Another old man, the Treasurer of the group, expressed the same sentiments. He said:

" The Chief may have caught and tied a tiger, but in the process has lost many claws and fangs himself."

Chapter Eighteen

Es trrt der Mensch, so lang er strebt.
(Johann Wolfgang von Goethe, Faust)

THE **THOUGHT** of the confrontation did not end with the closure of the meeting by Chief Bechongncho that afternoon. The president's description of Anuse's accusation as a mortal stab wound on the heart of the tribe could never have been more appropriate, for Beckongncho started bleeding right from the scene of the combat.

The night, weirdly silent, dark and mysterious, seemed interminable. Once in a while the breeze would rustle through the leafy branches of the trees and fall silent again.

The only permanent sound in Chief Beckongnho ears was the echo of Mr. Marcus Anuse's insults, his cynical hypocrisy, his shameless boldness, his foolhardiness. He passed the entire night a restless man. Reports on the activities of Anuse disturbed him. Thought on what Anuse was likely do in future pained him. Even more unsettling were the thoughts on what he needed to do to make it impossible for Anuse to repeat the embarrassing act. As far as the latter thought was concerned he had a lengthy discussion with his colleague, the SDO of Likume Central, who asked Beckongncho to leave everything in his hands.

There was much more to disconcert him. On the night after the party held in his honour at the residence of the SDO of Likume, Ephraim Njikem came to his room at the Rest House. There, after talking briefly on a few general things, he went straight to a point Anuse had mentioned in his talk which involved him, Njikem.

"Pa said a lot of annoying things this morning in fact," he began. "But your Highness, I just want to be sure, was he right in saying that you were actually imprisoned in Tetseale for eleven days?"

Beckongucho seemed to reflect.

"Yes, indeed. I was locked up there," he said abruptly.

Njikem nodded three times.

" You know I live in Tetseale," he said very softly, but with suppressed emotion. "And in fact, I should think that if such a thing happened to me in Sowa you would be the very first person to be contacted. At least you did not think me a rival for the post of Paramount Chief or District Officer of Small Monje. In fact, I have always wished you well, you know that."

Beckongucho looked into his eyes but remain silent.

"If such a thing happened to you in Sowa, and you told me first," he started to say, "there would be no danger because I know and you know that I can control my feelings better, which is more than can be said about you." That would have made Njikem even more furious. Beckongucho instead decided to try to persuade him in the simplest way possible.

"The situation was much more complicated than you would ever imagine," he began. "For one thing, I was not permitted to contact anybody I knew there. It did not look to me as though I would ever leave the prison alive."

"And after you left the place alive?"

"Ephraim, when a just man, an innocent man is suddenly seized from his sleep and put in prison and tortured and brought dangerously close to death for one week and released and thrown into the street, he cannot be the same person for a long time. It took me a very long time to come to myself, for my senses to function the right way. I just hope that I am finally behaving the way I used to behave."

Njikem tried in vain to understand and sympathize with his brother.

"But you should not have told pa that you slept with me without first talking to me about it," he pointed out. "That was just not right knowing what type of person he is."

" I told him nothing of that sort."

"But you certainly said it to somebody who told him," Njikem persisted. "You know how his ears are always sharp."

"I am very sorry about it. Very sorry," Beckongncho said.

" I was not really asking for an apology, Your Highness. I just wanted to have a few things clear in my mind, especially as you refused to receive me when I came to the village soon after your coronation."

Beckongncho tried to speak but, noticing that Njikem had not finished talking, he licked his lips and remained silent.

Njikem went on:

"You yourself have been the loser. I could not stand up to contradict him when he mentioned a point that you had deliberately hidden from me."

Again, Beckongncho tried to speak, but Njikem would not permit him.

"What makes me your brother? You will not receive me in your palace? You will keep secrets that threaten your very life from me? And I am your brother. In fact, it beats my imagination, it shocks me to hear people say that my brother kept his stay in Tetseale secret because he considered me a rival of the office of S.D.O."

"Ephraim, please," the Chief broke in. "Don't get unnecessarily hysterical. The office of the Paramount Chief or Senior DO anywhere has rival claimants. Even in Heaven. Nobody takes an exam to become that. By this I mean that it could have gone to you as well, if fate willed it, and you would have been sitting here where I am as both Paramount Chief and SDO of Nkokonoko Small Monje. But that does not mean that I saw in you a rival. No. Dismiss that thought from your mind. You should know better. And as for the refusal to receive you in the palace which you keep going back to everyday, you seem to deliberately shut your ears against my reasons. I talked to you about it, wrote to you about it and explained that the request you made was untraditional. You still do not seem to understand that certain obligations which tradition imposes on the Paramount Chief are extremely delicate."

***

Beckongncho did not get out of his room till 9.a.m the following day. And when he came to sit in the parlour he was informed that somebody wanted to see him. As he took his seat at the dining table a man was led into his presence.

The man was probably not quite forty years of age, but he had a much wrinkle face, the result more of hardship than of age. His hair was low, high cheeks slightly hollow, the temples deep and sunken. He had very sharp eyes that darted inquisitively from one corner of the house to the other. A slightly unkempt moustache ran above his upper lip which seemed to stretch into two deep lines that descended from both sides of his nose and disappeared into a beard that rose from under his chin. His lips were thick and dry and his teeth, when he spoke, looked large, slightly disfigured and coloured. He wore a thick black over-sized shirt which hung loosely over a blue pair of jeans that had faded much around the front of the thighs, the knees and the buttocks. The buttons of the shirt were large and white. When he entered he was bare-footed, having left his sandals at the veranda.

Beckongncho was stirring his coffee when the man came in. His voice was loud and sharp and he spoke with an air of familiarity rather than fear.

"That you wanted to see me, my young man?" Beckongncho asked.

"Yessa," the man answered from the corner where he stood. There was an elusive smile on his lips and eyes.

"What's your problem? Who are you?" Beckongncho asked.

"I am Ewusi Atanga James, Sa," the man said looking straight into Beckongucho's eyes.

Beckongucho's brows pulled together and he seemed to search his mind as he studied the visitor. "Never heard that name," he said looking at the man.

"True, Sa," the man said again with a smile. "But I know you fine, fine, Sa" he added.

" We met before?" Beckongncho asked.

"Yes, Sa."

"Sure?"

"Yessa."

"Where?"

"In Tetseale, Sa."

Beckongncho stirred his coffee and gulped down a mouthful as he continued to look at the man. Immediately, something inside him told him that he had really met the man before. But he could not tell where that was.

"You say you are who?"

The man repeated his names.

"Doesn't still ring bed," Beckongncho shook his head. "Where in Tetseale do you know me? Under what circumstances?"

"They called me **Protocol**," he announced, looking mischievously at the Elders who sat at the opposite corner.

"W-a-i-t a m-i-n-u-t-e.! Wait a minute," Beckongncho said, nodding and smiling. He beckoned to the stranger.

"Small Mammy, Small Mammy!" he called, turning his head in the direction of the corridor leading to the rooms in which his wives were.

The first wife emerged from the room and saw Beckongncho's eyes watering with laughter.

"You remember what I told you of the dark days in Tetseale?"

She nodded, reflected, smiled. "This is one of them. This is Chief of Protocol." The woman shook the man's hand. The Elders looked on, unable to make any sense of what they were beholding. The Tetseale tribulation was a secret which only the wife, Protocol and Beckongncho knew.

"So your real name was what?"

The man repeated. Beckongncho inquired about his other inmates. Ewusi Atanga James had met some only. Some had been tried and sentenced. Chief justice himself was serving a five year jail for money-doubling.

But how had Protocol discovered Beckongncho? Easy. Even before Beckongncho left Tetseale they had all heard about him. When he was appointed SDO, they celebrated in various corners. And as for finally rediscovering Beckongncho in Likume?
Ewusi himself was a *free-born of Likume*. He had just chanced on the occasion the previous day and thought he should pay a visit to an old friend.

Beckongncho had long put behind him the thought of his torture in Tetseale. He blamed not his inmates but those who sent him in. He thought of it now as a big joke that is best forgotten.

The tragic outcome of this reunion, however, was that Ewusi Atanga James persuaded Beckongncho to try and give him a job, anything. And before Beckongncho left for Small Monje, SDO Samson Ndong had promised the man who was introduced to him a job as a yard-boy.

Chapter Nineteen

If that the heavens do not their visible spirits
send quickly down to tame those vile offenses,
it will come. Humanity must perforce prey on itself.
Like monsters of the deep.
(Shakespeare: King Lear)

ON **WEDNESDAY**, two days after Chief Beckongncho's return to his palace in Small Monje, the committee of the Likume Elements of Small Monje met in an emergency session. That Wednesday was especially bright, though signs of storm could be sighted, gathering over the hills. That was a clear indication that heavy rain was not too far away. A whirlwind rose, circled on the dusty ground in front of the house in which the meeting was taking place, rocketed and disappeared into the branches of the encircling palm trees. Answering to the call of gravity, dry leaves, papers and rags which it had borne in its wake twirled grotesquely back to the flowers, the grass, the earth.

The agenda of this particular meeting was much unlike any other: there was only one item – Marcus Anuse's behaviour towards their Chief the previous Sunday. At that meeting Anuse was to be compelled to apologise for embarrassing the tribe and the Chief on the day of their Chief's visit. Anuse was also to be compelled to go home in Nkokonoko Small Monje and apologise personally to the Chief and beg for forgiveness.

The second point concerned Anuse's attitude towards his own workers on the previous Monday, the day after the meeting with the Chief. On Monday Anuse had summoned all his workers resident in Likume and the nearby districts and had warned them:

"Anybody who calls himself a worker under me will be dismissed instantly if it ever gets into my open ears that he has sent even only one white franc to that your so-called Chief-DO. If you pay it even in the dark, you know that Anuse will always know. You all know that Anuse is everywhere."

The committee found this threat disconcerting. ANUSE ENTERPRISES LIMITED   employed more than one hundred of their tribe's men and women. To allow him to carry out such an action would be dealing a staggering below to all the efforts they were determined to make to raise the sum of money their Chief had so openly pleaded for. And they had so earnestly promised to help! In order to maintain the unity of the clan as well as the respect of the throne, the Committee was once more unanimous in deciding that Anuse should be called upon to withdraw that cruel threat.

***

In keeping with the decision of the committee a general meeting was called. That Sunday Anuse was present, contrary to rumours that had circulated the whole week to the effect that he had vowed never to attend any meeting of his tribesmen any more.

The president spoke first. He announced the purpose of the meeting and why the committee had thought it necessary to call another meeting so soon - they met once a month. He went on:

"After all everybody can make a mistake. Our Chief cannot be so wicked as to refuse to forgive him. Then, lastly, I would also like to call on Mr. Marcus Anuse to tell us here and now, that he has withdrawn what he said to our brothers and sisters who work for him. This will enable them to contribute their own share for the rebuilding of our broken tribe and throne. What he said to them does not please us at all. Mr. Marcus Anuse, we would like to listen to you."

He resumed his seat and waited for Anuse to talk. Anuse had already been briefed of what had transpired at the last emergency meeting from which he had been deliberately excluded. He had learned that he was the subject of that evening. He had come very prepared to answer their charge.

In the room in which they held the meeting Anuse had a special seat, a rocking chair behind the executive table, facing the door. He was not a member of the executive. He was above that. As the president spoke he was leaning back, rocking the chair and proudly pulling at his gold-rimmed pipe, his elaborately decorated walking stick resting between his legs. He was dressed in his peculiar Sunday attire - a large expensive white three-piece *agbada,* very heavily embroidered in blue round the neck, chest and hands. The feet of the trousers of the *agbada* were also decorated in blue. On his head was a whitish blue cap, stitched to match, with a yellowish tassel dangling to the right of his inclined head. He was wearing a glittering pair of made-in-India slippers lined with something like tiger skin outside. His dark sunglasses hung round his neck on a glittering chain.

He did not rise at once when the president had finished talking, but pulled at his pipe for about a whole minute before putting it aside. Anuse was not the kind of man to quiver at what seemed to him no more than child's play. Shaking the tobacco out of his pipe by the stray, he rose majestically, straightened his dress, and coughed twice to clear his throat for his well-conned reply. He was going to say:

" It was not out of the influence of alcohol that I had spoken the way you had heard me speak to that your so-called Chief. So, let those who walk about with cotton in their ears take it out and hear: Marcus Anuse is not going to sell himself at a low price. By which he means that he will neither go to Small Monje for anything you are all thinking about, nor is he going to apologise to any meeting of lunatics such as you are. Then, to show you how seriously I consider this insult of yours by asking me to apologise, I am going to extend my warning.

" The other day I spoke of my workers. Today I shall extend that warning. If any man or woman who calls himself my worker, allows his sister or brother, uncle, aunt, cousin, nephew, niece or anything to send that their mother's anus which they call contribution to that your so-called Chief-DO Beckongncho, that man or woman will leave ANUSE ENTERPRISES LTD the very minute that Anuse hears it."

After that he was going to spit in front of them, walk out and enter his car and drive away without giving them any opportunity to persuade him.

But it was never to be. That speech was never to be made. He had barely opened his mouth to speak when a strange noise was heard outside. At first the people thought it was wind shaking the loose sheets of zinc on the roof of the meeting house. But it seemed to grow louder and louder, and come to stop abruptly. When they looked outside they all noticed to their consternation that it was a blue police van.

The tarpaulin had been removed, leaving the entire back bare. Four policemen in a police vehicle was not a rare sight at all in Likume. They were always on patrol because of the crime wave in that part of the country. But the arrival of four armed policemen just when they were trying to make amends for the insults on their Chief who was also a Senior District Office, startled even the absurdly indifferent amongst them. Could Anuse have invited the police to come and harass them?

There was a sudden catch of breath inside the hall where about seventy people sat. Two of the men remained outside, looking interestedly at a white PEUGEOT 404 which was parked in front of the house. It was Anuse's car. The two officers followed the corridor that led into the hall. At the door one of them knocked, entered and clicking his heels greeted very politely:

"Good morning, Sirs" He did not take off his dark sunglasses.

The president rose to greet him but fell back into his seat. It looked like he had merely missed his step, but that was not so. He was simply too frightened to control himself. He took a few trembling steps towards the visitor and answered for all of them:

"Good, good morning, Sa."

"We be very sorry to interrupt your meeting, Sirs. We de look for a certain Mr. Marcus Anuse. We learned that he is in here. The car outside looks his own, can we know if he is here?"

The voice was calm but there was something morbid and very sinister in its calmness.

The president sneezed, as if to expel the fear. Everybody averted the officer's stare. Somebody lowered his head and said to his neighbour:

"The kite and the mouse."

The man to whom he had just spoken jerked him with the shoulder, concealing a laugh. The kite and the mouse comes from a folktale in which a hunter crept behind the kite and caught it as its attention was buried in the trapping of a mouse that had just fled into a hole in a tree trunk.

To address the rich, omnipotent and ever-so-popular man a certain Mr. Anuse was an unpardonable offence against Anuse's dignity, even for an officer new in the precinct. It was sacrilege. Such an officer ought on his arrival to have been told about Anuse because he was the man who 'fed' the police force in Likume. It was sometimes believed and said that the protection of Anuse's person was a lesson that had already been incorporated into the body of instructions received by graduating policemen at the Likume Police College.

As if he had instinctively sensed danger well in advance, Anuse had already sat down when he noticed the policemen coming into the building. Now he rose with a self-assured pride and declared striking his chest:

" I am him, am Marcus Anuse."

That self introduction was not necessary because as soon as the officer spoke the people turned away just for a fraction of a minute and began turning back rather unconsciously, but nevertheless betrayingly, towards Anuse.

The other officer outside marched in too at the mention of the name. The one who had greeted walked up to Anuse, clicked his heels, gave a stiff formal salute and held up to his view a piece of paper.

"Is what?' Anuse inquired before the man had time to say he was under arrest.

"Under who?"

"You are under arrest."

Anuse pulled the falling sleeves of his large *agbada* over his shoulders and grinned. He had heard this sort of thing too many times before in his life.

"You are under arrest," the officer said for the third time, holding up the paper to the view of everybody else. "You are free to remain silent but if you choose to say anything it will be held against you in the court of law."

Anuse ignored the recitation, threw a cursory glance at it and looked away with offending pride. The two other officers outside marched in and stood each on either side of him. The look on Anuse's face immediately turned from proud indignation to fear. He was undergoing a brand new experience. The word "You are under arrest' had been said to him ten times and over in the past. But this had always occurred under circumstances in which he could negotiate with the captors. For instance, one incident had taken place in his store downtown.

He had offered a sum of money so big that the officers had found it stupid to repeat the words. On many other occasions they had met him at home in his house. What was common in all the past cases was the fact that the officers had come as if on a stroll immediately following a crime in which Anuse was rumoured to have been implicated. They were never more than two in number. But now in front of him he could see four policemen, armed, ordering him in public, and in a deadly serious manner.

"I, I am under that ya allest, why?"

" Instructions from above. They will explain to you. Our business is only to ask you to come with us."

"Then I am not going. I lefuse the allest." The officer who had spoken took in a long breath. Although they had come with instructions which would release the animal brutality with which their profession is usually associated, they had been wondering just how they would exercise brute force if Anuse yielded without any resistance. Inadvertently, therefore, Anuse had solved that problem for them.

"Do you recognize this seal?"

Anuse denied without looking at it.

"That is the seal of the State."

"I see," Anuse nodded but did not stir from where he stood.

"And do you recognize the signature and the stamp?"

" I don't."

"This is the stamp and signature of the Senior District Officer of Likume. The representative of the Head of State here." The officer spoke with infinite patience.

Anuse did not say anything this time. He was already freezing from his toes upward with fright but he still bore a certain measure of pride which forbade him to submit. Not before the people he ruled over like a king.

"Are you therefore ready to go or not?"

Anuse was silent. As though soliciting their intervention he turned to his tribemen:

"Are you people seeing how people look for trouble?"

Not a single muscle stirred on the face of anybody watching.

"You bastard idiot, gerout," the officer shouted through clenched teeth. His right hand was already behind Anuse's neck when he said this and he seemed to try to heave the man forward across the floor.

Anuse was a man of prodigious strength, had been a very good wrestler in his youth and even at sixty he could still instinctively summon some of his old tactics. His right hand was holding the edge of the table which stood in front of him. Had he known that the officers had come to take him not just out of Likume but even out of this life, he would have lifted the table with just one hand and killed at least one of the officers with it. But he made the fatal error of counting on the intervention of his people, all of whom only feared him, none of whom genuinely loved and respected him to the extent of risking his or her own life in this defence.

This point was greatly emphasized by the President's action. Very early in the scuffle a jug of wine fell down and broke. As though this was a more lamentable loss than Anuse's life he rose and very carefully began to collect the pieces together which he went and placed at the window sill, in order, perhaps, to give them enough room to fight. In his opinion and that of everybody else from the tribe, a contest between Anuse and a policemen was like a contest between gods and in which no mortal had any right to intervene.

As the officer tried to push him forward by pulling the neck of his grown, Anuse dogged just once and before he raised his head again he had moved one whole metre from the assailant who now found himself holding only an empty grown in his hands. The man threw down the dress and with the fury of a bull, charged towards Anuse. Face to face with his foe, the officer made a show of striking him with his raised hand. As he had suspected, Anuse shot out his muscular right hand to defend himself. The officer's right hand swung with lightning speed and struck Anuse a paralyzing blow with his baton on the elbow. Anuse uttered a sharp plaintive cry of unbearable pain, which made his tribesmen shudder in their seats.

By this time the three officers had joined their comrade. Beaten and kicked here and there toward the door Anuse refused to yield. One of the men seized him by the feet and began pulling. Anuse's hands clung to the edge of the table and he would not let it go. With one inexorable blow from the boot of his rifle another officer ground his fingers off the object. His lips swollen to several time their normal

171

size, and bleeding from all openings on his body, Anuse was beaten and kicked into the corridor. There he fell only to be kicked on and on until he rolled helplessly into the veranda. By this time he was practically completely naked.

As if they had been waiting and praying for that spare opportunity, as soon as the struggle moved to the veranda, and as soon as the last policeman left the small corridor the entire assembly of horrified natives emptied itself through the back door from whence those who had the nerve now watched the rest of the fight from over the backyard fence.

But not everybody thought Anuse guilty without trial. A passer-by vibrating with indignation at the degradation not just of a fellow human being but of a man he knew so well, stepped out of the stunned spectators and shouted with fiery defiance to the people over the fence:

"You don't protect people in your meeting?"

As if to excuse himself the President said:

"We don't know what he has done."

"Eh-eh!" the man cried out even louder than before. "Even if he has done what, you allow four people to tear through one hundred people and seize your king before your own eyes? Is that not King of Youths? The man who says his company is only for people from Small Monje? You cannot catch those rats and grind them to dust?"

The policemen heard him. But their orders might not have included the arrest of any other person, for one of them simply said:

"Why don't you come and show them how to catch and grind policemen?"

"Nye nye nye nye" the furious stranger mimicked through the nose. "It is only in a Small Monje meeting that you can show this ya madness. Try it in our meeting house and we shall show you that some mad people are more and than others."

The President of the meeting still did not make the important move. His causal prediction now seemed to have assumed physical form: Anuse was really bleeding

What this concerned stranger did not know was that the policemen still remembered that the people of Small Monje had killed six of their comrades not long ago and that the arrest of Anuse was the very first opportunity for them to avenge that hideous crime. In the presence of more than a hundred people, many of them passers-by who had stopped to witness the spectacle, the almighty Marcus Anuse, King of Youths, Managing Director of ANUSE ENTERPRISES LIMITED was hauled like a rejected bunch of bananas on to the back of the police Land Rover. Two policemen placed their feet on his bleeding naked body. Then they drove through the centre of Likume.

Part Four

Chapter Twenty

A soft answer turneth away wrath.
(Aeschylus)
Better old debts than old grudges.
(Prince Aldrid, *King of Nuthumbria*)

DURING THE first few months of his reign Chief Beckongucho virtually lived in the palace of Small Monje and drove to work in Bimobio country, a distance of twenty-three kilometres. It was here in the palace that he received a delegation of three men from his subjects in Likume two weeks after Anuse's lynching. It included the President, the General Secretary and the Treasurer. He was glad to see them and immediately went on to inquire about the object of their visit.

"His Highness, Mr. Marus Anuse has been arrested," the President said as if reporting the fall of a comet.

The Chief did not look agitated.

"It serves him right," he said, unruffled. He was looking at them as he spoke, and noticed a peculiar strain of disappointment that began to distort their faces. "Is that what you came to tell me?" he asked.

"Yes, it is, His Highness."

" I heard of it the very day it happened.'

The visitors looked at each other and then at the six or so Elders who were sitting with the Chief. Beckongncho said softly:

"My fathers, let me borrow a saying from the Ibos. They say:

"If a masquerade dances too high people will see its feet, and that's not good.

Mr. Marcus Anuse thought he was too rich to listen to a child talk to him. He thought Likume was too small a place for him to share his authority with any other human being. He thought this world is too small for him to control with any other human being.

That is not correct. He just needed something to make him understand that he was still a human being like you and I.

"I was in a position to prevent or even postpone that arrest. But he shamed me in public. A Paramount Chief and an SDO like myself cannot afford to be rubbed with excrement before the very people he is supposed to rule. When he spoke to me in Likume it was no longer Kevin Beckongncho he was insulting, it was the Government of this country."

"So what are we going to do, His Highness?" the president inquired.

" We who? And you mean do about what?"

"About the arrest of Mr. Marcus Anuse, His Highness."

The Chief's brows came together and the age lines of his face became harshly accentuated.

"What exactly do you mean?" he queried.

"When His Highness came down and talked to us we all were very glad with him. We completely agreed with him. And for this trip that I have come down with these two men like this, we had planned to come with something to make our Chief know that we did not just say Yes, Yes, so that our Chief should hurry back and leave us alone to do what we pleased. We had planned to bring what the blood of Small Monje, his tribe in Likume, can afford as mud for the rebuilding of the crumbling walls of our palace. But something happened."

Nobody interrupted him.

" The week after His Highness returned we agreed on a sum of 2000 francs for all the families. They were two hundred and thirty, not two hundred and twenty-five as His Highness noted. That was to have given us four hundred and sixty thousand francs. And we the Committee members were to have given 40,000 francs on top to make it five hundred thousand francs. That is what we would have brought to His Highness today. But this is all we have been able to get — one hundred and ten thousand francs."

He pointed to the sum of money which the Treasurer drew out of his bag. He also handed over a letter to the chief.

"And all the families have sworn that they will not add another franc again."

Beckongncho tore open the letter, glanced at it briefly, and looked at them without saying a word. A large bluish-green fly flew in, sat first on the knee of the President, dashed off, circled above the Chief's head, sat on his right shoulder and took off again. The Chief gently reached for his whisk on a side stool and waited until it flew to the table. He did not even wait for it to sit. In a lightning flash he struck it dead, its mangled body entangled in the long hairs of the whisk.

Mbe Fiege walked up to him and bowing down took the whisk and as he went to shake it away he said to himself.

"Why was it not that people could eat flies-eh? This one is a real big one."

"Mbe Fiege," the Chief called, "nothing stops you from carrying your pot to the latrine and frying all the flies there."

In spite of the seriousness of the situation, the people could not help laughing. But the laugh was very brief. The Elder returned the whisk to the side stool.

"Me and these flies in Small Monje!" the Chief said half to himself, half to his guests. "We will see who is who."

The President breathed out sharply by way of indicating that he had heard the Chief talk. The Chief now sat up again and said:

"You were there when my uncle spoke to me. For anybody less than myself, for anybody less than a Chief and less than an SDO it would not have needed another cause outside what he did to me for him to be arrested. And you are here asking me to use my good office for wrong purpose – to release a man whose very existence means the complete destruction of anything this tribe can ever be proud of. This is the measure of your gratitude to see me want to wash the throne clean again."

He blew his nose loudly.

"They have completely forgotten, His Highness," the president said.

'They who?"

"Our people, His highness. They have completely forgotten what Anuse said. Their suffering has made them to forget. Now they think only of his absence. Anuse said too many bad things. But the people do not remember them now because they are suffering too much…"

The Chief tightened his lips, nodded and asked with a haggard frown:

"How many of you here now are working with Anuse?"

"None of us, Your Highness."

"What did you say when the people came up to you with the idea of this letter?"

"They summoned the meeting on their own, Your Highness, and they decided what they wanted to have done. They had long forgotten about what Anuse did to you. It is as if a major artery has been cut in the tribe down the Coast, Your Highness, and the lifeblood of your people is draining away."

***

This was supposed to be the middle of the dry season. But once in a while Small Monje witnessed thunderstorms and very heavy rains. Even as they were talking one could see the sky darkening in the distance through the window. Thunder followed immediately and all of a sudden it looked as though a god had put his hand over the face of the earth.

"Who is there?" the Chief called through the door that opened to the back.

"His Highness wants somebody?" one of the Elders inquired.

A young girl of about eighteen came in from the back as if she had been expecting the call. She was one of the Chief's new wives and she was accompanied by a naughty little boy of about four. He was shirtless, shoeless, with a dirty khaki pair of shorts.

"Mengwi, bring me some kola there," the Chief ordered.

The young lady soon came out with kola nuts which she broke and showed the Chief. The small boy ran between them and seized one before the Chief stretched out his hand.

"Quick, put it back," the Chief shouted at him.

" I won't," the boy said jokingly as he placed the kola nut back on the saucer.

"You want to chop before the Chief?' The President asked by way of a joke. Beckongncho did not seem to be in good humour.

Some palm wine was brought with which they swallowed the kola nuts. Beckongucho munched in silence, looking from one face to the other. He felt reborn in his heart that corroding bitterness of his prison days in Tetseale. He would truly have died, just because of Anuse. The Elders were killed, just because of Anuse. Betong had died, just because of Anuse. The throne may never again regain its former lustre, just because of Anuse!

Tiny beads of sweat could be seen coursing gently down his cheeks and on his nose. His face now assumed after only a few second's reflection, a strained expression which made it look in the limelight as if he was shaking. A suppressed effort, possibly, to say something that will hurt many people; something, no doubt, which he found hard to give verbal form to. He had never looked more morose.

He needed money, just as a drowning man would need air. Yes, he also needed the respect of his people in Likume, he needed their love. As Anuse himself once said to Nchindia, a Paramount Chief of Nkokonoko Small Monje, who did not rule Likume was like a bird with one wing down. And it was Anuse himself who was the nerve centre of that population. Talk of releasing him? How was that going to be done without calling his own credibility to questions?

The procedure for him to be released was so plain as to make him look ridiculous. He needed to write to the SDO of Likume who had personally ordered the arrest:

Dear colleague;

I am very sorry to say that none of those things I told you about my uncle was true. I have fully investigated it all and I find him innocent.

I therefore think that my own personal honour before my people makes his release a matter of urgency. As one brother to another, look for ways and means by which we can set him free.

God willing, his colleague would oblige him and gain Anuse's release. But what problem shall he have solved? Couldn't his people guess how Anuse would behave towards him?

"I told you people that the shoulder can never grow above the head. Your Chief tried to have me killed, but I have proved to him that he is small. I am back where I belong, and I will show him whom I am...."

Who would be safe in Anuse's hands?

"The body of Mr. X was found floating in a river by his farm. The man who was making up stories about Anuse when he went to jail."

"The bodies of two policemen were found behind the market. Somebody identified them as the two men who beat Anuse on the day of his arrest…"

The reports would continue to pour in this fashion. He would be forced to contact his colleague again!

Dear Colleague:

I am very sorry that it was my first judgment of Anuse that was correct. When I asked you to release him I was merely yielding to a terrible pressure from my people and not facts which are even more startling now. For instance, the body of Mr. X which was found in a river was the body of the man whose incriminating evidence led to Anuse's arrest. Furthermore , the two policemen who were found behind the market were the same men who arrested Anuse at the tribal meeting. Anuse therefore had a hand in all the killings…

Nothing short of his kind of revelation would be needed to effect a second arrest. No. No. That was too high a price to pay just to remain in the good books of his Likume elements. He was not just the Paramount Chief of Small Monje. He was also the Senior District Officer of that area. The state held him in high regard and so he should not be the one to make them think less of him.

These people were indeed blind. Could they not see in the way the policemen treated Anuse that they knew he was never to come back? Even if by some miracle Anuse were still alive by the moment that they were pleading, they should know that it was good reason to let him die in prison just to secure the lives of the men who arrested him.

Was there no other possibility of getting somebody else to run Anuse's Company? Was there no possibility of ignoring the contributions from the Coast and using some of the funds sent for the development projects in Small Monje to pay back that pernicious debt? There ought to be a way out.

Like the captain of a sinking ship amidst mutinous crew Beckongncho looked round the room. All the confidence, hope, fortitude and determination that had sustained him all his life, and especially through those eleven days of torture in Tetseale prison, evaporated under the paralyzing effect of these opposing impulses. Yet he would not yield.

"My brothers," he broke the long silence, a note of obdurate pride vibrating between each word. "The mistakes I have made in my life can be counted on the fingers of one hand. And I have come out of every one of them having learnt some important lesson. Some mistakes should not be made because we shall never have the opportunity to correct them. I have read the letter and I have looked at the problem from all possible angles, and I have decided differently. I will not detain you here even for this night. You will return to our people in Likume who sent you, with all that they sent you, if you do not think that they will be glad to hear that you left anything behind. And when you get there, call everybody together who had a hand in the drafting of this letter and tell them that the Paramount chief and SDO of Nkokonoko Small Monje has read their letter and after due consideration has said No to their request."

Initially he had intended to add:

"The tribe of Small Monje existed long before we ever heard of Likume. We cannot therefore let the tribe sink in order to save Likume. Tell them that if this tribe is to stand, it should not be with the help of blood money. Tell them that this tribe is big enough to stand without Anuse."

But he simply dismissed them without giving them any opportunity to dissuade him.

Chapter Twenty-One

Yet with great toil all that I can attain
By long experience, and in learned schools,
Is for to know my knowledge is but vain,
And those that think them wise, are greatest fools.
(Sir William Alexander, Earl of Stirling:
The Tragedy of Croesus)

CURIOUSLY ENOUGH, the firm dismissal of the Likume Delegation did not exactly set the seal on the fate of Marcus Anuse and his followers in Likume, nor Anuse's relationship with Chief Beckongncho. It was to be only the beginning. The delegation visited the chief on July 3ʳᵈ. On October 24ᵗʰ Chief Beckongncho attended a seminar in Tetesale where he was expected to give a talk on 'The Role of Chief's in Civil Administration." Participants for the seminar were lodged in the Parliamentarian Flats, a 22-room eighteen-year old, unpainted structure which was previously used for the housing of Parliamentarians. It now admitted Senior Civil Servants on mission, for 10.000 francs per night, which was half the regular charge.

Beckongncho arrived in Tetseale on Sunday 27ᵗʰ October in the afternoon and spent the rest of the evening preparing his paper for the following day. On Wednesday 30ᵗʰ October the participants had a day off. It was during this period that Beckongncho decided to visit his brother Ephraim Njikem.

When he entered Njikem walked up to him; knowing that he could not shake his hand, he stood some distance from him and said:

"I am very happy that Your Highness has come. I had been wondering how I could get you."

Beckongncho smiled gently, walked up to the large armchair his host showed him and as he sat he said softly:

"Ephraim, the palace has not yet moved from Small Monje. You should have no difficulty knowing where or how to get me." Then he went on to ask: "How is the family?"

Njikem looked thoughtfully at Beckongncho and without answering the question he said:

"As I said, if you do not release Pa, inevitably, you will have problems."

"So how are the children? How is your wife? How is work?"

Njikem hesitated for some time and said off-handedly:

"They are all well, if anything happened you should have known. They are okay."

"Brother, you continue to amaze me," Beckongncho began. "Sincerely, I come to visit you on my own, and you receive me as if you had invited me for a private discussion. There must be some way of doing things, which indicates that we can place ourselves in other people's position. You don't even want to know why I am here, when I came , and things of the sort…"

" I am sorry," Njikem said.

"That is hardly the point," Beckongncho said. " I was merely pointing out."

"I just got carried away when I saw you," Njikem told him. "It is something I have been turning over and over in my mind…"

"So what is this thing on your mind concerning pa?"

"Pa has to be released."

Beckongncho asked for a drink.

"Something cold. A sweet drink, " he added.

"We have some syrup which I use to drink my whisky and things of the sort," Njikem said. "But they can get you Coke or Fanta across the street."

***

Two women came out of a taxi at the gate and hurried across the passage by the window next to where the chief was sitting. It was bright outside, but they looked soaked to the marrow. They ran to the back of the house without talking to anybody.

"That's what you wanted," Njikem shouted.

"That was my wife and house girl, Your Excellency," he said to Beckongncho.

"You don't need to introduce my own wife to me," Beckongncho said. "I will recognize her even one mile away in the dark."

" I told them not to trust this town." Njikem said, "Rain must be falling cats and hens in Eborakum," he said. "As we were saying," he resumed. "Do you know where Pa is now?"

"Get me the syrup and ice-cold water."

Njikem brought the syrup and a glass from the cupboard himself. Beckongncho held up his glass until he felt the syrup was enough. Njikem then poured water into the glass until it was full.

Beckongncho himself stirred the syrup until it blended completely with the water; Njikem put a few drops of the syrup in his glass and poured some shots of whisky on to it.

"Cheers," Beckongncho said.

"Cheers, Your Highness," Njikem said.

Beckongncho held the glass to his lips and when he lowered it there was only the green coloration of menthol syrup at the bottom.

"Surely Your Highness was really thirsty."

" As you can see," Beckongncho said. He cleared his throat briefly and said:

"This is how you receive a man. Now we can talk. It looks like every time I meet you I am coming to answer a query."

"It is no query. I said Pa has to be released."

"Do you know who arrested him? Do you know why he was arrested? Do you know where he is now?" Beckongncho inquired.

"I know that he was arrested in Likume. I know that he is here in the Tetseale Central Prison now. I also know that his arrest came after he confronted you in public."

"Let me also tell you what you may not really know in the matter, Ephraim. His attack on me was merely the last straw. It was the SDO for Likume who ordered his arrest. SDO Samson Ndong of Likume is a cousin to the Governor. I mean the Governor who was removed during the crisis which led to my appointment as SDO.

"Some say it was through that relationship the SDO got to be appointed. Pa went about telling people that it was he who had caused the man's removal, that the Governor took money from him but left him in the rain just because others offered more. By other here Pa was naturally referring to me; that the Governor had teamed up with the company commander to blow the Small Monje crisis out of proportion; that after Ngobefuo and the others had been taken away the Governor continued to keep the troops there because he could make huge personal gains from the monies allocated to take care of the soldiers since his brother was given the contract to feed the soldiers.

"Even if this were true, Pa should not have been the one to say it. When I came down to Likume during that my first visit I had it in mind to try to talk to him about it. But you remember how he took on me. Pa would listen to nobody."

"Your Highness, let me say this before you refuse. You can succeed as an SDO, but fail as a Chief."

Beckongncho looked at him. He felt insulted.

Njikem nodded and said: "True. I know that if I was working in your office you would have long transferred me to some remote corner so that you can do things the way you like without any interference. But as a Chief you cannot throw away any of your subjects. You cannot transfer anybody. You are condemned to live with them and swallow their shit."

Beckongncho looked first at Njikem and round the house.

Njikem was a man of flashy taste. Anything relating to Hollywood fascinated him and you made no mistake about it the moment you set foot in his parlour. Directly opposite the main door hung a larger-than-life portrait of **Diana Ross.** There was also one of **THE BEATLES** on the same wall. To the left hung one of **Mohammed Ali**, one of **Malcolm X** and one of **Marcus Garvey**. To the right, over the dining section hung half portraits of **Pélé** and **Sean Connery**. He knew the names of the latest records in French, English or Lingala by rote.

In dress he stitched his shirts and trousers in the latest fashion. A dandy of the first order, when Beckongncho came in he was wearing a silk-like shirt with all the buttons undone, save for the last one, thereby exposing a broad hairy, muscular chest.

His hair-do was in the latest Afro-cut. He was wearing a pair of blue jeans with baggy legs, à la mode and a large leather belt bearing the name TEXAS in bold lettering in front. A gold chain hung round his neck with a small plate bearing the initials of his names E.N.S On his right arm he wore a wrist chain, the colour of gold, but probably merely an alloy.

Insignificant as they may seem these remained some of those elements of taste which made him and the fastidious Beckongncho such uneasy bedfellows! A faint smile of contempt settled briefly at the corners of Beckongncho's mouth, when Njikem mentioned the word shit.

'That's the way you see things," he said.

"That's the way they are," Njikem said firmly. "Everybody thinks, in fact, believes, and says openly that it was you who sent the police to come and arrest Pa. And I learned that you turned a deaf ear to a delegation that came from Likume to plead for him. Because, as you say, Pa is corrupt, that Pa is rotten.."

"You make it sound as if I am accusing Pa wrongly," Beckongncho said.

" Your Highness," Njikem pressed. "Take your mind back some thirty years ago and I'II show you something."

He rose and went into his room and soon returned with an album which he flipped open to the first page.

"Do you recall this picture, Your Highness?"

Beckongncho looked at it.

"Of course, I do. This is me, this is you, this is Pa. I know it. I have one of them too.

"Do you recall the year it was taken?

"Mmmmmh…" Beckongncho reflected.

Njikem told him.

"That is the year in which Pa Anuse gave money so that we should be admitted into GTTC, the day when names of people who had passed the entrance exam were dropped from the list and ours inserted. And you went on to pass the scholarship exam. It is true that the fact that we eventually did so well indicate that we deserved to be on the pass list in the first place. But we were not, and Pa bought our places, God knows for how much."

Beckongncho looked straight at Njikem and said:

"Can you lower the music a little, it is a bit too loud for my liking. You are saying something serious. You could even put it off."

Njikem walked to the stereo set and lowered the volume a bit, but did not stop it.

"What point are you trying to make now, bringing back the past?" he asked Njikem.

***

Mrs. Njikem came out of the room at the back. She had changed her clothes and looked dry. She came and, curtsying, greeted Beckongncho.

"My own wife," Beckongncho said. "You passed before the Chief without saying a word?"

"Your Highness," she pleaded. "Let me confess that if I knew that you had seen and recognized me I would have come to greet you like that. I was ashamed to stand like that. The rain caught us in the market and when we came and saw sun here we were really surprised."

"O.K, mammy, go you. We are discussing something."

It was she who brought kola nuts and proposed lunch which Beckongncho turned down on grounds that he was being expected at the FLATS.

"I want to say, Your Highness," Njikem began again, "that you cannot make a crab walk straight. Pa Anuse was born corrupt, rotten, as you would say. He might be so, without ever seeing anything wrong with being so or feeling so. He has always believed in bribery, which we all know is a crime, a sin even. But think of what we would be today if he had not done something evil. Out of some evil, some good can come."

"I am listening, Njikem," Beckongncho said. "If good comes out of evil it does not make evil good," he added with an undertone of selfrighteous pride.

"Perhaps. look at the English society whose sense of morality we praise to the skies! How did the Englishman come to be so moral?"

"How did he come to be so moral?" Beckongncho asked.

"Through respecting its important criminals. For instance, when Francis Drake attacked merchant ships and killed people and stole their goods, he was knighted by Queen Elizabeth the First. He became Sir Francis Drake. Robin Hood the Robber is virtually a saint in English history."

Beckongncho could not conceal a laugh in which one discerned a strain of superciliousness.

"Seriously," Njikem went on. "Through bribery and other petty evils Pa was able to set up a business that employed half our tribesmen in Likume, many of whom may not and will never believe in any of his ideals. But because you hate bribery, because you want to wipe all evil people from the surface of the earth, you have taken a measure that has destabilised the entire tribe in Likume.

"The children of those who worked for Anuse cannot go to school anymore. And who knows whether amongst those poor miserable children we are not killing the future saviour of the tribe? Women have abandoned their husbands because they can no longer take care of them. I was in Likume when you yourself described the Likume elements who had turned out to see you as the blocks on which the tribe was to be rebuilt. Now you yourself have scattered the very blocks on which you wanted to rebuild."

Beckongncho felt uneasy at the force of Njikem's accusation. He said:

"Njikem, I have told you that I am not to blame in that regard."

"Before we proceed in this thing that I am saying let us go and you see Pa for yourself," Njikem said. "After that, if you still think he should die there, all for you."

"Where?"

" I told you he is now here in Tetseale Central Prison."

"Since when?"

" Some six months."

" I did not know he had been transferred."

Njikem said nothing else.

Chapter Twenty-Two

As flies to wanton boys, are we to the gods;
They kill us for their sport.
                              (Shakespare: *King Lear*)

MADE UP of a population of at least one million Tetseale was not only the seat of government but the economic capital of Ngong-Nchem. In a curious way it always seemed to reflect the spirit of Ngong-Nchem itself - stupendous, sprawling, and with a lifestyle of boastful arrogance enveloping an inner decay and rottenness. Tetseale has over the decades provided both the inspiration and subject matter for musicians.

For instance, a few of the more popular lines say:
"Tetseale is full of enjoyment,"
If you are tired of Tetseale, you are tired of life."
"Teteseale is a land flowing with milk and honey."
'Teteseale is a land of endless opportunity," and the like.
Some are not so optimistic. They say:
"Teteseale is a melting pot," that
"If your woman leaves you for Tetseale, forget about her and go back to the village for another one."
"If you want to hear and see smell, go to Tetseale."

But these contradictions were not just words in songs, they were stark realities. In Tetseale you found the tallest as well as the shortest buildings, the healthiest as well as the dirtiest environments, the wealthiest as well as the poorest people, the newest as well as the most out-moded structure, vehicles or fashions in dress; the shortest as well as the longest cars, the most beautiful as well as the ugliest ladies, the blind, the half-blind, the lame, the half-lame, the lepers the cripples, the mad, the naked, the inconceivably human!

As Beckongncho and Njikem drove through the centre of that city under the sweltering heat to the Central Prison, it was as though all the contradictions of its life had come out to be seen, heard, smelt, touched, praised, condemned, all at the same time! Hawkers taking advantage of the traffic congestion forced their wares through open car windows, thanking those who brought, shouting deprecations at those who refused to look at them, persuading those who looked a trifle undecided; big business tycoons, big company directors or bloated Ministers slouched in comfort in double-chins behind Mercedes 400's.

There were the motor-cyclists also, the bicyclists, truck pushers with bare dark torsos that glistened in the sunlight. There were the pedestrians under umbrellas or large straw hats or bushy hair. There were the pigs and goats that had either just broken loose or had never been confined; half-eaten foods, exposed excrement by the roadside, a dead chicken or dead dog here and there, discarded horns from slaughtered cows, old radios and TV sets.

They all greeted Beckongncho and his brother as they threaded a precarious passage through the streets. The distance they had to cover was less than eight kilometres. But it took them two gruelling hours under the sun that poured its piercing rays on all.

"This city has never ceased to amaze me, Ephraim," Beckongncho remarked. "Each time I pass through here it seems as if every other person and everything had planned to be out on the same mission."

"Hmm," Njikem breathed sharply. "Everybody here is a prisoner of some kind. You hate the place, but you cannot leave it."

That was about the only exchange that took place between the two men since they left the house.

The Central Prison was a maximum security prison. Covering a ground space of about a hectare, you could not tell how large it was unless you were watching from the air. All that visitors saw was a cement wall reinforced with stone and having iron gates and a small window with massive iron protection on either side. A guard received you at another small stone building, immediately outside the gate.

"I am Kevin Beckongncho, the SDO of Small Monje," he said by way of introduction to the guard who asked for their identity cards. "This is my brother Ephraim Njikem. We have our father under detention here from Likume. We would like to talk to him."

That kind of introduction was sure to work against them, and would have complicated the mission. For example, the guard seemed to instantly take offence. When people came in cars to prisoners or detainees, the guards could be sure that they would gain nothing. In cases of that nature they could really make it impossible for you to see anybody. They could claim the prisoner was very sick or that he had been sent to do a job somewhere. On the other hand guards could squeeze as much as 1000 francs from visitors arriving on foot. That explained why they were never so excited to receive rich or important visitors.

Beckongncho and Njikem might have had to wait for a very long time had not the Superintendent of the Prison come out to leave just at the same time that they were trying to gain access into the prison. It was the Superintendent who greeted first, and it was he who urged a guard to attend to them immediately.

The guard grumbled silently, but went and did what they wanted.

"What is his name?", the guard asked.

"Pa Anuse. Mr. Marcus Anuse."

The guard took their identity cards. Speaking through a phone he asked another guard inside the gate to let them in. When they came they had to introduce themselves again and tell the purpose of their coming. The guard led them to a waiting room and showed them where to sit.

***

When Anuse was taken away to the police he was sixty-two. But because of his wealth and the care he took of himself he could have passed for forty or there about. He always ensured that there was no trace of grey hair on his well-oiled head. He kept his hair generally low and kept side burns which he trimmed very carefully to just below his cheek bones and even carried a small regular comb in his pocket with which he constantly put it in order. He was a very hairy man by nature but the only traces of hair on his face were his thick eyebrows, eyelashes and a carefully trimmed line of dark hair abut one millimetre thick which ran just above his upper lips.

He was very heavily built, a fact that was accentuated by his good living. That was the picture which still hovered at the back of Beckongncho's mind and they sat there waiting for him.

***

It would be wrong to think that Beckongncho was a wicked man, or that he was merely egotistical. The problem lay in the fact that he was something of a perfectionist, a man who took every responsibility of his seriously and took time to ensure that nobody put unnecessary obstacles in his way. When he endorsed the arrest of Anuse it was because he saw in Anuse the representative of the *nouveau riche* who posed the greatest threat to the throne. He wanted to let the people know that he would not pardon anybody who dared to mess around with an office as sacred as the throne.

However, in spite of the damage he knew Anuse had inflicted on the throne, what he saw in the Central Prison that day brought back to his own mind, for the very first time, his own suffering at the hands of an unjust system. It made him rethink his decision, however expedient it had been.

A scarecrow-of-a-man followed the guard as they emerged from an inner room and walked across the open space that separated the various sections of the prison yard. He was tall with bushy hair and a nest of beard that had not seen a blade for months. His head over skinny shoulders looked like an inverted calabash. In spite of the nest of beard his jaws looked shrunken and squeezed beneath the naked check bones. His forehead was all lines and cracks, his eyes retreated under his protruding brows. His ears did not look like part of his body but something pinned to the sides of his head, just behind his high cheek bones. His neck was a bundle of veins and dry skin stretching between the chin and bare shoulder bones. He was shirtless, and you could count his ribs which rose over the cavity of his belly like a cage. He walked as if he had developed a million boils under the soles of his feet! When he was led to the visitors Beckongncho asked with disbelief.

"Is this Pa?"

Njikem did not answer.

It was Anuse himself. With eyes blinking as if he had emerged from a darkness in which he had been confined for a very long time he managed to recognize the two men. He looked steadily at Beckongncho.

"Chief, nobody is God," he said unrepentantly. " I have not died." Then he turned to Njikem: "My child you are welcome."

Beckongncho looked at Njikem and in his looks one could read the question: "Do you say I should work for the release of a man who treats me with such disrespect?"

You would think Njikem read Beckongncho's mind, for, looking away he said:

"It doesn't matter."

Beckongncho took excuse and walked back out of the waiting room and went to stand by Njikem's car until the latter came to join him. As it usually happened when the two men were concerned, for some odd reason, Beckongncho's frustration became directed not against Anuse but Njikem. Did Njikem mean to prove that he was more capable of handling his subjects than the Chief himself? Was Njikem hoping to claim some credit for the release of Anuse? That would not work! Before Njikem knew what was happening. Anuse would long have been released.

***

SDO Samson of Likume was supposed to be attending the seminar too. But Beckongncho had noticed that he was absent throughout the first part of their deliberations. When he returned to his hotel later that evening and learned that the man finally came he immediately went to see him. The man told Beckongncho that he could not come earlier because he had not been well the previous week, and that when he felt better the doctor suggested a few days of bed-rest, an occasion which coincided with the commencement of the seminar.

"At any rate," he went on. I sent word to the Minister explaining why I would not be around at the beginning."

At this point Beckongncho told him of his problem. " I want us to forget what my uncle did in the past and seek ways and means to have him released."

SDO Samson must have been about five years older than Beckongncho. He was also older in the service, very much older. Having undergone professional training in the School of Administration, he had served as Sub-District Officer for two years and was now in his sixth year as Senior District Officer.

He knew how new Beckongncho was in the administration, but he always treated him with great respect. He enjoyed listening to Beckongncho outline plans for the development of his district and how he hoped to realize them. Sometimes he envied Beckongncho's sense of planning and organization.

"For me I proceed by trial and error," he would say. 'Whatever works best is the best for me."

But, as soon as Beckongncho brought up the subject of his uncle he sat pensively for a whole minute, visibly disturbed. Finally, as though he had not heard Beckongncho speak he asked:

"Did you see my letter?"

"I didn't." Beckongncho said rather sourly. Why had his colleague not responded to his question? Did the letter contradict the request he had just made?

"What was in the letter?" He inquired worriedly. "Anything to do with my uncle's release?"

"Well, no" the man replied. "Anyway, why this sudden decision to have your uncle released?"

Beckongncho thought he should press on to know what the letter was all about. He had noticed a rare coldness in SDO Samson's attitude towards him. But since the man himself had said there was nothing particularly serious, there was no point insisting. He would first of all finish with his own case.

Anuse's predicament assumed a new reality for the first time.

"I went to see him this afternoon," he began. "He looked terrible. So terrible that if anybody else saw him in that state it would hurt my relationship with my people among whom I am becoming more and more unpopular. I did not know he had been transferred here."

"He had," SDO Samson said.

Beckongncho noticed the carefree manner of the response, but decided not to take offence. He went on:

"My people seem to have forgotten all that he did. All they know is that his entire business has collapsed. His workers idle, starving, and that I am the sole cause. I am sure it was Anuse we wanted to punish, not the people."

The man smiled faintly and asked:

"How could we punish Anuse without punishing the people? When you take away the driver of a vehicle it is obvious that you want the passengers to walk on foot. It stand to reasons."

"It stands to reason," Beckongncho repeated to himself and remained silent.

"Anyway," the man began a bit softly, "we cannot go on arguing like this. It will take us nowhere. The long and short of it is that since he is no longer in Likume, things are likely to be complicated. Had you thought of this while he was still in Likume it would be just a piece of cake. First thing, how are the authorities feeling about him?"

Beckongncho bit his nail and remained silent.

"Anyway, if you were able to see him it means they don't treat him as a V.I.P."

Beckongncho looked across at him with questioning brow.

"I mean a Very Important Prisoner," SDO Samson explained. "That's how they call political prisoners."

'By the way, why was he transferred here?" Beckongncho asked.

Again there was a knowing smile on the man's lips, a smile which seemed to imply that Beckongncho had not yet understood the intricacies of civil administration.

"This is an election year," he began. "Any detainees of influence are not allowed to be held too near their homes."

Beckongncho nodded and was about to go away when SDO Samson said abruptly:

"And, there's something I have to say." His voice was unusually sober.

Beckongncho returned to his seat, eyeing his colleague in silence.

"And what is it?" he asked at last.

"It has to do with the letter I sent to you."

"Yes," Beckongncho nodded. "What about it?"

"For how long had you known the gentlemen you introduced to me in Likume last year when you came to talk to your people?"

"Which gentleman?"

"The one whom you said wanted a job of any kind. The man who was made yard boy at the District Office."

"I told you I did not know him much. I told you the troubles I went through prior to becoming Chef and SDO, and how I spent a long time in detention. I told you he was one of those who helped get food for me. What has he done?"

"A seven-year old daughter of my first Assistant was defiled. Since that happened he has not been seen. The deep-freezer in the

Rest Hose also disappeared the same day he disappeared."

SDO Samson looked distraught.

" I am extremely sorry to hear that, and I am even more sorry that it makes you treat me with such suspicion."

" I have not treated you with suspicion," SDO Samson tried in vain to defend himself.

" I know how you have always treated me," Beckongncho said. "It is different from what I have noticed this evening. The gentleman was not my friend. He was a helpless gentleman I met in distress, a gentleman I thought we could help. If you said no, I could not have insisted, and I could never have owed you any grudge for refusing. The fact you accepted indicates not that you loved me but that you understood his problem. If he has turned out to be what he has turned out I can only say I am sorry to be connected with it. I don't keep company with thieves.'

"I have not said you do."

"But it was implied in the very careful manner you went about it. You made it sound like my best friend has betrayed you, rather than that a rascal has betrayed both of us".

He went back to the Central Prison and asked for Anuse to be brought to see him. When he came he said: "Pa, just get ready, arrangements are afoot to have you released. You have suffered enough."

Anuse threw his hands open and with the most insulting show of ingratitude said :

"Do as you want, Nobody is God."

***

Notwithstanding Marcus Anuse's impudence, Beckongncho proceeded with his plans to gain his transfer and eventual release. Having already made the vital presentation at the seminar on the second day, it was easy for him to obtain permission to be absent for a few hours on Thursday.

He took this opportunity to get in touch with the Prisons Superintendent who was the key person to contact in effecting Anuse's transfer to Likume as the first step towards his release. It was the same very understanding and cooperative man whose intervention the previous day had facilitated their seeing Anuse. The man listened attentively, understood Beckongncho's circumstances and promised to do all in his power to ensure that it succeeded. He advised:

"We need to be very cunning in explaining why he must be transferred to Likume. You cannot say it is because the Chief of his village wants him to be sent there."

Beckongncho looked perplexed. The man went on:

"Usually one of two things need to be done – a Ministerial Order or a Medical Report."

"Which of them is easier?" Beckongncho inquired. " I don't have a long time to be here, and the sooner he is out the better for me."

"There is no easy one. A Ministerial Order takes about one month to obtain. A Medical Report may take about one week. But it can take more than a year to get a doctor to give a certificate to ascertain a disease that somebody does not have."

Beckongncho paced around pensively for a whole minute. When he finally spoke it was quite unlike him. He spoke like one of those corrupt DO's he had so often condemned:

"Is there no shortcut?"

People had often asked him such a question when they found themselves corned in complicated bureaucratic procedures. And whenever they asked him the answer was obvious: "NO." He knew the answer could also be "Yes" So he was not surprised when the Superintendent said:

"Of course the procedure can be accelerated. Every route has a shortcut," the man added after a while.

"So what is the shortcut?"

The man rubbed his forefinger against his thumb. Beckongncho pulled his brows together in momentary surprise.

"Of course," the man read his fears instantly. "You cannot by-pass the Minister without spending money."

"About how much are we looking at?"

The allowed Beckongncho to guess for himself.

"I will pay anything for him to be moved to Likume. That man needs to be released. I shall never mean anything to anybody from my tribe if that man is not released. Even if it means paying one hundred thousand francs, I wouldn't mind."

"I shall see what I can do," the man said after a long reflection. "When would you have liked to have him transferred?"

"If that can be done even right now, I should be very grateful. The only problem now is that I do not have money. I have only fifty thousands in my pocket. If I give you this now, how much more will be required?"

"Fifty, of course," the man said as if they had already agreed on the cost.

***

The seminar was to end on Saturday. On Friday Beckongncho came to see the Superintendent with the rest of the money. A medical file had been prepared showing that Marcus Anuse had *Kutusfera Kutusfera*, a disease the Superintendent simply described as "very bad sick." He was being immediately referred to the Special, Dr. D. Boloja in Likume for urgent attention.

The very morning that the vehicle conveying Anuse to Likume left, Beckongncho also left for Small Monje, "to put my house in order," he told SDO Samson, "before I join you down for us to battle with the bail."

***

Sometimes, some things don't just work out right. The Land Rover in which Beckongncho was travelling back to Small Monje must have been about twelve years old. But that in itself did not give any cause for alarm. Brand new vehicles had often run into all sorts of embarrassment on the untarred, stony, Tetseasle-Small Monje stretch. It was a distance of less than five hundred kilometres, but vehicles had been known to spend weeks in gutters or in the middle of the road.

Beckongncho and his driver had travelled for six hours, covering about two hundred kilometres, when they had the first of some five breakdowns. That occurred at Opiodb, and they would have to ravel another full day to reach Small Monje. The driver complained of the wheel-bearing and the brakes binding. But that too gave no cause for alarm because the driver was an accomplished mechanic himself and knew how to take care of petty problems of

202

that nature. As the man laboured to get the car going again Beckongncho took advantage of that to listen to the afternoon news.

It was 3 pm. Nothing of consequence was said beyond the usual messages of support to the Head of State. It was the Death Announcements which usually came after the Newscast which alarmed him. The very first announcement hurt and confused him at the same time. It said:

The death has been announced of Chief Marcus Anuse in Tetseale. The Biongong elements in Likume are hereby informed that the remains of the Chief will reach Likume around mid-day tomorrow. He will be laid in state in his Likume residence tomorrow evening. Burial takes place on Monday at 4pm.

Anuse dead! In Tetseale? But they had left for Likume when he left Tetseale. Had all his efforts been in vain? And why Chief? Had Anuse received in death what eluded him in life? He would be told later that Njikem had described him as Chief in order to facilitate the release of his corpse for an honourable burial like all other dead prisoners.

At Koneji where he was to spend the night at the Rest House he managed to get Central Prison on the phone.

"It is true, Sir, there was an accident. Two warders died," he was told.

Beckongncho asked to be put through to the residence of the Superintendent of Prisons. The man confirmed the disconcerting news.

"Where did the accident occur?"

"At Mukuno,"

"Not Tetseale?"

"Mukuno."

"But the radio said Tetseale. Mukuno is nearer Likume, one hundred kilometres to Likume, two hundred from Tetseale. Why would they say Tetseale and not Mukuno?"

'There might be a mistake. Perhaps it is because at the time of his death he was still technically under the jurisdiction of Tetseale. I think that's why."

Beckongncho held the line for a very long time without saying a word.

"Hello" the superintendent called.

"Hello" Beckongncho responded. "That man's death means something to me," he said after a long pause.

"Very sorry," the Superintendent said.

"Where is the corpse?"

"All the corpses were brought back here. They are in the mortuary."

"Who made the announcement concerning Mr. Anuse?"

"Probably the gentlemen with whom you came to the prison yard the other day. I don't know how he got the news of the death but he was one of the very first persons to reach here when the corpses arrived. I hear he has arranged for the body to be put in the fridge."

Beckongncho breathed out simply.

"Did he know of the plans to have him released?"

"I told him. He was asking me why he did not know the plan."

"And what did you tell him?" Beckongncho asked nervously.

"Tell him? Do I know why he did not know about the plan?"

"I'll see you," Beckongncho said and hung up the receiver.

He had other worries: how was he going to confront Njikem? How were his people to know the efforts he had made to gain his uncle's release? It did not matter that he had lost one hundred thousand francs on a lost cause. He must clear himself. He would leave for Likume as soon as he arrived at Small Monje and find a way to clear himself before his people.

Chapter Twenty-Three

For the want of a nail the shoe was lost,
For the want of a shoe the horse was lost,
For the want of a horse the rider was lost,
And for the want of a rider
The battle was lost
And all for the want of a horse shoe.

(The Grimm Brothers)

BECKONGNCHO LEFT for Likume with two Elders the day after he got to Small Monje. They arrived in Likume at about 9p.m the very day, luckily enough, without any serious breakdown. He did not go to Anuse's Compound. He decided he would discuss a few things with his colleague. S.DO Samson first when they came together.

"That my uncle is dead," he announced mournfully.

"Yes, too bad," SDO Samson shook his head. "I only heard this morning," he lied. "Accept my condolence."

Beckongncho thanked him, but for all the show of sympathy, he could still sense a note of indifference in the man's voice.

"Good riddance," SDO Samson said.

Beckongncho looked up at him with dismay.

The man seemed to understand the surprise.

"The death solves your problems, I suppose,' the man added.

"It only complicates them," Beckongncho said, sighed and took in a long breath in which one could detect profound weariness.

"How?" S.DO Samson asked.

"You see, as I said in Tetseale, although I have not at any one moment seen anything wrong with his arrest, the pressures on me to negotiate for his release are enormous. It was in order to ease some of that pressure that I consulted you to cooperate with me."

" I know."

"But now he is dead. It will help if my people know the extent to which I had gone to effect his release when he died."

"You intend then to go there and inform them or what?"

"Not me," Beckongncho said. 'They won't listen. Even if they listen, they will not believe me. I seem to have that feeling."

"So what exactly are you insinuating?" the man asked, his lips curved upward in cold distaste.

Beckongncho's hands had been folded over his belly as he spoke. At this juncture, with his left elbow over the back of his right hand which still lay over his belly he pulled at his lower lip for a whole minute and said;

"That is the favour I am asking you to do for me. I would like you to talk to them about it. I want somebody in authority like yourself. Somebody who will be easily believed."

The SDO put his left hand to his mouth and shouted 'Whooooooo!' Then sitting back he said:

"Is there nothing else you can ask from me? Anything else but that."

Beckongncho shook his head. He was not just asking for the sake of it. He had a problem. He told SDO Samson.

"I have always hated to make inordinate demands on anybody. Before I ask a favour I give the issue due consideration. So much so that if it is denied I never know how to ask for another."

'Then I am afraid that in this particular case you have not given the issue due consideration."

"What makes you think so?" The man's outright refusal injected a note of desperation into Beckongncho's thoughts. An unredeemed dreariness had crept into his voice.

"I think so because if you did you should have known that your people know and say that I personally ordered the arrest of your uncle. I have received threats in writing to that effect. If you gave the issue due consideration you would have seen it for yourself that it is suicide for me to stand and announce that the man whose arrest I ordered was on his way to being released through the efforts of SDO Beckongncho when he died.

"What do you think they would imagine has motivated me to make that declaration? I see it as something that should come up during a conversation and not from the pulpit. As I said before, ask another favour. Something that will not make me look like a fool."

There was something in the man's tone towards Beckongncho which the latter interpreted as an aversion. He tried to persuade SDO Samson:

"I said I cannot, and the reason is simply that I now find myself in a very delicate situation. Such as I have never felt before. Had Pa Anuse reached here safely, I should never have made this hard demand. While my people are writing to tell you that you personally arrested their brother, they are also telling me that I was the one who ordered the arrest. They have told me that. They therefore believe that just one word from me would have been enough to open the prison gates and set him free. You and I know that the situation is not as simple as that. But they don't. The fact that he had not been released just means that I had not given that all-important word. They don't know about the effort I made to gain his release. That is my worry".

"My worry, dear colleague, is why you think I should very easily follow a corpse into the grave," Samson said.

A cold sense of defeat stole into Beckongncho's mind.

"You are beginning to sound more and more offended," he said, "which makes me feel ashamed and hurt. I apologise sincerely if what I have said offends you. I said it because , for some reason, I thought you were the one persons to solve that problems."

"I am also sorry," the SDO said, sincerely sorry, if my refusal offends you. And furthermore," the man went on a bit more sternly. "You've not asked me whether that your *psycho-friend* has been caught or not, or whether his stolen deep-freezer has been recovered or not. You have not inquired about the health of the little girl who may have suffered an irreparable psychological damage. At least when we ask for favours from others, we should also take their own welfare into consideration. I am being asked questions I can't answer."

Beckongncho stood silent, hurt, ashamed, guilty, angry. That explained the lack of cooperation on the part of his colleague., he thought. Partly, perhaps.

"I am sorry," he said with almost child-like humility. "Actually, that should have been the first thing to do. Forgive me," he pleaded. What a price to pay for helping a helpless creature, he thought.

The SDO for Likume took out a packet of cigarette from his drawer, pulled out one and put it between his lips. He did not light it, and he did not say anything to Beckongncho.

Beckongncho went on contritely.

"I usually do not forget or neglect my obligations to anybody, big or small. If you find me careless as you do now, it can only mean that I am going through a crisis that makes my mind difficult to function as well as it ought. You see the extent to which that my uncle's death is affecting me?"

The man struck a match and held it to his cigarette until it lit and began immediately to pull at it. He did not talk.

"What are the latest developments on the issue, in any case?" he asked.

"We are unable to trace the whereabouts of the man. The parents of the girl are anxious to know more about him. They intend to institute a case,"

"I know no more about him than you do," Beckongncho said firmly. "You should actually be in a better position to know better as his employer. You should have a file on him. Before a man is employed I would imagine that we know where he comes from, his relatives or parents and the like."

"But when such a person commits a crime and escapes you cannot go back to the parents to ask whether…."

Beckongncho would not allow him to finish talking.

"So the best source of information is an innocent passer-by who in a gesture of sympathy and goodwill took mercy on him and recommended him for a job?"

That was the last the two men ever saw of each other. But as far as Beckongncho was concerned there was one last card to play. His self-confidence completely drained, he sent a note to Njikem who was at the funeral.

Dear Brother,

The death of Pa has come as a severe blow to us all. I came down this afternoon and intend to take part in burial. The tradition, you know, forbids me to see the corpse. You may have been told that through my efforts following our last discussion, he was on his way to being released when he died.

In spite of what had transpired between him and myself, I feel obliged to let the people know that I had not only forgiven him, but arranged for his release when fate stood in my way. I would like you to do this for me at his burial.

Your sincere brother,
Kevin.

Njikem's reply brought the Chief very little relief, to say the least. He wrote.

Your Highness;

Thanks you for your note which I have just received while we are seriously engaged in last minute arrangements for our father's burial. If you had made any plans to release him, I am not aware of that and cannot therefore talk on an issue I know nothing about. If you are sincere about what you are saying, what stops you from coming down yourself and announcing your good works? Perhaps there was something to gain from acting in private, which I fail to see.

I may never know why you keep your thoughts shut against me.

Sincerely yours,

Ephraim Njikem.

Chief Beckongncho was undaunted. He would attend the funeral. He would put off that cloak of SDO and Paramount Chief and talk like one brother to the others. He would go, for better or for worse. He knew the family might not receive him. But he would go still.

When he arrived at the scene the following day, it was just as he had feared. Nobody rose to meet him. He came when they had lowered his coffin and were making speeches in praise of the deceased. He stood silent until the last speech was made, by Njikem, then he literally forced his way through the thick crowd to the centre and began with an air of mournful sobriety:

"If there is anybody here who blames me over my uncle's death, I accept that blame. He is dead, yes, but I would like you people to know what I had done. I had made the necessary contacts and arrangements. He was on his way to being released and, had this misfortune not occurred, he would have been free by now."

He was virtually talking to himself because he was fighting to speak above the noises that came from every corner.

Suppressing an indignation that had swollen to the verge of violence, the president of the Likume elements thought that he could answer him:

"Why had you to wait until he was dying before you made your arrangement?"

"Eeeh hhe," those who heard him wondered aloud.

The president turned to the choir mistress and asked her to give them one more song. He knew that Beckongncho had not finished talking. But that did not matter.

The choir mistress intoned a song, waved her hand three times and the choir took off:

"I am married to Jesus, Satan leave me alone…"

Beckongncho departed the way he had come, without anybody paying special attention to him. Some rascal even shouted;

"Murderer, murderer," to his hearing.

One of the Elders who had come with him muttered;

"That's why we said his Highness should not come."

"That's why Your Highness needed to come," Beckongncho said. Just then heavy rain came down dispersing all but those remained to fill the grave and trample on it.

Beckongncho.

Chapter Twenty-Four

The robb'd that smiles steals something from the thief;
He robs himself that spends a bootless grief.
(Shakespeare: *Othello*)

WHEN BECKONGHNCHO left Likume he was sure that he had lost all authority, love and respect as the Paramount Chief. He vowed he would never set foot there again. He vowed he would not go down to the Coast again unless on a very important official business. The humiliation in Likume, he knew, would not be a secret for long. People in other provinces would soon know and would be driven to treat him with the same dishonour.

What he could not fathom was the extent to which the loss of authority down the Coast would affect his position as Paramount Chief of Small Monje. He thought of this the whole length of the journey back.

The Elders behaved differently from what he had expected. They looked happy. They hated the fact that their chief had been treated with scorn. They hated the fact that their chief had even gone down to attend the funeral. But they liked what the trip had done for them back home. Fuo-Nchumbe put it very tersely:

"Finally the dad feather has fallen from the wing of the eagle.'

They were all unanimous in seeing the loss of Likume as a blessing in disguise. Akendong said:

"Sometimes when a sick child dies we thank God. Likume has been draining the Chief's energies. His Highness thought so much of Likume that they even seemed to forget that his palace is here in Nkokonoko Small Monje. Look at me here in Small Monje. I have never gone anywhere. And what do I lack?" he ended up pointing to his bare feet and bedraggled loin cloth and jumpa."

Beckongncho felt relieved that they had not made the injury worse for him. He still remembered that some had disapproved of the very idea of going down. They had reminded him that as Chief he was forbidden to see a corpse. He had assured them convincingly that he would not attend the wake keeping and that he just wanted to take a load off his mind. He was happy that they had not made mention of the initial objection to his going and how he had appeared at the grave side. But he knew there would be a problem.

The payment of the fine imposed on Small Monje would have to be shouldered squarely by him and a few able bodies. The Elders of the council would not be long in discovering that Likume was not only a bad feather that had fallen from the wing of the eagle, but the wing itself, a right wing. In his efforts to raise money to meet up with the compensation Beckongncho would be forced to resort to measures which would in due course compromise his dignity in the eyes of the administration.

***

One evening, several months after Likume broke away from his grip, Chief Beckongncho was sitting in Council with his Elders in the palace when he was informed that some visitors wanted to talk to him. It was just about 6 pm dusk already, in Small Monje. All the Elders of the Council were present.

Immediately to Beckongncho's right was Bejaah, almost as tall as Beckongncho himself, verging on seventy or just a little over seventy. His hair was all grey, or actually white. Generally of a very moody disposition, he was a very keen listener, very patient, though of very strong convictions. He never interrupted anybody, even if he knew the speaker was talking in error. He would make his point only at the end, when his opinion had been asked. Unlike his predecessor, Ngobefuo, he was tolerant to a fault. He was a very good judge of character. If he saw a man and dismissed him as a thief or a fraud, further investigations usually proved him right or nearly always so. Always with his pipe in his hand, he was carrying a small raffia bag by his side containing the horn of a buffalo, a small roll of tobacco and a snuffbox. He had one bad habit though;

212

he was always clearing his throat too, as if his nasal cavity was blocked. Beckongncho loved and respected him the most amongst the entire Elder.

Next to Bejaah was Fiege-Dje. He was a boon companion of Bejaah, but a very different kind of personality. Very fickle, and very unpredictable, he did not seem to have any fixed ideas about anybody or anything. He would praise and condemn the same person in almost the same breath. He was always begging for something. So much so that whenever anybody who knew him well took out a kola nut or some tobacco he showed it to Fiege-Dje first, just to be on the safe side and enjoy his own property. But he had many redeeming features: he could run errands for anybody, and even in his sixties he enjoyed serving people, especially the Chief. Some people said behind his back that he usually ran errands or served people not out of natural altruistic motives but because he knew that if the service produced any profit he would share in it. This was not completely true because he never stood to ask for a reward after a service. He just liked keeping people happy. Furthermore, he never complained about anything, and when he drew attention to a situation as he usually did, it was more out of a desire to let people know what was happening than that he hated what he had seen or heard.

There was also Fuolebe: not tall at all but with a forehead that would have suited a great academician better than a village Elder. Compared to all the other Elders

he was always very neat in dress and fastidious in taste. Like Beckongncho whom he admired to the point of idolatry, he made a fetish of brevity and precision in speech. He hated wasting time, and was most impatient with irrelevant talk. He seemed always to want to finish a topic and go elsewhere. Thus whenever Beckongncho felt like making an allusion that took him a bit out of the topic under discussion, he always began by saying, "Let Fuolebe bear with us this small digression..." He was probably in his mid-sixties.

To Fuolebe's right was the fabulous Fuo-Akeumbin. He was a little taller than Beckongncho, but completely bald. He was always in the traditional outfit: a black raffia cap with a red feather on it, a well-embroidered jumpa over a blue-black loin cloth. There was no known local musical instrument or drum he could not play, and play very well, from the xylophone to the balafon, from the flute to the guitar. He was always in the company of Fuo-Akendong, not just because he was married from that family, but because the two always had something to talk and laugh about. It was hard to tell who of them was the joker, but they were always laughing together. He never stopped talking about the days of the Germans when he went to school. But all that he seemed to have retained from the German school days was the letter S which he added in free variation to every English word. For instance, mans, mes, yous, todays, comes heres, hows dos yous dos, goods monings, gives mes wasters, sits downs, etc etc, were perfectly normal forms of speech for anybody who took German Education seriously. Actually he may have been confusing German with English Education. He was, however, capable of taking a very serious look at a situation and suggesting ways of getting out of it or preventing a critical outcome.

Next to Fuo-Akeumbin was Fuo-Akendong. He was just about the same age with Fuo-Akeumbin, but he was of a heavier build. He had very small eyes that darted constantly from one object or person to the other. Perpetually on the humorous side of life he would treat the most serious and delicate situations with disarming levity. But he was very perceptive, very honest, and had no problems switching from light-hearted humour to outright seriousness. He was enormously popular among the people, a fact which Beckongncho exploited whenever he wanted to know something about anybody without asking the person himself.

Directly opposite the Chief was Fuo-Nchumbe. His was of a very philosophical disposition. Very quiet and accommodating, he was not known to have ever quarrelled with anybody. He was very generous, but those who did not know him well thought him snobbish and selfish. He believed that there were always two sides to an argument, and also that the minority could sometimes be correct, if only they were given the chance to their ides.

There was also Komia and four others, but these five constituted the cornerstones of Beckongncho's empire. He consulted with them whenever the situation arose. Unfortunately he did not meet with all of them as often as they would have liked.

It is not that Beckongncho was a dictator. Just that he always avoided entangling himself in issues of a controversial nature that would require the intervention of others. He worked very hard, and the Council had so much confidence in him that it simply allowed him to do things his own way, unless he sought their help. It was at these five principal Elders that Beckongncho was looking when he stated the purpose of the meeting.

***

There were three things he had intended to discuss with the Elders: the Chief's farms and animals, the question of his succession and the future relationship between Small Monje and Likume.

He had already finished discussion on the farms: the defunct Co-operative Unions were to be revitalized, Self-Reliance groups were to be formed through which a means would be sought of setting up an enterprise to collect produce from the farms and arrange for its sale outside Small Monje; all the women had to do was harvest their cocoyams, have them weighed at the Self-Reliance Cooperative Office and deposited there. After the sales they were to report back for their monies. A small amount of money was to be deducted as handling charges. This along with other levies would be used to set up a scan water project – a German firm had already been contacted to that effect.

The question of his succession seemed tied to that of the Chief's wives. Of the seventeen wives of the throne that had escaped to the coast, eleven had been recovered, seven of whom had given birth and one was pregnant. It was when Beckongncho became Chief that he learned that Chief Fuo-Ndee had become impotent during the last eleven years of his reign, which was exactly the length of time during which Mme-Nji, his youngest wife had lived with him. Mme-Nji was one of the very beautiful women Nchindia had abandoned. But she had remained in the palace.

When Beckongncho came to power his own wife was five months pregnant and eventually gave birth to a baby girl. Even if the baby had been male, he would still not have a strong claim to the throne. Mme-Nji was among the very first women on whom Beckongncho exercised his new role as the Paramount Chief. And when she gave birth it was a male. Many other women delivered male children during that period too. But the point of discussion was that it would be a special tribute to Mme-Nji's fidelity to give her son the strongest recommendation as the next possible successor. The lady herself had long been chosen his Mafuo. After Mme-Nji's first son, the sons of the other women were to be considered, depending on the conduct of the children and their mothers and even uncles and aunts. Beckongncho's own children before the crowning only stood a chance if the Elders ran into a particular problem in choosing from amongst the above-mentioned groups.

It was at this point in the discussion that the visitor had been announced. Beckongncho went on with the meeting for some twenty more minutes before coming to meet the man in the waiting room.

"Evening, Patron," the little man greeted, holding out his hand.

"Good evening," Beckongncho answered but did not shake his hand. His position as Paramount Chief forbade him to shake hands, especially in the palace where he wielded all the authority his title entailed. The visitor would interpret this in future as a sign of snobbery.

" Can I help you?" Beckongncho asked.

" I am Bruno Jean-Pierre Monhga."

Beckongncho nodded.

"Assistant Chief of Service of Controls in the Ministry of Finance."

Beckongncho nodded, and said:

"My pleasure, Mr. Bruno."

"We are here on mission," Bruno said. "The Provincial Auditing Committee is going round, that is why were are here."

Beckongncho looked the man straight in the eyes.

"Surely it cannot be that you have come to audit me here and now," he said. "In the palace here I am the Paramount Chief. And for all I know, you don't audit chiefs."

"No, er, er, that is not what I mean," the man said hesitatingly.

"Any way," Beckongncho said, "Let them serve you a drink. I am at a meeting with my Elders. I'll be with you soon." He went back to meet the old men.

***

The third point of discussion did not take long and they were not all unanimous on the Chief's argument. He said it would be self-deceit to think that Small Monje could survive without Likume or other Coastal cities. Then very slowly but forcefully he told the attentive assembly of Elders:

"History is seldom a good judge. When Anuse confronted me the whole world was watching. When he insulted and disgraced the Provincial Governor, the whole world was listening. Nobody approved of his actions, that is why when they came to take him away, nobody rose to defend him. But not too long from now, not many of those who saw and heard what he did would be alive.

"What history will record is the fact that Beckongncho cut Likume off from Small Monje. It will not record the detailed circumstances under which it happened. History will never record the personal differences that existed between Anuse and Beckongncho. History may not record Anuse's private ambitions to be Paramount Chief of Small Monje and his plans to eliminate anybody in his way. History will not record the extent to which he went to destroy Chieftaincy in Nkokonoko Small Monje. All that history will record is the fact that, Kevin Beckongncho, cut Likume off."

" So what is His Highness saying ?" Bejaah asked.

"So I am saying that, should I not be there tomorrow, let him who sits on this throne make peace with Likume and the Small Monje elements in the Coast. My split with Likume is total, but personal, and I am too close to the event to turn round and say I am sorry. Let he who comes after me say he was no party to what happened and so he would not honour my stand point. Let him bring Likume back to fold."

There was a long silence.

"I did not tell you this, but as I mentioned in Likume during the burial, I had made all arrangements for Anuse to be released from prison so that he could take over the leadership of his business. But he died."

He sat back and waited for questions.

There were none. But the fact that he rose and went to meet his guest without any contradictions did not mean that everybody was in complete agreement. In the mind of many of the Elders, all those projects requiring the intervention of Likume were too small a price to pay for the power they would continue to have if Small Monje continued to exist in splendid isolation. They thought the Chief was once more giving away his powers, as well as theirs. But they did not know how to contradict Beckongncho. Perhaps it would be best to wait for the coming of that other Chief.

***

"As we were saying," Beckongncho began when he went back to meet his guest. He had never met the man before, but he seemed to instantly detest him.

"We are auditing all District Heads, DO's and SDO's," the man said.

Beckongncho nodded silently.

"So when do you start?" he asked when he noticed that the man had finished talking.

The man did not answer the question directly. Instead he chose to explain his strategy:

"You see, Chief, all auditors are not the same. We know we handle very delicate issues, some of which can even send people into prison. Some wicked auditors would just come to your office and take you by surprise. We are different. We give you time to, you know, put things together."

" I appreciate that," Beckongncho said. "This is actually the first time I am being threatened with auditing as SDO, perhaps that is why I am not quite aware of the procedure."

"What I have told you is not the procedure. It is what we do when we want to favour a man."

A suspicious smile lingered at the corners of his mouth.

" I see," Beckongncho said to himself.

The man's next point disturbed him. He said:

"We shall be looking into the levying of taxes in your area, the distribution, the payment of compensation for the damages that were done here during the trouble, how much has been paid in, by whom, and so on and so forth. Things like this, if you do not know beforehand, can create problems."

Beckongncho tightened his lips and looked at him again. The man's presence reeked of blackmail, and he could smell it in the air. The compensation had not actually been paid and the levying of taxes was irregular. Not that he personally stood to gain by the irregularity.

"How did you come by such information?" he asked.

"It is our job," the man said with a knowing smile. "We know these things. Nothing under the sun can hide."

Beckongncho stared at the man for a very long time, determined not to look afraid or panicky.

"So what do I do?"

The man did not answer. He expected Beckongncho to understand. And, indeed, Beckongncho understood but chose not to show it. Did he expect Beckongncho to rush to his office and fool around with his files which he kept always in order? That would be ridiculous! He had not gone out of his way to do anything so outrageous as to need to buy off the auditors. He could always explain himself if they found something abnormal.

"Where are you spending the night? And by the way, where are the others?"

"We are four of us, plus one driver." The man ignored the first part of the question.

"Where are the others?"

"Up at the gate, in the Jeep. The Chief of the mission is there."

Beckongncho looked at the man for a while with an admixture of hatred and contempt.

"Why did you all not come down?"

"I did not know how long I was to wait."

"And why did you not tell me the head of your mission was there? You gave me the impression that you were the leader?"

"Well," the man shrugged.

"Again, where do you intend to sleep?"

"Where you choose that we sleep."

Beckongncho was beginning to feel more and more irritated.

"The Rest House is there. I'll find somebody to lead you there, and we shall only talk in the morning."

***

The information which Bruno took back to his chief of mission did not favour Beckongncho. Beckongncho was not ready to influence the outcome of the committee's findings. He had refused to shake hands with the messenger sent to him. He had refused to come out to meet the chief of mission, or even send something to

219

clean his eyes and oil his hands. He had chosen to send his driver to arrange for their accommodation.

What this meant was clear in their minds: either Beckongncho did not care about whatever happened to him following the findings of the auditors, or he kept a faultless record. The former was likely, the latter impossible. Not with all the rumours which had made the mission necessary! They went to bed that night determined to find many things incriminating in Beckongncho's record.

When the auditors left without saying a word to him Beckongncho knew that they were up to some mischief. And true to his fears, the auditors' report submitted to the office of the Provincial Governor was cruel. The Governor invited him soon afterwards and asked him three questions: the first concerned the compensation. Why had Beckongncho to make the Bimobio contribute when the crime was committed by Small Monje? Beckongncho's explanation was simple: half the population of Small Monje was made up of women and old men with no real source of income. The Small Monje Elements in Likume and other coastal towns had refused to pay.

The second question had to do with the levying of taxes. He had been instructed to increase the taxes for Small Monje as part of the fine imposed on them. He had chosen to increase the taxes uniformly for Small Monje and Bimobio, why? Beckongncho explained that he had been anxious to clear the Small Monje compensation problem from his records in order to concentrate on more important issues, and since the monies raised went into the Government coffers and not his own or those of Small Monje he did not think he had acted wrongly.

The third question had to do with the diversion of funds for the development of his province into the account for the compensation imposed on Small Monje. Beckongncho's answer was the same. It was one way of accelerating the clearance of the pernicious debt.

The Governor asked him to return to his job. He did not mention the word misappropriation of Government funds. The word hung over every statement that he made. And before he left Tetseale, he knew his days in the administration of the Civil Service was numbered.

Beckongncho told himself that he was nobody's fool. Would never be! He returned to Small Monje on the 9th of February. The 11th was a national feast day on which he had to officiate at the opening and closing ceremonies and the award of prizes. On the 13th February he was back in Tetseale to see the Minister of Territorial Administration.

***

He waited patiently until it was his turn, then he knocked and went in. The Minister was glad to see him. He was always glad to talk to Beckongncho. He was the same man whose intervention had converted Beckongncho from a mere Headmaster and a local Chief to a Senior District Officer.

The Minister showed him where to sit and immediately inquired:

"So what news from your Small Monje end of the World?"

"No news Your Excellency,"

"No news is good news," the Minister said. The ghost of a smile flashed across Beckongncho's visage.

"So what can I do for you this time?" He was talking and turning over the page of an open file in front of him.

"I'd like the Honourable Minister to read this," he said holding out a long khaki envelope to the Minister. The man took and placed it in the IN-COMING tray and looked across at Beckongncho. He seemed to deliberately avert the Minister's eyes.

He picked up the letter and using his letter knife tore it open along with the width. He pulled the letter out and asked:

"What is it about?" There was trepidation in his voice.

"Well, Your Excellency, read it," Beckongncho sounded bold and even condescending, but not visibly impolite.

"Is it a summons?" he asked half-smiling without suspicion.

"No summons, Your Excellency." The Minister stretched out the letter and read to himself.

Office of the Senior
District Office
Bimobio's & Small Monje,
Lower-Middle-Best Province,
12ᵗʰ February,1969

The Honourable Minister
Of Territorial Administration
Ministry of Territorial
Administration,
TETSEALE.

SUBJECT:
RESIGNATION AS SENIOR DISTRICT OFFICER
Your Excellency,
I shall continue to be most grateful to you personally for giving me the
opportunity to hold the office of Senior District Officer for the past two years
and a half. However, I must say with a heavy heart that it is becoming more
and more impossible for me to reconcile my responsibilities as Senior District
Officer with the aspirations of my people.
I am therefore, by this letter , and with all due respect, resigning the office.
Most Respectfully Yours
Kevin Beckongncho.

The Minister read it over again, then raising his head and looking sternly into Beckongncho's face said:
"No. You cannot resign."
Beckongncho did not respond.
"This has never happened before. Ever".
His nostrils seemed to distend and vibrate ominously.
Beckongncho still did not say anything.
"Do you know what this letter means?"
" I do. Your Excellency," Beckongncho responded very politely.
"What do you think it means?"
"That I can no longer act as SDO, Your Excellency,"
"It means more than that," the Minister said very softly. "And I have the impression that you do not know the full implication of this act."

Beckongncho changed the position of his feet, supported his chin in his left hand and looked on, silent.

"When you moved from Headmaster to SDO," a monstrous concession I initiated, you earned in addition to your salary, a huge duty allowance which you are aware of. True or false?"

"True Your Excellency," Beckongncho's tone was a bit indifferent.

"If you are dismissed as SDO, you lose only your duty allowance, but you retain your salary. But when you resign as SDO, RESIGN, for goodness sake! You lose your Civil Service status, your pension etc. etc."

The Minister folded his hands and sat up, looking at Beckongncho, somehow expecting him to withdraw his letter.

"Your Excellency is looking only at the financial aspect of it," he said.

"It is the most important aspect in the whole thing."

"Well," Beckongncho shrugged. It was too late, he thought. He had already submitted the letter. If he withdrew he would never command any respect in the administration of the Government. They could dismiss him the very next day, or send him to some remote corner of the country. The resignation would stand. It was a decision he had thought over very well. He would not therefore change it on the spur of the moment.

"Besides, and most serious of all," the Minister resumed, his face devastated with rage, "it is a slap in the face of the administration. You are by this careless document reducing a carefully worked out machinery of the state to a joke which you could choose to belong to or not to."

He looked at Beckongncho. His face remained expressionless.

"I would like to advise you as a personal friend to go back and reconsider this letter and the decision that prompted it."

He looked again at Beckongncho. When Beckongncho was sure that the Minister had finished talking he said with calm decision:

"Your Excellency, that is all I came down here to tell you. I came down in the administrative Land Rover with the driver. I would like to know from Your Excellency whether I should take it back to Small Monje or leave it here."

The Minister, taking Beckongncho's response for an insult, stamped his first so hard on the desk that his private secretary came rushing in.

"Get out of my sight," the man shouted. The command was not actually directed at Beckongncho. But both him and the secretary went out through the same door.

Five minutes later he summoned his secretary and asked her to call Beckongncho back. When Beckongncho came he asked him to sit down. It now dawned on him that Beckongncho had made up his mind irrevocably.

"If you are so decided…"

" I am decided, Your Excellency," Beckongncho interrupted the Minister.

The man paused for a long time. He did not appreciate Beckongncho's rudeness in interrupting him. On his part Beckongncho noticed the anger on the Minister's face.

'I am sorry, Your Excellency, I did not mean to interrupt you. I did not mean to be rude."

"I was saying that if you are so decided," the Minister resumed.

Beckongncho was silent.

"You must have to wait until a suitable replacement for you is found."

"To this I have no objective, Your Excellency. All I ask for now is that the records should indicated that from this day, date and hour, as I leave this office, I am no longer SDO of Nkokonko Small Monje and Bimobio area. If that is agreed, I can hang around my office till a new SDO is appointed."

Chapter Twenty-Five

Quem Deus perdere vult, dementat prius.
(Anonymous)

ON HIS return to Small Monje Beckongncho summoned a meeting of his Chief Elders where he told them the move he had just taken in order to allow himself enough time to concentrate freely on affairs of the tribe and throne. The old men praised and thanked him and later that same evening they all went to the shrine where a special thanksgiving prayer was offered to *Akeukeuor*.

His letter of resignation was submitted on Saturday February 14th. He returned to Small Monje on Monday, February 16th, the day he met his Elders and offered the prayer. On Tuesday February 17th, he went to his office where he summoned a meeting of his junior and senior staff and informed them of his resignation. He handed over the running of the district to his first Assistance SDO, pending the appointment of a successor from the ministry. He had therefore not kept his word to the Minister.

Nobody knew how to react to his resignation because it had never been heard of before. Not that he looked like a man who could not do such a thing. Quite the contrary. One of the chief clerks remarked that of late he had noticed that Beckongncho hated his job very much.

On Thursday February 19th he was informed that a new SDO had been chosen to replace him, and that the official handing over ceremony would take place on Saturday February 21st. He was also given a copy of the programme, which he studied carefully:

8.00 am   *The Provincial District Heads and Sub-District Officers arrive Senior District Office.*
9.00.a.m   *Arrival of Paramount and Sub-Chiefs*
9.300 am   *Arrival of New SDO and Commissioner of Police*

10.00 am   *Arrival of Secretary General in Ministry of Territorial Administration.*
Singing of National Anthem.
Official opening of ceremony
Speech of secretary General
Speech of In-coming SDO
Speech of Out-gong SDO
HANDING OVER
CLOSING REMARKS- by S.G
ENTERTAINMENT.

"Where do I come in here?" Beckongncho inquired.

"Second item on the programme," the Chief of protocol told him. "Under Paramount Chiefs and Sub-Chiefs. Any problem?"

"The problem is that when the Paramount Chief comes in, nobody else is supposed to arrive," he said with insolent pride. Trapped in his own decision, Beckongncho had come to detest anything and anybody that had something to do with the administration of the country.

"What!"

"Yes, I come last."

"That is you want to come after the Secretary Genera?"

"That is where I belong.," Beckongncho told him firmly.

"When you were SDO, when did you usually come in?"

"I came in where the SDO came in. I could not come in as SDO, run out, change into the Paramount Chief dress and come in as Paramount Chief."

***

That same afternoon Ephraim Njikem visited Beckongncho in the palace. He immediately told Beckongncho why he had come:

"I have been very worried by this your dismissal thing in the papers. What really happened?"

"Whose dismissal?" Beckongncho inquired.

"Yours," Njikem opened the paper, the national daily THE STARLIGHT and showed the article in the column under society.

The caption said.

SMALL MONJE AREA:

Beckongncho read on:

The newly established Provincial Auditing Committees mean business. In the wake of their exercise, heads are beginning to roll. The first casualty following the exposure of fraud and blatant misappropriation of Government funds, is SDO Kevin Beckongncho who was relieved of his post by Presidential Order no. 321/sb/M.b/T. of 16th February, 1969.

Beckongncho went over to the shelf in his sitting room and brought out a file which he threw open, took out a copy of the letter he had submitted to the Minister of Territorial Administration and showed Njikem.

"I was not dismissed, Ephraim. I resigned," he said calmly. "I took this down myself. Looking at the date, 12th February. What this means in effect is that your Government dismissed the SDO of Small Monje and Bimobio four full days after he had tendered in his letter of resignation. Look at my travelling warrant."

He showed Njikem. Quite naturally, Beckongncho expected Njikem to look indignant. Instead, Njikem only looked dubiously confused, which kept him worried.

"But how did the newspaper men come by the idea of your dismissal?"

"You are asking me a question I cannot really answer.'

Beckongncho returned the file to the shelf and sitting back down said:

"It appears to me that you are bent on believing the papers and doubting me. Would you rather see me dismissed than resign?"

Njikem did not answer immediately. Beckongncho expected that if he had guessed wrongly Njikem would deny at once. Njikem's silence confirmed the lingering suspicion that Njikem did not quite wish him well.

"Tell me, Kevin," Njikem implored with infinite earnestness. "Let me call your name for once..."

"It's no insult Beckongncho cut in. "That's what I'm called."

"What exactly do you begrudge me for?"

"Who said I begrudge you?"

"You do."

"How?"

"There is no important secret in your life which I share. And I hide nothing of mine from you..."

"Ephraim," Beckongncho pleaded. "Human beings are made differently…"

"They are, Your Highness. But you treat me as if I am God's unsuccessful attempt to create a person like you."

Beckongncho looked at Njikem for a while. Was Njikem thinking of the secret manner in which he had gone about gaining the late Anuse's release?

"What exactly has prompted you to say so?"

"You took your resignation letter down yourself?"

The tone made it a question.

"That's what I said."

"And you don't think I needed to know something of this nature? Even if it meant giving me a chance to make a suggestion you would not take, I think I deserve better treatment."

Beckongncho did not know whether to take Njikem seriously or otherwise. After turning in his letter of resignation he had made three attempts to see Njikem but none had been successful. The first time he had seen Njikem's RENAULT 16 in his parking space at his office long before he drove into the compound. When he actually entered the compound proper he thought the blind in Njikem's office window opened slightly before closing again. He thought he saw the shadow of somebody, most probably a lady, pass from Njikem's office into the general office .

Then when he came to the office and asked to see him the lady who received him said curtly: "I no dey, sa."

"Are you sure?" Beckongncho asked.

"Why not?" the lady said.

" You think he must have gone far?"

'I don't know, sa," the woman responded.

"I am asking because I see his car outside there," Beckongncho said.

There was no answer.

"Well," Beckongncho said, "wherever he is, please tell him when he comes that the Paramount Chief of Nkokonoko Small Monje tried to see him." His conclusion quite naturally was that his brother for some unknown reason had deliberately refused to see him.

Ephraim listened to Beckongncho's explanation intently. He knew deep in his heart of hearts that not too long ago he had actually refused to see Beckongncho in his office in Tetseale.

"They were trying to use me to suppress our people's demands," Beckongncho resumed. "I seemed to have become an agent of oppression in the eyes of our people. Young men were arrested down the coast under the pretext that they had uttered defamatory statements against the Government in my presence. Worst of all the Government would not listen to whatever I had to say about how we could pay the fine that was imposed on the tribe.

"They sent people to audit me who had made up their minds that I was guilty in many respects," Beckongncho said. "They had ideas I could not change. They would have sacked me in the long run anyway. I decided that I could as well leave with honour on my own rather than wait to be thrown out with ignominy. This throne needs a Chief more than Small Monje needs an SDO of its own."

Njikem had come ready to answer Beckongncho on his refusal to come to his aid at their uncle's funeral. That was one reason he sounded so aggressive. Unfortunately for him Beckongncho decided not to bring up the matter. He thought he could appease Beckongncho, so he told him:

" I must write a rejoinder," Njikem broke in as if he had not been listening at all.

"A rejoinder to what?" Beckongncho inquired.

"To the article claiming that you were dismissed. I will also attach a copy of your resignation letter. It will be great news for the private press."

Beckongncho laughed and told him it was not necessary.

"The public must know the truth?" Njikem insisted.

"Do me this favour," Beckongncho pleaded. "Let things remain just the way they are. Our people know I resigned. My workers know that. You know it, I hope. If the media, the true source of the truth has abdicated its responsibility to inform, if it has chosen only to misinform the public, I think under the present political climate I can use my time better than refuting lies and insisting on truths that are obvious even to infants. I think Small Monje has made enough headlines already."

***

Perhaps Beckongncho's guess was right, and Njikem must have decided not to receive him on that fateful day without knowing how important the visit was. He must have been still smarting from the annoying manner in which Beckongncho handled the Anuse problem, especially his exclusion from plans to gain the release and his request that he, Njikem, should talk in his defence at the burial. Beckongncho asked him whether he did not see the letter he left with his wife.

" I never saw any such thing," Njikem responded in a tone which made it sound like Beckongncho was merely fabricating an excuse.

"On the 13th of February I made three attempt to see you - twice in your office and once at your house. In the end I gave your wife a letter to give you. Had you decided to meet me on that day this resignation would be no news to you because I was looking for you to tell you about it."

He was looking at Njikem as he spoke and he could see guilt written all over his face.

***

Despite the fact that Beckongncho had written a letter, Njikem was actually hearing it for the first time. Mrs Njikem had done precisely as Beckongncho had demanded: She had put the letter on the dining table where Njikem would see it as soon as he came home. She was behind the house when Njikem returned from work and asked for his lunch. The house girl who had set the table had put the letter in a file on the shelf since she had not been told of the urgency of the message. Mrs. Njikem had also forgotten to remind her husband about it. Consequently Njikem was hearing about the resignation for the first time.

Upon his return to Tetseale Njikem would eventually find the letter, but that would not make him trust and respect Beckongncho any more than before. The reason this time: Beckongncho had chosen to inform him about the resignation only after he had deposited his letter with the Minister. It meant Beckongncho held him of so little account that he did not think he, Njikem, could make a suggestion that would make him change his mind.

"But this resignation itself," he began, "whose advice did you seek, or as usual you did not think anybody could say anything sensible about it?"

Beckongncho breathed out sharply.

"You don't consult people's views when you want to do right things, when you are responding to an injury, or when you are forestalling a humiliation. I could see it coming. I consulted nobody whatsoever. Nobody."

"So what's the situation as of now?" Njikem asked vaguely.

Beckongncho raised a brow of uncertainty as to what he implied.

"Has a new SDO been appointed?"

Beckongncho nodded.

"Certainly. The Handing over is even on Saturday."

"After tomorrow?"

Beckongncho nodded.

"Then why don't I hang on and witness it?"

"As you like it," he said indifferently.

***

Did Beckongncho say he did not mention the resignation issue to anybody whatsoever? That was a white lie. Small Mammy knew about it and, had she objected to it, Beckongncho should have rethought his decision. Small Mammy was Beckongncho's first wife. Her full name was Francisca Songakap. Her intimate friends called her Frank, Franka and quite often Frankie, or Franky. Beckongncho never called her anything else but Small Mammy. Some would say the appellation grew out of the fact that she was very small in stature. She was hardly more than 1.4metres. But it is closer to the truth to say the appellation grew out of the very intimate relationship that existed between the couple in their married life.

Nobody who did not know them before Beckongncho became Paramount Chief and SDO would find much to substantiate this claim. Although Mrs. Beckongncho was not exactly the kind of woman to be readily sent for a beauty contest, she had charm in the best senses of the word. With fairly pronounced but not exaggerated features she had a slightly pronounced forehead, expressive roundish eyes, a gently protruding nose with fairly open nostrils. She had a mouth not too large, not too small but whose most permanent characteristic was a broad friendly smile. Her voice, in spite of her smallness in size, was loud and she always spoke as

231

if she either had a slight hearing defect, or assumed it in others. Not many people had visited Beckongncho without complimenting him or his wife about her hospitality. She would feel hurt if a visitor left without having a bite or a drink. And in her little black handbag which she always carried with her, there were always a few kola nuts for any friend of the family she might meet on her way.

Some men, mistaking her open-handedness for frivolity, had ventured to make a pass at her, an act which had earned them an enmity so bitter that they had never visited the family thereafter. She had spent two years in a technical school before abandoning it because her parents could not afford the fees. And after she was married to Beckongncho she preferred to stay at home and take care of her family than pursuing an endeavour whose result seemed rather unpredictable. She had done some typing in college, but she chose to become a seamstress, a job in which she had distinguished herself as being very painstaking and competent. Her neighbours, customers and apprentices in Sowa judged her differently.

Some thought her hypocritical and pretentious, some thought her proud and others thought she was servile and stupid. All these judgements grew from her reactions to their perennial subject of conversation - MEN. And her reactions, dubious as her mates may have found them, were conditioned by her attitude towards her husband. She was not an adulteress, never suspected Beckongncho of adultery, and so was never interested in stories of adultery which the other women dwelled on so frequently.

Many women who believed that no woman can survive by sticking to her husband alone saw a streak of hypocrisy in this attitude. She never asked to see Beckongncho's bank account, though she believed that he always saved enough to take care of the family problems. Beckongncho never particularly cared to know how much she made a week or a month. But he was happy when she brought two hundred thousand francs every four months as her share of their women's *Njangi*. He would take and put it into the Credit Union. If she needed anything, say a new machine, Beckongncho provided it without submitting her to any undue interrogation. If Beckongncho needed money for some emergency she would give without making him lose his status of husband and head of the family. Between them therefore money was not a factor.

Stories of men squandering salaries by buying clothes, fridges and even houses for free women did not interest her and made little sense to her. There was a particular notorious neighbour, a certain Domestic Science Mistress hell-bent on converting Francisca.

She claimed that a week never passed without her receiving a beating from her husband, even though she said she has mastered all the wiles in the lives of men. She never mentioned Beckongncho's name directly, but she swore by the names of all the known gods that there was no headmaster who did not make a pass at his female staff - married or unmarried. Her method of curbing or controlling her husband's nocturnal activities was simple:

"As soon as salaries come, I call Fred, we sit down, I remove money for food, for the children, for drugs, for my hair. Then I give him 4,000francs – 1000 francs a week. I take the rest to the Credit Union."

"For me I don't know how much H.M earns," Francisca would say.

"It means you don't know how much he gives to women outside?"

"I don't know. Do you know how much Fred gives?" she would ask.

The wise woman would shrink in defeat. And thus Francisca continued to live with Beckongncho. Their relationship was built on mutual trust and respect. Beckongncho trusted her, never made her feel she was being watched and never questioned her if she delayed in returning home from the market or a meeting, which she scarcely did. The idea never crossed his mind that Small Mammy might have taken undue advantage to go and see a paramour. It was inconceivable.

They lived so peacefully that her attitude towards life was directly conditioned by that of her husband. If her husband loved somebody or something she did not take long to find it loveable. If he hated somebody, that was the man to hate. She was the key to Beckongncho's success in life. Beckongncho now had four children with her – two boys and two girls. Before he become Chief they had two children a boy and a girl. Since becoming Chief, they had added another girl and a boy.

***

When Beckongncho got news that he had been made Chief and showed an interest in the position, she helped him realise the goal, and when he was finally crowned Chief she helped him enjoy the office. She did not feel threatened by the fact that Beckongncho's love will diminish with the increased number of wives. And indeed she remained close to his heart as a very special person. It was only when Beckongncho become SDO that she felt miserable. She hated ceremony with all her soul and in as much as she would have liked to attend parties with her husband, she found her place by his side being taken up gradually by other women. Inevitably a jealous sense of exclusion set in which strained their relationship somehow.

She was the only person and the only woman to whom Beckongncho gave a hint of his intention when the auditor left. He told her.

" I expect something embarrassing to happen to me soon, Small Mammy."

"What kind of thing? Your blood is shaking you again?" She asked. She remembered that many of the important events to happen in his life had always been preceded by a feeling of uneasiness which he always communicated to her.

"This SDO thing will not leave me. Whether it is because I did not go to the National School of Administration, I don't know. There are certain things I cannot stand." He did not tell her precisely what his fears were. But when he returned from seeing the Provincial Governor, he told her:

"Small Mammy, I'll no longer be SDO here,"

"They want to transfer you?"

"They could do that, or anything else they want. But what I know is that it won't be something good."

"How do you know?"

"I know. I can judge situations. If they transfer me from here, I'll never be able to exercise my full authority here as Paramount Chief. I may never be able to realize any of the goals I have set up for this tribe. They may even go further. They may even dismiss me."

From experience Francisca knew that before Beckongncho voiced his fears he had judged the situation so thoroughly that to question is to doubt or insult his intelligence.

"So what will you do?"

"I'll not wait for them to transfer or remove me. I'll remove myself. You may now remain, the wife of the Paramount Chief not SDO."

"If it will bring you shame, leave it. Forget about how I feel. You know that my happiness is our happiness, and your sadness my sadness." She had only one worry.

"What will the Elders say? What will the other wives say?"

"As far as I am concerned, those are no problems. The Elders don't even know what it really meant to be SDO. They see it as something that disturbs me form discharging my duties as Chief. As for the other women, I don't need to explain." So the issue ended and Beckongncho left for Tetseale knowing that he would be answerable to nobody for the decision he had taken. A Biongong proverb has it that:

"When a man sees you in the morning and greets you with a smile, it means a good woman sleeps behind his bed." Believe it.

Chapter Twenty-Six

A man at whom everybody points,
dies without being ill.
(Mieder and Dundes:
The Wisdom of Many)

A **S FAR** as the handing over ceremony was concerned Beckongncho stood very firm on his decision. It will be recalled that when the programme of the day's activities was first presented to him on Wednesday 9th February, he insisted he must come last. The Protocol Officer had thought otherwise and had left without convincing Beckongncho, nor being convinced by him on the order of arrival.

That Saturday the ceremony began at 8.am as originally scheduled. By 10 am when the Secretary General arrived Beckongncho had still not come. The Chief of Protocol told the Secretary General what Beckongncho had told him a few days before. A messenger was dispatched immediately along with a policeman to go for him in the administrative vehicle.

After some ten minutes when the vehicle returned to say Beckongncho was already on his way and that he had said he would not come in the vehicle the Secretary General ordered the ceremony to start. Somebody intoned the National Anthem and they began singing.

O Fatherland of the fields green.
Of the mountains high and of the seas
Raised you are from the labours of the hands,
That through the goodness of the heart,
That through the goodness of the heart,
That through justice for all,
In the forefront of the nations of Africa
We, thy children, the breast of thy earth.
Should with pride they name forever brandish.

O, Father, O Fatherland, O Father, O Fatherland,
That we the breast of they earth.
Should with pride, Brandish,
Should with pride, Brandish,
Forever brandish,
In the forefront
Of the nations
Of Africa.

They had hardly sung this first stanza when a bugle was heard in the distance. Loud drumming and singing followed. As if that was the sign they had been waiting for, the natives in the hall immediately forgot about the National Anthem and jumped out and began singing towards the direction of the bugle and drums. The forces of law and order were helpless in holding them back. The singing of the National Anthem had to be abandoned.

Twenty minutes later calm, order and Paramount Chief Kevin Beckongncho arrived at the ceremonial ground. Far ahead of him danced three masquerades, immediately behind the masquerades walked three of the Chief's younger wives – Songakap was one.

Behind the three women rode two men on white horses. The men were Fuo-Akendong and Fuo-Akeumbin. Beckongncho himself rode on a palanquin borne by six people with six others walking besides them to relieve them as soon as the need arose. Two other men rode black horses behind the Chief – they were Folebe and Fontchu-mbe. One bugler, now with swollen lips and silent, walked behind the rider. When they began he was in front. But the was now tired, exhausted.

When Beckongncho was lowered from the Palanquin in front of the hall, he was immediately led to where he was to sit. He walked gracefully, in no hurry, and waved to the crowd at every peace.

The Secretary General glanced at his watch for the fourth time and Beckongncho had not yet sat down when he gave orders for the Anthem to resume, and it was sung to the end.

The Secretary General proceeded with the ceremony in bitterness. The handing-over was done. During that time which he painted the life history of the new SDO-Akanfo Condre in glowing colours. He did not talk about Beckongncho except when he said, "When an SDO is dismissed, his place cannot be left vacant."

The new SDO talked briefly, made one reference to Beckongncho's dismissal and promised not to repeat the errors of his predecessor. He accepted that he had heard enormity of the task ahead of him, but that he was counting on the total support of the people of Small Monje and Bimobio in the extremely tough task that lay ahead of him.

Beckongncho's speech was even briefer. After the usual respect to all the dignitaries present he began very undercurrent of calculated arrogance, cynicism and sarcastic irony.

"I am most thankful to the Minister of Territorial Administration here represented by his Secretary General," he began, "for ever giving me the opportunity to know what it means to be an SDO in a place as unpredictable as Bimobio and Nkokonoko Small Monje. My successor, we have been to be that, or even more, to be sent here, because he will require all the experience. I give him my blessings, in the hope that his own presence will make the one important difference to this phenomenon we call Small Monje. I don't know how I came to be the SDO of this area. Yet, I gave it my best shot, but as you have all been told, the Government thought differently and **dismissed** me." Njikem almost rose to protest, but realizing that he was reacting that way alone, he made as if he was merely adjusting his seat and sat back down silent, confused.

As Beckongncho pronounced the word **dismissed**, he smiled to himself to give the word the ironic twist that it deserved. Some, like Njikem, would miss the irony and take the word at face value and, long after his death, would never reconcile Beckongncho's claim of resignation to the public acceptance of dismissal which the papers had carried.

"So no hard feelings," he went on. "The great English poet Lord Tennyson put it well long ago when he said:
The old order changeth, yielding place to new,
And God fulfils himself in many ways.
Lest one good custom corrupt the world."

He ended, but perhaps not as firmly as he had begun. His eyes seemed to cloud and he spoke with a little hesitation towards the end as though he was suppressing grief.

Nobody clapped.

The Secretary General served himself a drink of imported water, conferred with the new SDO very briefly, and then he rose to talk again. He thanked the people for turning up in such large numbers and hoped that it was an indication of the massive support the new boss could expect from them. He formally crowned the new SDO "with", as he said "the powers conferred on me."

Had the ceremony ended here, people would have had little to say to each other in remembrance of the day, and many wished it had ended there. But, not only did the Secretary General choose to speak, but he went on to say the one thing he should never have said at that particular time and to those particular people. Like a football coach speaking to his team to bring them to order, he warned:

"I want to insist that there is no higher authority on this land on which we are standing now, than the Government whose representative is the SDO."

He pointed to the new SDO, then stamping his fist on the desk and raising his voice to give his words a more serious import he added:

"So nobody, I say nobody, whatever he thinks of himself, should ever arrogate to himself the respect and honour due the Head of State or his representative."

Beckongncho knew that the bit referred to him very personally, and he was quick to notice the silent disapproval that seemed to rise from various corners of the large hall.

The other Chiefs also looked very disturbed in their seats.

"Yesss," the Secretary General said loudly. "I mean what I say."

A momentary silence fell, profound, pregnant and ominous. There was a slight murmur at the back and at the distant corners as from children, indignant at an insult from an adult, but afraid to stand out and protest.

The hall in which the ceremony was taking place was about twenty meters long and about ten metres wide. The Secretary General and the rest of the Government officials sat on the stage that rose about a meter above the level of the main floor.

To the left of the stage was one of four doors, through which the officials could enter or leave without interference from the crowd. Another door opened at the far corner directly opposite the stage through which natives or members of the audience could leave. A third door exited to the right along the length of the wall. Almost at the edge of the stage stood a table and three chairs from which the people were talking. To the right of the chairs, very close to the wall was the kingly seat to which Beckongncho retreated after he had finished talking.

Behind him stood two of his youngest wives. Each of them wrapped a loincloth over the breasts in the traditional fashion, wore a bunch of beads round the neck and several bangles on either arm. One held his fly whisky and the other his walking stick.

After Beckongncho had spoken and returned to his seat at the corner he fixed his gaze over the Secretary General and the new SDO. He was not looking at them at all, but through the open window above them. He was looking at the palm trees swaying from side to look at the morning breeze. He did not lower his eyes to look at the Secretary General or to answer him. After all, he thought, he had not been asked a question.

It was in this charged atmosphere that all of a sudden something went wrong, and brought the ceremony to an embarrassing end, and gave to the history of Nkokonoko Small Monje a new twist. When nature calls, even kings must answer, at once! Even before he came into the hall Beckongncho felt like urinating. He thought he could resist the urge till after the ceremony. But because of his own delay in arriving, the ceremony turned out to be slightly longer than he had anticipated and the longer he stayed the more acute that desire became. And now the Secretary General's poisoned words converted it into a physical pain that called for instant attention. He rose and walking behind the chair of the Secretary General held up his right index finger and said:

"If you don't mind Sir, I'll be back."

As he walked out the situation was instantly misunderstood. First of all, the Secretary General did not quite understand what he had said, and the Chief could not stand to repeat what he had said. As far as the people were concerned, they did not like what the Secretary General had said. They did not think anybody ought to stand higher than their Chief in Small Monje. If they had their way they would have shouted down the man who in direct contravention of their tradition of public speaking, he stamped his fist as he spoke to them.

241

In their poisoned and perplexed minds, they thought their Chief had merely read their thoughts and risen in protest, a move they applauded by rising with him. Even Njikem in the front row was not exactly sure of what Beckongncho had said.

Some said he had warned the Secretary General that if he heard that rubbish again he would deal with him. When the people rose amidst much murmuring the Secretary General whispered to the Commissioner who in turn asked a policeman to call back Beckongncho. The man, one of those who had guarded Beckongncho as SDO for two years marched up to him and in a stentorian voice asked him to go back.

Beckongncho brushed him aside with the back of his hand. A second policeman went up on his own accord. Before he got there some ten men were on them, brandishing weapons, ready to do battle. Beckongncho left the hall and went into the toilet at the end of the building and before he re-emerged his two wives had followed him with his rug and walking stick, his palanquin had also been brought. Nearly everybody except the Secretary General, the SDO and other Government guests had left the hall and were waiting to see what would happen.

As though acting under a spell Beckongncho climbed onto the palanquin, three masquerades jumped out of the tall elephant grass, followed by two drummers and the horsemen.

"Yeee-hohoho, Yeee-hohoho," the people sang as they carried their Chief away.

Njikem remained glued to his seat. He did not know whether Beckongncho's behaviour was an accident or a premeditated act. When he left the hall eventually he returned to Tetseale without meeting Beckongncho.

Epilogue

TO EVERY man upon this earth,
Death cometh soon or late,
And how can man die better
Than facing fearful odds
For the ashes of his father,
And the temples of his god?
(Lord Macaulary:
Lays of Ancient Rome)

THE CIRCUMSTANCES of the death of Paramount chief Kevin Beckongncho remain one of the unsolved mysteries in the annals of that principality. One morning exactly eighteen months after the installation of the new SDO, Fuo-Akendong was still sleeping when at about 7 o'clock a native knocked at his door.

"Have you heard?" the stranger asked.

"Heard what?"

"That our Chief is no more. That Beckongncho is gone."

"Gone how? To where?" Akendong gaped.

"Who said?"

"The radio." In reality, the Provincial Radio Station had announced at 6 O'clock that:

"The Provincial Governor of the Lower Middle-Belt announces sorrowfully the death of Kevin Beckongncho after a protected illness."

After a protected illness? Beckongncho had never been known to be sick. He had never shown any signs of feeling or looking sick. And why did the announcement come from a Radio station? The death of a Chief was never announced until his successor had been got. And even so, it was only done through the **Nteuh**! There was something most strange. Akendong walked to the Chief's hut. The doors were open. They entered cautiously at first and when there was no sign of anybody anywhere they called aloud.

243

Still no answer.

They passed through the sitting room to the backyard. Chief Beckongncho was indeed dead.   Among the numerous projects Beckongncho had mapped out for Small Monje had been the rebuilding of the palace. In esteem the throne had regained its greatness as of old – before Nchindia. But the walls of the palace were crumbling every rainy season. According, each time the opportunity presented itself he had cement blocks made. A wall behind the **Ndle-ndee** was lined with some of the blocks as a means of protecting them from the rains until such a time that they would be put into use. Some nine pieces of plywood had been put against the blocks and sticks pinned at angles against the boards to keep them in place. The blocks exerted such pressure on the boards that if anybody accidently tripped on any of the sticks supporting them they could come crashing down on him. It was not an area of the palace that people frequented. Not even the Chief. And if the Chief ever passed there at all, Beckongncho was not the kind of person to ignore the danger of passing there, especially at night.

Yet, Kevin Beckongncho's disfigured body was removed from under the rubble of the blocks that morning. As the **Nteuh** was struck to assemble the shocked natives, questions were asked, but without any answers. Was it suicide? It could not be. Beckongncho could not possibly do that. Who first discovered the incident, and what had he gone to do there so early in the morning? Who sent the information to the Governor? Such a man must have witnessed the act, must have reported to the SDO who alone had the facility to contact the Governor or the Radio Station. Could somebody have been hired to kill Beckongncho? Some said Beckongncho received two guests late the previous evening.

Among those who came down to the palace there was nobody from the District Office. How then did they get the information. Beckongncho himself had said that he could not co-exist with the new SDO in Small Monje. But it did not mean that he would kill himself.

The security report which the Secretary General had personally presented to the Minister of Territorial Administration and the Delegate for Internal Security had also indicated that the new SDO and Kevin Beckongncho could not co-exist in Small Monje. As a matter of fact, Chieftaincy was to be wiped out from Small Monje.

Just how had this been effected? Had Beckongncho been drugged before being led to his death? If so by whom? Had the Government once more infiltrated the internal security system of the Paramount Chieftaincy of Small Monje? The new SDO was in no position to answer any questions concerning the death. But he was in a position to ban any public demonstrations concerning the event. No investigations were to be carried out by any individual or groups of individuals on the death of Beckongncho. He would not be mourned for.

There was more bad news for Small Monje: a release from the Ministry of Health declared that the stream behind the palace, what the Elders called the River of Forgetfulness, was the breeding ground for Malaria, Typhoid and Sleeping Sickness. The palace and its immediate environs were therefore declared unfit and unhealthy for human habitation. Caterpillars would come from Tetseale to raze the palace to the ground and the area transformed into a Research Centre for Infectious Tropical Diseases. If any Elders thought the new arrangement displeased them they could construct a new palace on their own at least five kilometres away.

Beckongncho's successor was only an infant. A regency would have to be set up in the new palace. The Secretary General's inhuman suggestion to the Chief of Internal Security, the Government's swift and merciless response, together with the fears of the people of Small Monje had finally collided in the form of clubs and a brick wall over Beckongncho's head, killing him and also killing Chieftaincy.

But that would not be the end of the story because on top of the verbal threats and anonymous letters to the SDO of Small Monje, the Middle-Belt Provincial Governor received a letter that brought the Small Monje file from the archives back to his desk for urgent consideration.

The Biongong Elites,
C/O General Secretary,
Ephriam Njikem,
Ministry of Mines & Power
Tetseale.
30th March 1969.

The Minister of,
Territorial Administration,
Ministry of Territorial
Administration,
TETSEALE,

Your Excellency,

LETTER OF PROTEST

We the elites of Nkokonoko Small Monje and the Bimobio area write to express our disapproval and total condemnation of the extent to which your ministry has seized upon itself to systematically trample on the very pride of our land. Not so long ago, Small Monje hit the headlines of the news for the execution of their Chief, the District Officer and a Reverend Father. The issue would appear to have been laid to rest without an accusing finger pointing to the District Officer who personally masterminded the desecration of the land by the theft of the statue of our good. Right now, we have lost our Paramount Chief – Kevin Beckongncho – the man who for purely personnel reasons resigned as SDO of the area, and an act which the Government chose to call dismissal. His death which was first announced not by the Elders of his palace but by the Provincial Radio Station has raised many eyebrows of suspicion. This suspicion has been accentuated by even more blatantly provocative acts on the part of the SDO: that the Chief must not be mourned for, that the palace be moved ten kilometres away and be reconstructed at the expense of the natives, that the Ministry of Health has declared the area was infested with deadly diseases. We write to remind your Excellency that we know the mineral potentiality of Small Monje and the entire Biongong. We know that the story of the Research Centre for Tropical Diseases is fake because of the plans long conceived for using part of the palace grounds as the site of a Smelting Industry. We believe that these plans could, with time, have been realized without killing a Chief or faking a medical report to move his palace. Accordingly, we would like to warn in the strongest terms possible that all plans to exploit the bauxite deposits at the expense of Small Monje and Bimobio rather than to their advantage will end in smoke, UNLESS THE FOLLOWING CONDITIONS ARE MET:

1. *An independent report from experts from the World Health Organisation on the veracity of the Ministry of Health's claim of the presence of RICKETTSIA PROAWERIT AND RIPANOSOME*
   - *an allegation put forward as an excuse for moving the palace.*
2. the immediate lifting of the ban on the mourning of our Chief.
3. *The setting up within one week of an independent Commission to establish and publish the precise cause of the death of Chief Beckongncho.*
   Such a Commission, we suggest, should be made up of an Archbishop, a retired magistrate and a lawyer, a representative from your Ministry and Internal Security, and Amnesty International.
4. *The cancellation of the ridiculous threat of moving the palace.*

Finally we would like to inform Your Excellency that Saturday the 19th of June has been set forth for the mourning of Chief Kevin Beckongncho in the traditional manner which befits his status as one of the greatest Chiefs in this area. We appeal to you to use your good office to ensure that we act under full security. Copies of this letter are being sent simultaneously to Amnesty International, the Paramount Chiefs of Biongong, the Provincial Governor, the Chief of Internal Security and the SDO of Small Monje-Bimobio area.

The letter bore seventy-two signatures on a separate sheet. The story of Small Monje may not have reached its final end yet. Or?

The End